THE RELIC HUNTERS

OTHER TITLES BY DAVID LEADBEATER

The Matt Drake Series

The Alicia Myles Series

The Torsten Dahl Thriller Series

Stand Your Ground (Dahl Thriller #1)

The Disavowed Series

The Razor's Edge (Disavowed #1)
In Harm's Way (Disavowed #2)
Threat Level: Red (Disavowed #3)

The Chosen Few Series

Chosen (The Chosen Trilogy #1)
Guardians (The Chosen Trilogy #2)

Short Stories

Walking with Ghosts (A short story)
A Whispering of Ghosts (A short story)

THE RELIC HUNTERS

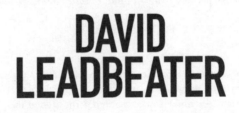

THE RELIC **1** HUNTERS

DAVID LEADBEATER

THOMAS & MERCER

Text copyright © 2017, 2018 by David Leadbeater
All rights reserved.

Previously self-published in Great Britain in 2017. This edition contains editorial revisions.

Published by Thomas & Mercer, Seattle

www.apub.com

Amazon, the Amazon logo, and Thomas & Mercer are trademarks of Amazon.com, Inc., or its affiliates.

ISBN-13: 9781503902473
ISBN-10: 1503902471

Cover design by Ghost Design

Printed in the United States of America

For my beautiful daughters, Keira and Megan, and my
wonderful, supportive wife, Erica.
"Memories to keep, and to keep making."

CHAPTER ONE

"Look at the mad monk."

He heard these words often as he walked by. Spoken by unenlightened scum, wandering pointlessly with their unwashed children. These ignorant cattle, followers of the herd, bleating through life without the slightest inkling that every day, their every step, their every breath, was being judged, controlled, and manipulated.

He would happily snuff them out, even without an order from his master.

But not today. One surprising event had already occurred this morning, and he was about to be the author of at least one more, at least to the outside world. The earlier event, a true shock indeed, was hearing the unease and disarray in his master's voice. A first, and probably last, for this life.

He scanned the road quickly, assimilating every scrap of information offered by his surroundings. The path that followed a slight incline up toward the front of the Archaeological Museum of Athens was clogged with tourists and gawkers. It was loud, colorful, and upbeat. That would soon change. He kept the grave smile to himself as a man and woman barged past his right shoulder.

The words of his master ran incessantly through his brain: "My son, focus fully on the work at hand. You can bask and bathe in the light, but only with the full illumination of focus. If you want to swim, focus on swimming. If you want to run, focus on running. If the moment is dark, confusing, or unclear, focus on your objective. And you will always have an objective, Baltasar. Always."

The couple continued along their way, laughing loudly, oblivious to the muted monster in their midst. Baltasar took his time to thread through the crowd, focused. Ahead, the tall, round pillars that fronted the museum's edifice extended toward the entrance and two sets of wide steps. The moment was approaching, then. He would have to be quick.

Baltasar could see the appeal of archaeological mystery, but was happy to destroy this museum on even the most whimsical order from his master. Obedience was everything. Loyalty and trust kept him alive. The Archaeological Museum of Athens housed the relics of yesteryear to entertain the world of today and tomorrow, but Baltasar recognized only his master's words on the subject of the past.

"Only four things matter from anyone's past. The words you spoke. The barbs and bullets you loosed. The life you led. The opportunities you squandered. Remember, it is too late to complain when the chance has already passed you by."

Everything else was flotsam, designed to make the herd lose focus.

Baltasar headed directly for the entrance, feeling a steady flow of adrenaline. Frequently, the jobs he carried out required him to remain incognito; today, though, there was no such need. Today, the requirement was for speed.

Baltasar had spent a lifetime honing and enhancing the man—the weapon—that he had become. Still evolving, still advancing. The black bristle at the side of his head and the thick topknot along the middle were as much an identity as his given name. The yellow elastic band he used to keep it in place, the same. The wounds that decorated his body—the scars that had been handed out, mostly by those who had trained him, but never his enemies—gave him peace. Often, he would trace them in the dark, remembering their provenance and the lessons learned. They were the blueprint of his education, the road map that had brought him where he was right now.

Baltasar was an intimidating man—tall, broad, grim of face. But his visage was offset by the humble black robes he wore, diminishing any threat he posed in the eyes of all but those who knew his identity.

Ahead, beyond the entrance to the museum, he was faced with three different doors. Straight in front stood the door to the Prehistoric Collection, but Baltasar knew he should use the door to the left. Initially, this led to the Sculptural Collection, followed a circular route, and presented dated Greek sculptures and others heavily influenced by ancient Egypt. Interestingly, at least for Baltasar and because of what he knew about the mission at hand, a bronze statue of Zeus could also be viewed along his route. At the rear of the museum sat rooms where private and temporary exhibitions were held. It was toward this area that Baltasar set his feet. Feet that had trodden a thousand different paths.

Found and purchased at a Far East flesh market at the age of six, he had only ever known the world as his enemy. Thrown from one evil master to the next, he had tried running, again and again, until they decided to break his spirit. Before this could be accomplished, a new man entered his life. Nobody knew his name, but he was known as a connoisseur of the slave markets, a man who bought infrequently and never resold his purchases.

"These weak men need you to worship them. They need to dominate you to rise above their own nauseating fears, to prove to themselves that they are strong. But come with me . . . come with me and I will show you that divinity is earned a different way. All sin can be repented. No self-flagellation, no seven Hail Marys, no amount of bowing and kneeling can make you truly great, truly at one with God in this world. It is no longer in his image."

Baltasar had warmed to this man, seeing in him a desire to aid and teach, a quality that promised restraint before violence, something new.

"I am yours."

"I do not ask that. I will never ask that of you. First, understand that there is no god beyond the one we create. There is no salvation greater than that which we make. There is no afterlife, no eternal redemption beyond the legacy we leave. I am not an easy man. Not a fool. The things I ask of you will be dire indeed. But you will have one thing, I promise . . . one thing above all else."

Baltasar had leaned forward. "Yes?"

"Family. I will give you a family. If family is truly a feeling of fitting in."

The seed had been sown, the die cast. Baltasar had found true purpose and enlightenment. The next twenty years of his life were full, content. And as the master said—some of the tasks they asked of him were beyond appalling, but family came first.

Baltasar was mindful that he could never leave his master, but that too was a comfort, a safety net for all his sins. He was dimly aware that he'd been raised to be different from most other people: few morals, no taboos, and utter obedience to the point of banishment. He would never question an order.

A circuitous route through the museum brought him to the private exhibition rooms, behind which he knew stood the various laboratories where new artifacts were stored and examined. The entry doors were behind an airport-style metal detector and a basic keypad. No guards were evident, though the area was watched over constantly by a cluster of security cameras. Baltasar wasn't worried. In truth, words like "worry," "burden," and "insecurity" held only vague meaning for him. The path provided. The master provided. All was well. Baltasar's love was not blind, as some said. It saw enough. It saw everything that kept him on the right path.

Baltasar visited the restrooms, lost the robes, putting them into a backpack, and changed into jeans, a black T-shirt, and a baseball cap. A total transformation. Dressed in the strange outfit, he felt a moment of inappropriateness bordering on betrayal, but the robes would never be far away.

He passed through the detector, needing no weapons, cell phone, or money. He jabbed at the keypad in the correct manner, a servant of a man who could attain the code to any keypad on the planet in a matter of minutes. Expecting the doors to open, he breezed easily through when they did so.

Beyond, lay a rectangular open-plan room of cubicles, each with its own desk, computer, and set of drawers. At the far end were the "clean" rooms, to which older, more important relics found their way. Baltasar had been informed that the object he sought would be there, almost certainly inside the middle room of the three. Of course, he had never expected the workplace to be empty, and he wasn't disappointed. Three sat at their desks, heads down, lost in their jobs. Another stood by the water cooler, contemplating his plastic cup and the grimy window in front of his face.

Baltasar picked up half a mug of cold coffee from a desk and strolled through as if he'd just started work. One older lady gave him a glance before looking away. The man by the water cooler never moved. Baltasar reached the middle clean room in a matter of seconds and faced his first obstacle.

The standard lock with no key.

Breaking it open would be easy, but noisy. To try the handle and find it locked would draw attention. There was only one course of action.

Kill all witnesses first.

Pausing for a few seconds, Baltasar pulled down the neck of his T-shirt and traced one of the old wounds on the skin below. Scar tissue, ridged and angry; it was pure white stitching now, but oddly comforting. It reminded him of past days when he'd still been fully unaware of the master's true plan for him. Another scar ran across his stomach. Baltasar lifted his T-shirt now and traced that one, pressing hard. The pressure cleared any white noise that might be buzzing around his brain.

The man by the water cooler was staring at him.

Baltasar smiled, picked up a letter opener, and leapt at the first worker. Head down, focused on their task, they never even looked up before the shiny silver edge dug deep into their neck and ripped its way to the right. Then the blood was splashing, the life ebbing. Pain was a secondary sense to shock, at least at first. Baltasar was already leaping away, seeing the water-cooler guy opening his mouth to scream. The letter opener flew true, flung with incredible dexterity and strength, and lodged as far as it was able into the side of the man's neck. Another expression of shock. The plastic cup fell to the floor, splashing its contents across a pair of patent leather shoes. Then Baltasar was there, withdrawing the letter opener quickly, then thrusting it back into place.

Again and again and again.

Eight seconds had passed.

Spinning, he saw the old lady regarding him with disbelief. The only other person left alive, a man wearing a bright-red hoodie, was clearly about to make a break for the exit.

Baltasar allowed the body to fall to the floor beside the water cooler and continue bleeding out. Of course, he knew that even a trained operative such as he had little chance of stopping the man now rising from his desk, so an alternative had to be sought. In an office space as cluttered as this, many items came to hand. A keyboard wasn't heavy or accurate enough unless he achieved the perfect shot, and in this environment it was unlikely. He almost went for the thick-rimmed trash can, knowing its heavy impact would send the now-running man sprawling, but then spotted a far better substitute.

A severed head.

Baltasar hefted it, moved it to his right hand, and took aim. The old lady took a deep breath and almost screamed, appearing more worried about the head than her life. Baltasar hadn't thought she'd think that way. Still, he let loose the severed skull, wondering briefly if his action might have some classic meaning, and then watched as it smashed against the man's right cheekbone. The effect was immediate, eliciting a squeal and diverting his run straight into a desk. He hit hard, knees striking wood, legs folding, chin coming down and bouncing off the surface. Baltasar didn't stop for one second. The discreet vibration of the timer in his pocket had already told him that he had less than ten minutes.

Baltasar used his momentum to grab the edge of the desk, swing out with both feet, and kick the old lady hard in the chest. He was back on his feet before she even hit the floor. The other man was still groaning. Baltasar could leave them both in a stupor, but couldn't take the slightest chance. Another weapon then appealed to him.

The sword was old and damaged. The point was useful, however, and, despite its age, was still sharp enough to kill both coworkers. Now, Baltasar had the lab to himself. He returned to the locked door, forced it open, and quickly entered. The object he sought was right there, next to a microscope and a discarded pair of white gloves. Unstrapping the small backpack, he pulled on gloves of his own and placed the object gently inside the receptacle he'd been given. Then he sealed it.

Shrugging the backpack onto his shoulders once more, he looked around one last time and was ready to go. He started a countdown in his head. Four minutes. Barely enough time, but flawless timing was essential. Crucial to almost every mission. Timing was the difference between a clear escape and an ignominious capture. Working fast, Baltasar made a good job of concealing the bodies and the blood even though he didn't have to. The alarm must not be raised—not here, in this room. He then exited the lab, passed through the detector, and moved fast along the halls. Nobody gave him a second glance. Baltasar desperately wanted to change back into his robes, but knew they singled him out. The civilian costume would have to do, for now. Many innocents milled about the museum, lost in their own worlds.

Young and old. Foreign and local. Priceless works of art before their eyes. Baltasar passed a few moments reflecting on the fact that there were many ways to steal relics, objects of incredible significance, but there really was only one way to ensure that theft was never discovered.

The organization his master worked for had done this before. Very loudly. Very publicly. In their wisdom, their infinite intelligence and depth of cunning, they knew what worked best.

The main doors were ahead. Baltasar felt another vibration inside his pocket. He had less than thirty seconds.

Athens was barely visible through freshly cleaned glass. The city would never be the same.

CHAPTER TWO

Baltasar jogged down the double set of steps, feeling the first tremor traveling through the concrete and up his legs. This wasn't the warning pulse, though. This was the real thing. It was the sensation of a mini earthquake, and those that it touched froze in place, eyes widening, body language suddenly hesitant. He saw them turning toward each other, looking for some kind of explanation, some solace perhaps, but not a single one of them had an answer.

Not the crowd heading straight toward him, eager to see the museum. Not the bus drivers collected down the road, smoking and drinking and talking about life. Not the school kids to the left, so close to the entrance that they were in danger already.

Another shudder, this one deeper, stronger. Baltasar kept walking, and then felt the earth move once more. It felt like an earthquake to be sure, and that was good. Mimicking the herd—because he knew a man walking away and not watching was considered unnatural and would be spotted later by the police—he stared back at the museum as he continued forward. He forced a look of concern onto his visage, maybe even fright.

The museum's vast multicolumned façade lurched. Mortar crumbled from the many joints, and a large piece of rubble sheared away from one wall. Windows compressed out of shape and shattered. He saw glass exploding in every direction, no doubt littering the swelling floors. A tidal wave seemed to pass through the building, raising its enormous bulk, then letting it resettle, but the damage was already done.

A column began to fall away from the front, looming over tourists and then crashing into their midst as they scattered. The ground shuddered as the column burst apart. Debris shot far and wide. Another column began to sway. People streamed out of the front doors, screaming, waving their arms, and trying to pull loved ones along. Many fell in the panic, trampled. Others fought and punched and embraced their baser instincts. Baltasar knew this was normal—many would regret it later; a few would not.

The trees that fronted the museum were shaking, the earth turning. Incredibly, people were taking shelter beneath, turning Baltasar's phony look of amazement into a genuine one.

"One of the greatest museums in the world," his master had said, shaking his head slowly, regretfully. "A poor choice we have, but our path is greater. We are worthier. It all comes down to our greater good."

Baltasar now saw firsthand the complexity and depth of his master's belief.

It was truly breathtaking.

The lengthy wings at both ends of the entrance began to crumble. The roof collapsed. Screams of terror and death curdled the air. Invaluable collections of artifacts were destroyed. Men, women, and children flew past him, trying to escape the area. Baltasar thought that might be a very good idea. He walked faster, stopped to blend in, then ran for a while. He looked erratic, scared. The pack on his back that contained the small, insignificant artifact that had triggered this staggering event looked like every other pack on every other back.

The artifact inside was safe. His master would be pleased. Baltasar took one more moment to study the crumbling edifice of the museum, the crash of stone columns, the madness of panic. He listened to the rumble and groan of the earth, the terror in the air. He smelled utter fear and gasoline and powder. He saw pluming dust, chunks of rubble still collapsing. The rumbling had stopped, but the hell that followed was only just beginning.

Baltasar imagined a nice journey back to the homeland, the easy bus that would eventually get him there. A long trip, but the right trip. Incongruous. Safer than flying because the man he worked for couldn't accept the minute risk that an aircraft might crash and kill everyone on board.

And they would lose the artifact.

At least if a bus crashed, Baltasar stood a chance of surviving.

He wondered what the master was doing now, and if he was thinking about his return in approximately forty-eight hours, perhaps even discussing it with an equal.

Then he saw the time of day and knew they would be deep underground, in uniform, headdresses attached perhaps, knives gleaming and maybe already streaked with blood. The symbol they worshipped would never let them down—but sacrifice was required. The chanting would be deepening, growing more feral. The fires would be raging.

Baltasar slipped away from the horrifying scene of devastation, unable to keep the smile of pleasure from his face.

CHAPTER THREE

In Hell, a man should know his place. In Hell, a man should know the full extent of his sins. And in particular, the ones that brought him there.

Guy Bodie tried to keep it together. Ten days was a long time to share this desperate dance with a thousand devils, but his convictions told him help was coming.

Most of the time, though, he just didn't trust them.

The environment itself was unsettling. If you didn't see the high walls with the barbed wire and lookout towers, you might think you were walking through a small Mexican town. Tiny shops plied a trade. Market stalls sold perishable goods, clothes, books, secondhand bed linen, bottled water, packets of sweets that he only recognized from his youth on the streets of London, and more. Men milled everywhere, beaten, despondent. But then, so did women. And children.

It was the oddest prison Bodie had ever found himself in.

There were ways to make money in here, but he hadn't been made privy to any of them. The American dollar stash he'd been lucky enough to have on him was dwindling. The clothes he still wore were dirty and unwashed, much like himself. The beard was growing. He figured he had enough money to last five more days on rations, maybe six. The ten days he'd spent here already had yielded a blueprint of the grounds: gates, entrances and exits, guard towers, offices, and the dens where gang bosses, mafia dons, and heads of drug cartels continued to manage their businesses. He saw where the prostitutes came in for the live-in guards, every Wednesday; where the drugs came and went; where the weapons were exchanged. It wasn't that he was a master spy—although he was considered by many as the best in the world at his chosen trade—but more that nobody attempted to hide what they were doing. Nobody cared.

That told Guy Bodie at least two things.

First, the authorities knew what was going on, and accepted it for whatever reason. Second, he was never going to be released. This particular trip to Mexico was one-way. And, if current and recent appearances were anything to go by, more of a minibreak than an extended vacation. *Why am I here?* It had been less of an arrest and more of an abduction, and his close-mouthed captors had been less than chatty. It couldn't be because of the last heist, as he'd never even reached the place he was supposed to be casing.

Bodie was no stranger to loneliness; in some ways he embraced it. Loneliness was one of his oldest friends, a place in which he could dwell and not fear. But prison was not lonely. It was a zoo, replete with all manner of animals, most of them looking for the best way to kill you.

An old man had watched him pass by the first day, then, on the return journey, snagged his hand.

"You stick with your own," he grated, eyes rheumy and narrow against the blazing sun, but clearly focused. "Them." He nodded to a corner of the yard where Bodie saw other English or American folk. "Ain't nobody else here for you. They'll kill you."

Bodie wasn't that easy to kill, but he wasn't about to paint himself as a target either. "Thanks for the info. Did you see who brought me here?"

The old man squinted. "What kinda jackass accent is that?"

Bodie grinned at the sweating creases that formed a slight smile. "London."

"And the teeth?"

"All my own. Big, bright-white choppers run in the family."

"Wish I'd been given a set like that. Woulda never needed a flashlight."

"Heard that before."

"I'm sure you have. And yeah, I saw the guys that brought you in. Same fuckers that bring everyone in." He pointed at the watchtowers. "Them fuckers."

"Guards." Bodie had been afraid of that. It meant he was here in at least some kind of official capacity and hadn't just been deposited in the first available hideout. "Bollocks."

"Dogs?"

"Nah. Just bollocks."

"You people and yer bollocks." The old man chuckled, which became a cough that wracked his ribcage. "You make me smile."

Bodie bowed just a smidgen. "At your service. For a short while anyway."

"You seem like a carer. Ain't no place for you here, boy. You change, or you ain't gonna survive."

Bodie blinked in surprise. Despite his outer demeanor, the man had seen right through him. "Don't worry," he said. "I'll kick you when we're done."

"Good."

"I realize we're in Mexico." Bodie cast a glance around at the concrete squat structures, the sandy, earthy ground, the blue skies, and the high, flaking walls. "But I was hurting no one. I was minding my own business—" He stopped himself from saying "on a recon trip." "So, I know I wasn't taken far, but where the hell *are* we?"

"*El infierno.* This is one of the worst kind of hellholes, my friend. Vices in here are worse than out there." He nodded over the walls. "No law. Run by a madman, a warden who *wants* to be here. Nothing is too immoral. Nothing is too depraved. This is the eighth circle of Hell, London man."

Bodie took a breath. *Shit. Worse than I thought, then.* "And where does Lucifer hang his hat?"

Those eyes again, focusing, gleaning. "Why'd you wanna know that?"

"Always good to know where the boss lives."

Bodie allowed himself another small smile, remembering the phrase from his early light-fingered days. The boss was well-off, and usually a dick, so made for a nice, easy target. Nobody stood up for the boss.

"Not sure I agree, but take a right after the marketplace. At the end of that street there's a high step up to an open doorway. Careful though, London, you won't get three paces along that street without a knife pressing to yer throat."

Bodie nodded, thinking, *Not my idea or memory of prison, but at least it's unique.*

"Speaking of knives." The old man unfolded a sleeve in which lay half a dozen small, handmade shivs. "I have a stash of these nearby. They still have their uses in here. Especially for quiet work."

Bodie studied the razor blades, trapped between two lengths of wood and secured with plastic ties. Easy, small, barely detectable, very concealable. "How much?"

Back then, ten days ago, he'd had time. He'd expected help. His people? Surely they knew where he was. They'd track him down. They were the fucking best, for God's sake.

But now?

Bodie studied the skies as the sun started to flatten across the horizon. At least, what he could see of the horizon. Not much, unless he climbed onto one of the low buildings' roofs. Which was also permitted. Trouble was, at night the roofs offered a kind of pecking order. If you wanted to go up there, you had to be prepared to fight.

Bodie stuck to the streets, surviving. Outlandish sounds filled the steadily falling night. Screams and howls and the sound of gunfire.

A man chuckling incessantly. A woman groaning in pleasure. The whispered persuasions of incessant drug use.

Bodie made his way back to the area he'd deemed safer than anywhere else, pushing a coughing man out of the way and threading through a group of unwashed, stinking youths. Nobody gave ground here; you put your head down and barged through.

Like London in the summer, he thought. *Or Paris every day.*

The prisoners he'd grown used to seeing looked up as he passed them by on his daily route. No recognition, no nods or smiles. They didn't want to be associated with him, and he hardly blamed them. Two men had attacked him on the second day, for no obvious reason. Bodie had showed them the error of their ways, without injuring them permanently. He wouldn't do that anymore.

Always the smoother road. Always the softer option.

A man who had seen the effects of the misery he wrought always faced a point of no return. Continue, and fall without end. Or change your ways, adapt, and try to win. Bodie had been taught by the best, and was now always careful to ensure the innocent never became tangled up in his crimes. But he was unconcerned as to the welfare of criminals. The team he'd assembled was unique—it contained all the elements of a comprehensive unit that audacious, adept, victimless crimes demanded. They were thieves. They were relic hunters.

But none of that would help him in here. Around him, men shifted. Men groaned. A young woman walked by, long skirts sweeping the filthy floor. A young boy slept curled up in the outer corner of a doorway.

Bodie sat down on a set of steps, concrete to his back, a wide space in front of him. Any man or woman in jail faced the intense mental stress of having to be ready at all times. Just watching for enemies every minute, every second. Bodie knew you could develop a certain mind-set—a sixth sense of sorts. You could even sleep. But you had to be prepared to do damage at the slightest advance, the smallest provocation. You had to make other prisoners believe it wasn't worth bothering you.

Here, however, the rules were different. Take the four inmates approaching. In most civilized prisons they'd be closely guarded and wearing prison uniforms. Here they wore jeans and torn T-shirts, had heavy boots, and carried weapons. One bore a long scar, another grinned to show all gums and no teeth. Bodie rose quickly, now embracing the solitariness as those close to him scurried away. In a matter of seconds, he summed up an odd situation.

The men were Mexican. They didn't know him. Hellhole—as he'd decided to refer to the prison—was merely a place for him to die and disappear. Somebody had taken a contract out on his life.

"Hey, guys," he began. "You speak English? *Inglés?*"

Two looked blank, but Gummy and Scarface met his eyes and slowed. "I do," one said with a heavy accent. "You pay me thousand extra I make it quick, not slow like we were told."

"Who told you to make it slow?" Bodie asked the chatty one. No point being antagonistic.

"The boss." A shrug. *"El jefe."*

"Ahh." Bodie smiled. "Now we're getting somewhere. El jefe told you to make it slow. And who told el jefe?"

The men all exchanged a glance and then a laugh. "Nobody orders el jefe."

"Sure they do." Bodie knew the fight was coming and had already evaluated all four men, the surroundings, and any objects he might use. When they stared in bewilderment, he rubbed his thumb and forefinger together.

"Money talks."

He tried a new tack. "There's a man named Jack Pantera. He's *my* old boss. A grand, old-school thief. He'll set you up royally."

But they looked to be done talking. Bodie readied himself, but then the biggest of the four stopped and stared hard.

"Man," he whispered in awe. "Are those teeth real? 'Cause if not, I'm gonna have me a new set."

Bodie grinned wider. "Bask in the light, asshole. Bask in the light."

He was moving even as he spoke, using the environment to fight, as he used it every time he carried out a new job. First, he targeted the big guy, moving in and dancing away, leaving three fast strikes in his wake. He tried to jerk the length of metal pipe from the man's hand, but the meaty paw held on tight. The body did spasm hard, though, wracked with pain.

Bodie used the steps to get some height, then jumped on top of Chatty, landing an elbow atop the man's shaven skull, forcing him to his knees. Bodie would have liked to finish him there and then, but didn't have the time. The other two were already upon him, and the big guy was recovering fast. Bodie used the fallen man, thrusting off his bent back to gain momentum. A simple punch to the throat and Gummy fell, clutching and gasping.

Scarface hit him hard, but Bodie expected that. You didn't get out of a low-odds skirmish like this without taking some damage. Somehow he smothered the baseball bat that the guy swung, taking a hit on the forearm but diverting the main force of the blow. The guy hit hard, though, leading with the shoulder, smashing Bodie backward and almost off his feet. Here again, Bodie knew what was behind him. No trip hazards, no hard corners, just a flat wall. Bodie hit it, feigned an injury, looked punch-drunk, and then slipped away just as the attack came in. The baseball bat struck concrete, clanging, its wielder overbalanced. Bodie stepped around, delivered two elbows and a kidney punch, and sent Scarface sliding down.

Bodie grabbed the dropped bat.

The giant was back on his feet now, along with the one Bodie had skull punched. The metal bar whistled down and Bodie parried it with the bat, fencing now and wishing he'd had the time to relieve this man of his weapon earlier. The bar came again. Bodie deflected it at the ground, then stood on the ragged end. The big guy ended up staring him in the face, almost point blank.

Bodie flashed the smile, the one that dazzled.

"I'm gonna pull 'em out one by one." The metal bar fell, muscles flexed, and Bodie was pulled into a bear hug. Scarface grinned as if to say, "Well, that's that, then. Nobody ever survived one of those." Bodie could believe it. The breath was forced quickly from his body. The nerves around his ribcage flashed warning. Pain like fire exploded inside his head. Something was creaking inside, and he didn't like to imagine what it might be.

The giant's lips were crushed to his ear.

"Ish end fer youuu." Barely intelligible, but Bodie caught the drift. It was time.

The small shiv he'd bought paid for itself. Letting it fall into his hand, he drove the razor blade up again and again, perforating the giant three, four, five times and making his eyes widen, his strength ebb away.

"Fooled you," he said as Scarface's visage crumpled.

The giant collapsed. Now, Bodie knew this had to end fast. His own strength was failing; his element of surprise was gone. Skipping past Gummy, he brought the baseball bat down hard on top of Chatty's skull. Spinning, he flung the bat and caught Gummy across the cheekbone, sending him sprawling. Scarface was lunging fast now, when Bodie whacked him across the back of the neck, wincing as the crack of broken bone split the night.

Sadly, he would have to end these men. It had been a long time since Bodie intentionally committed violence—past events had led him to commit only victimless crimes—but he knew as well as anyone that they'd been set a task, a mission, and could not return to their captain with anything less than a win. They would keep coming, but if they never made it back, it should give Bodie another day. Maybe two while the man who paid for his murder made some kind of reevaluation. So Bodie did what he had to do.

To survive.

Nothing moved in the shadows. The prison still spewed forth its nightly distractions and diversions, its screams, loud music and flashing lights, its hooting and hysterical laughter, its gunfire. But where Bodie stood, and all around, only silence and shadow.

The bodies lay cooling where he left them, so Bodie relieved them of small weapons, cash, and anything else that seemed important, and then strode off, nursing wounds, to find another corner to lay his head, one thought flashing across his mind like the urgent, bright-red letters on a giant billboard.

I have to get the hell out of here!

CHAPTER FOUR

Acapulco Bay sat pretty beneath the midday sun, glistening seas and sandy beaches perhaps not quite taking enough attention away from the worn hotel facades, signifying that this '50s Hollywood glamour spot may have lost much of its attraction and fame, if not its natural finery.

High-rise hotels dominated the southern end of the bay, minimal in luxury and at maximum turnover. Tourists tended to stick to the hotel beach, or the small strip that ran around the bay, paying top dollar for generic, well-organized trips rather than opting for a spur-of-the-moment wander around town.

Cassidy Coleman dipped her toes in the warm pool water, her lithe, bronzed body glowing with oil and sunlight, reflective Ray-Bans turned exclusively in a single direction—straight at those people she currently labeled her dithering, incapable teammates, her thoughts vectoring along a single pissed-off highway.

For fuck's sake, these guys are supposed to be good? Just give me a name. A place. A body to go fuck up.

Eli Cross glanced over. "Cassidy, we're doing our best here. Doesn't help you firing eye daggers."

"Four days to find him. *Four days.* Now, five more and you still don't have a plan? Get it together, dude, or I'm just gonna smash right through the front door."

"That might actually be the only way," Jemma Blunt said. "There's nothing regimental about this prison. No routines to plan around. We're not talking a supermax here, Cassidy."

"Nah, it's not that simple," Sam Gunn said. "If this were a supermax we'd be sorted. It's the *lack* of proper security that's the problem."

Cassidy snorted. "Friggin' geeks. Interrupt their daily routine and they're all at sea. You do know I could kill you with my big toe, don't you?"

They all threw a glance across. "You're already killing me," Cross said with a hint of impropriety. "With that body."

Cassidy gritted her teeth. "This is not the time, dude. This sure is not the time."

Cross changed his attitude quickly. "You're right," he said. "So just gather round. We need to talk."

Cassidy looked around the pool, unable to shake the peculiar feeling that what they were doing here was wholly wrong. The leader of their little family was rotting inside a Mexican shithole while they wallowed under the midday sun, dipping their toes in a pristine swimming pool.

She took a moment to study the others, gauging their commitment. Cross was a career thief with a wealth of experience and the nounce to get out of almost any scrape. He was Bodie's oldest friend—at least as far as she knew. Jemma Blunt was a top-notch cat burglar-cum-outstanding mission-planner, recommended years ago by Cross himself. Some of her operational tactics and blueprints were copied, implemented, and improvised by thieves and authorities worldwide. Sam Gunn was a tech genius, no doubt handy with security systems, the youngest and least forthcoming member of the team. And then there was Cassidy Coleman—a paradox in herself.

At seventeen she walked away from a safe home, but a home in which she'd not been welcome. She never saw her parents again, fell in with a bad boyfriend, became homeless for a few years, and was helped by an older man with good intentions who then died of a sudden heart attack at a comparatively young age.

Cassidy again tried to turn her life around, finding a full-time job and using her streetwise, hard-learned skills to get noticed. She studied the art of fighting, using her new talents to grab bit parts in movies, which showcased her abilities and natural beauty. She wanted to get ahead, driven by past failures, driven to rise above. In the end, though, she returned to old habits. The movies dried up, or the offers were lesser, and Coleman entered the underground street-fighting scene, making quite a name for herself before meeting a man named Guy Bodie.

And here they were, many years later.

Cassidy had wanted to go all out to save him, storm the prison with guns and swords and tanks—everything they didn't have and Guy Bodie would never have sanctioned. Jemma had insisted they have a plan—it was her job and she did it to perfection, the best in the world. Sam Gunn had convinced her he could hack and piggyback and "black hat" his way through the prison's systems to make their incursion foolproof and safe. Eli Cross, with his experience and excellence, had backed them. Now . . . well, now they looked shakier than a drunken man on a pogo stick. But family was family, and this was the most authentic one she'd ever had.

Home is a feeling of belonging, Bodie always said.

It rang truer with her than everything she ever learned in school.

She rose, pulled a towel around her, and padded over to the plastic table. Wet footprints charted her path. They had deliberately chosen the area where nobody wanted to be, unshaded and scorching hot. As Eli said in his thick Southern accent, "It's a goddamn sight better than my crappy room."

Yeah, but was it right, *sitting here when their leader was wallowing in prison?*

Cassidy shrugged the guilt away. Jemma and Gunn were the morally precious ones, not her. Both, she expected, because they hadn't yet shrugged off the trappings of youth. They hadn't seen it all, not like her.

"What you got, simpletons?"

Gunn regarded her with hurt. "Here." He jabbed at a computer screen filled with a blueprint of the prison. "And here. Both trafficking points. We think drugs, guns, other weapons, whatever. But it's the weakest entry point."

"How the hell do you know that? You haven't even set eyes on the place."

"That's my job, if you remember." Gunn looked even more hurt now. "I might not be deadly with my fists like you guys, but I sure can smash up a keyboard."

"Indulge me." Cassidy took a long drink of bottled water, the sweat around her neck trickling downhill as she tipped her head back. "I'm not just the muscle, you know."

"Nah, you're the distraction too," Cross said, smiling.

"Google Maps gets us started." Gunn imitated a lens zooming in from afar. "Diagrams from the planning office, very old, get us a bit further. But that's kids' stuff, and basically unreliable. For the real cream you have to troll a little. Y'know. The dark web?" He spoke it like a narrator might intone the name of a horror movie.

"I know the dark web," Cassidy said. "It's full of what you English might call 'boring wankers.'"

Gunn ignored her glance. "It's also full of extremely nasty shit, hard to navigate and even harder to crack from a remote terminal like this one." He tapped the Apple. "Give me a little credit."

Cassidy leaned forward. "I'll give you credit when your plan helps get Bodie back."

"Basically, I found the men that work for the man that runs the prison. He tells them what he wants. They find it and send it through. And of course they communicate using computers. It's the best way for a man that isn't a prisoner living *inside* a prison—running it, guards, local councils and all."

"And that took four days?"

"The info's not just lying around. There's no Dark Google. You have to coax it out of people by making a few digital friends. Most of the time, the only way they let you in is if you hack something they can't."

Cassidy tried to get her head around that. It sounded like a rite of passage. The new boy proving he was as good as the old boys. "Focus on Bodie," she said. "What's next?"

"That's where I come in," Jemma said. "Gunn is the hacker, I'm the planner. We use Sam's intel to procure something valuable, something they want, and approach this 'trafficking' gate. Then it'll be up to you and your silver tongue to get us inside."

"Tongue or fist," Cassidy said. "We'll be inside about three minutes after we arrive."

"That'll do. Now, we have a rough idea of where Bodie will be, judging by the way they group off in there. More Gunn intel. I believe, at night, with Eli's and your skills, Cassidy, we can make our way to that area unseen. If they send a guard or two with us, we can handle that. The disorderly way they do things inside makes me think they might never even be found . . ."

"What about the elephant in the room?" Cross asked.

Cassidy stared at him, eyes expressing her bewilderment. "What the fuck—" She glanced over her shoulder just in case.

"Bodie disappeared right in the middle of our last job. No explanation. No communication. How do we know he ain't right where he wants to be?"

"Bodie lives for this group," Jemma said. "This life we love, stealing relics from people who can afford to lose them. It's his chosen life, and he's our boss."

"I know that. But it ain't easy to kidnap Guy Bodie. I'd say it's easier to kidnap SEAL Team Seven. What the goddamn hell happened? We're flying blind."

Cassidy saw the logic, understood it. But Bodie had sacrificed so much for them, so often. "He's more than worth the risk."

Cross nodded, smiling again. "I guess he is at that."

"A major pro planned it," Jemma said. "Of that I'm sure."

"In our line of business," Cassidy said, "with that skill set? That's a pretty short list."

"Right, well, let's get Bodie back first and then worry about who tried to vanish him into a Mexican prison," Cross said. Even for a team with their resources—contacts around the globe and a monetary fund to draw on, their chain of informants, their experience, and their separate skills—it had taken all that and a good slice of luck to locate Bodie. In particular, the "corruptibility"—as Cassidy called it—of the Mexican government helped.

Jemma cleared her throat, shading her eyes from the bright sun. "Where was I? Well, we get in, locate Bodie, handle a few guards. There's no perfect plan here, because there's simply no sense of routine to the prison. No curfew. No lockups. The inmates have free run of the place, 24/7." She held her hands up, then rubbed her temples. "For a plotter like me, this is Dante's vision of Hell."

"Just get me in," Cassidy hissed. "I'll do the rest."

"She means *us*," Cross corrected.

"Course I do. So when do we go?" Cassidy fidgeted and checked her watch, ready to move in that very moment.

"Gotta check it through first," Gunn replied. "One more chat on the web. One last box to tick. I think, if you can be ready for tomorrow night, we're a go."

"It's a night mission, Cassidy," Cross explained to her disgusted look. "And we can't go tonight."

Cassidy couldn't think of any reason why. "New season of *Vikings* starting?"

Jemma laughed. "If it was, do you think we'd be sitting here now?"

The team smiled, warm with each other despite their differences and mismatched personalities. They all felt better now that they had a plan, of sorts. Now that they knew where their leader was.

Cross caught Cassidy's attention and offered her his arm. "This Southern gentleman would like to spend all afternoon purchasing weapons. What do you say?"

The tall, muscular redhead rose to her feet fast. "Fuck, yeah."

CHAPTER FIVE

Baltasar stayed low and unobtrusive as the bus rumbled its way out of Greece. The false documents were perfectly in order, and he never once worried they would fail him.

Though the bus was the preferred mode of transport for his master, Baltasar would actually have liked to walk, to hitch lifts, to hop off and on when possible, but it was a long twenty-six-hour journey to get where he wanted to go. His master was unwilling to risk an air crash or rely on the train, and a bus journey went unnoticed, like a heart skipping a beat.

Until someone destroyed the Archaeological Museum of Athens.

Still, Baltasar had gotten out early; the bus had left as the dust still plumed skyward and emergency services raced to the site. The timing was snug, but no more than what he was used to.

How fast could the Greek authorities turn shock and horror into inquiry and examination? It might be an issue, but it was the rare occurrence his master could not control.

Cap pulled down, T-shirt bagged out, face turned toward the window, Baltasar rode the bus in disinterested silence, but his ears picked up everything. One of his many scars, long and narrow, ran into view from under the sleeve of his T-shirt, distracting him for a while as he fingered its ragged white length. Comforting; it took him back to the old days.

But not now. He pinched the skin hard, knowing every faculty he possessed should be focused on his environment. Instantly he knew someone had seen him hurt himself and looked over; he stared the youth down until he looked away. The bus rumbled on through a falling darkness, bound for its one and only Greek stop before crossing the border.

Larissa was coming up. Baltasar knew the bus station would offer up a few newcomers, spit out a few travelers, hopefully the woman with the strong body odor right behind him. The streets were gray, dark, barely lit. Those who walked the sidewalks this night might be doing so with a little more trepidation than usual.

Larissa's bus station resembled a thousand others the world over. Baltasar wasn't unduly worried as the vehicle slowed, the brakes loud and grating, until he saw half a dozen police cars waiting. He saw a cluster of uniformed cops, several suits, and then a surprisingly large assemblage of military on the platform. Immediately he spied the guns, the stances, the expressions. They weren't prepared to storm the bus, they were here to search it.

Relax. They can't possibly know it was you. You have changed into different colored clothes, so even if someone did report a man leaving the scene, they couldn't easily connect it.

This was a search then, no doubt because it was the very last bus to leave Athens. Understandable, really. Procedural. And if it was more . . . then he had his skill set.

Heads rose and necks craned. People swiped at the windows, cleaning them with dirty fingers. Baltasar cast a glance upward to where his backpack lay jammed into the luggage rack. The robes were long gone, discarded when he changed clothes, and would be replaced when he reached home.

The single worry was the map.

A police officer came on board, flashed a badge, shouted that they would be detained until further notice and until a thorough check of the passengers and bus was undertaken. He cited the Athens museum destruction as the cause, and thanked everyone for their understanding. People moaned as people do, their lives derailed by someone else's suffering.

One man complained the loudest and was the first to be escorted off the bus—to some makeshift interview room, Baltasar assumed. He saw the hours stretching ahead and settled himself to learn a new character, one he'd already prepared: the seasoned European traveler, dropped out of college several years ago, and drifted along ever since. Content. Harmless. Not even worth searching.

He wondered if a search of every passenger was mandatory. This idea was confirmed when a woman was marched off in a different direction. He then wondered if they might be picking out single passengers. A worry, but something he couldn't affect. The legend the master had created for him would hold up.

Every passenger was checked, apparently at random. Baltasar slowed his breath, made quiet meditation. The bus became noisy, kids screaming, passengers complaining. Somebody started playing music until a loud woman's voice told them to shut it off or else risk being force-fed the device.

The police worked methodically and carefully, but rarely offered any help. Baltasar wondered how many other buses were being stopped. Medicine was asked for, as was water. In the end, Baltasar's turn came, and he followed a police officer off the bus with his luggage and no protest.

Two hours lost already, and they weren't even halfway through the passengers.

"Sit."

A skinny woman in uniform directed him to a battered plastic chair, its black seat scarred with age. Baltasar nodded and sat facing two men across a stained table. Two mugs of steaming coffee sat atop it, one for each man, but they didn't offer him anything.

"ID?" one asked, a buck-toothed older man with salt-and-pepper hair. "Where are you going?"

Baltasar handed over a country ID and met their eyes. "All the way."

"Germany? What is your business there?"

Salt-and-Pepper talked, while the other man ran his ID through a portable scanner. His eyes reflected flashing images on a computer screen. Baltasar made sure to look at him, confident in his ID and training.

"No business. I am just sightseeing." Baltasar spoke perfect Greek, English, and German, but made them barely passable.

Standard questions came at him steadily, questions he was well prepared to answer. He endured it all to remain unsuspicious.

Finally came the search.

Two more men with wands and wandering hands. He removed his shoes and socks. They patted him all over, and of course had no idea they were looking for a map. This was the real reason the museum had been demolished. The map was concealed inside the backpack, inside a plastic pouch, inside a sheaf of tourist guides and other similar maps of ancient European sites. Some had been aged to look similar, as collectible tourist maps often were these days. Only an expert could tell the difference.

The cops leafed through the pouch, appearing worn out from the hours-long interrogation and search. They found the pack of leaflets, flicked through them, and found nothing untoward. They weren't looking for leaflets. With a shrug, Baltasar was sent back to the bus and another interminable wait.

Time wasted. He ought to inform the master. The six-hour mark passed. Baltasar became irritated for the first time since they stopped.

The master shouldn't be made to wait like this. Was there a way to hurry it along? Not without drawing attention to himself.

Baltasar would endure the wait because his master and others in the organization told him this was the only way to achieve their goals, just as he'd helped rob and ruin the museum, just as he'd committed a thousand treacherous acts before . . . and would again.

CHAPTER SIX

Guy Bodie ached, not just his body, but mind and soul. Bruises were fleeting, but damage collected over a lifetime gradually became a hanging, immovable weight. The world had not been good to him, and he felt it owed him at least one favor.

No sign of it here, though, in this place, at this time. The old man who'd helped him out with the shiv was gone, replaced by a family of four. Bodie spent a little time searching nearby, but there was no sign of the old-timer. He veered away from the scene of the previous night's battle, staying mobile and taking little rest.

Occasionally he smelled himself, and the scent was on the verge of overripe. What was normally skin shaven to within a millimeter of fresh blood had sprouted bristles across his face. Bodie had expected some kind of contact—even if his team had started off ignorant, surely they would have tracked him down by now.

Has something happened to them?

Impossible to say, so best not let it cloud the issues at hand. Bodie didn't mind the loneliness—growing up, he'd welcomed and sought it—but in here it was a death sentence. The few Europeans he'd found either wouldn't speak to him or didn't understand him. Of those, one Englishman only repeated what, earlier, an American had told him.

"Get away from me, man. They got you marked. They got you spotted. They takin' you outta here in pieces, man, so best make your peace."

Bodie would have preferred a little help, but good friends were hard to find. Impossible, actually. He was the prison jinx. *Might as well have leprosy.* Those he stepped close to either gave him the dead eye or shuffled away, depending on their outlook.

Bodie managed to buy food, though, and water. He figured the cash would last another few days. The dog-eat-dog environment of prison told him he should steal more, but he had long since stopped committing crimes that left victims in his wake.

It struck him again now, as the sun blazed hard on top of his head. A day long ago when he'd been forced to confront the woman he robbed—seen the fear, passion, and despair in her eyes and etched in every line on her face. The depth of it had told him right then that it was not worth it. More succinctly than any prison stretch would ever do.

That was why he'd quit being a criminal, a clever but guilt-ridden thief, and turned to victimless crime.

Observe your victims, see what you put them through.

Alone was good, but Bodie somehow then started to build a family. In conflict, unlikely, contradictory, but something that promised a new depth. Often, he enjoyed working with the team and sharing their camaraderie more than he enjoyed the job they were on, and the outcome.

A bit of introspection here? Was he expecting to die?

In truth, the odds weren't good. But Bodie possessed resources most people couldn't reach. There was always a way to even the odds. He found some shade from the beating sun, a place to rest and watch everything, attune to his surroundings. A woman passed by, dragging her young son by the hand, clothes dirty and eyes blank as if they already knew they would never leave this place. Bodie knew the Mexican cartels ran most of the prisons, even used them to train new soldiers and fill their ranks.

Bribery and crime on a massive scale. But still, it worked for them. Youths sauntered past without noticing him under the shadow cast by the wooden lee rising above him. He was well tucked away. He heard them talking, cursing, laughing. A watchtower rose above all, its guard stuck in one position, mirrored sunglasses glinting. The prison was loud, vertiginous noise swelling at every high wall. It stank too, of rotten vegetables and litter, of sweat and dirt, of blood recently spilled. Bodie sensed it all, staying still and quiet, knowing a wall at your back was about the best you could hope for in a place like this.

His mentor, Jack Pantera, had been Bodie's role model, and trained him well after Bodie had made an effort to hit what he thought of as the illicit straight and narrow—the area of a victimless crime. There were many ways to make illegal money, it seemed, without bringing harm to innocent people. Jack Pantera was a master of one, and pulled Bodie into his fold, teaching him all he knew.

That was years ago. Now, Bodie used everything he'd been taught and everything he'd learned since to stay alert and alive—the observational skills, the patience, a way to recall faces and read body language. The afternoon was waning, but that just meant it was time for more of the crazies to come out. By far, the worst kind of animal in here was the nocturnal kind.

Fights broke out in an area between buildings to Bodie's right; he only saw the dust caused by their scuffling feet. Women talked to the left, kids running around their ankles. Two gunshots rang out, unnoticed by the majority. Bodie's position included a direct line of sight to the long, narrow street that led to the big boss's residence. In an hour of study, he saw nothing openly move, but noticed glints at the windows, curtains moving in unnatural fashion, and dark shadows shifting—enough to mark out at least a dozen watchers. At the far end—the actual house—all was cast in shadow: barred windows impenetrable, steel doors untouchable. Nothing moved inside the glass or on the balconies; nothing moved around the roof. Bodie sighed with a touch of frustration.

Questions beset him like a deadly plague.

Maybe he could ask the seven guys heading his way right now with purpose in their gait.

Exhaling noisily, he rose, walked forward a few steps, still with the building at his back and the shade covering his face and body.

"Hey guys, I have a question. Who the hell put me here, and why am I here?"

The leader, a man with so many facial tattoos he looked blue, slowed. "You don't know?"

Bodie shrugged. "Hard to find that out from men who won't speak."

Laughter came from the hole between the tattoos. "Ah, that is great. Just great. The big, bad thief, best of the best we're told, stands clueless, as uninformed as the public, ignorant as a lamb on its way to slaughter. I—"

"Wait." Bodie held up a finger, paused a second, then shook his head. "No, thought I heard Shakespeare for a moment there. My mistake. Went all misty-eyed. Please continue."

"A man about to die," Tattoo Face's right-hand man growled. "Make all the jokes you like. It will only hurt more."

"Remember this . . ." Tattoo said. "You are alone right now. Totally, utterly alone."

Bodie saw his point. "Nice of you to remind me." He wasn't ready yet, so he drew out the time and gave them pause for thought. "I have people on my side. People out there who I have faith in, who I trust to have my back. They *will* be here." He nodded at the wall. "Eli Cross—a forty-three-year-old redneck who made a Saudi Arabian prince lock up his own son for the crime of burglary. Eli took the Fabergé, but the son rots in prison. Of course, Khalid was sympathetic to terrorists too . . ." Bodie raised a brow. "Then we have Sam Gunn—techno geek, preener, intelligent, and geller of hair. Weird kid. Has all the hallmarks of a ladies' man, yet I'd bet my bollocks he masturbates to Justin Bieber songs. Once hacked the CIA and sent a dozen field agents, countrywide, to a dozen different zoos. Specifically, the monkey house. You work it out. Then there's Jemma Blunt—job planner extraordinaire, good thief, with deeper morals than a nun and a soldier's sense of honor. You'll want her at your next breakout party, believe me. Finally we have a big slab of dynamite—Cassidy Coleman. You'd better watch your backs, boys, because they would never leave family behind."

He paused, rethinking. "Don't ever tell Cassidy I said that about her. She'd hang me out to dry. The muscle, the distraction, the killer in every single way you can imagine. I once saw her heft a drug kingpin to knock four guys off their Harleys, then stuff 'em, bikes and all, down an abandoned well." Bodie shrugged. "Probably still there."

Tattoo Face had been listening, and now nodded without emotion. "They with you right now? Here?"

"Ah, no. Not really."

"So it will be *you* that is hung out to dry. Dropped down the well. Sent to the monkey house, yes?"

Bodie bit his lip and smiled, sensing the guy hadn't fully understood. "So long as I don't have to tug it to Bieber, I'll take that."

Another hesitation, and then Tattoo Face had had enough. His lieutenants were waved through, and they came around both sides, together, weapons raised. Bodie was pleased to see only one gun, but it was the gun he needed.

He would have to tackle them three at a time. Bodie was ready. First he brandished the shiv, mostly to breed uncertainty and make somebody think twice. The man who slowed slightly interrupted their flow. Bodie could focus on the two frontrunners. His second tactic was to run *at* them, taking them by surprise.

Pocketing the shiv to ensure he didn't lose it, he ran inside the first man's baton swing, jabbed at the throat, and then spun, elbow smashing the second man point blank in the nose. Blood spurted, followed by a gurgling scream. The first man tried to shake it off, the second looked up to the skies, eyes watering. Bodie grabbed him by the waist, employed his strength to fling him around and into the upcoming third man. They tangled, both went to their knees.

Bodie was under no illusions. This was going to go against him, and fast. Surprise didn't last, and prisoners would always come back for more. Tattoo Face went for him, but Bodie still had a plan. Earlier he'd filled the empty plastic water bottle with small stones; now he used it as a weapon, cracking the leader across the cheeks with a hefty swat. The impact stopped the man in his tracks, made him grunt and clutch his cheek. Bodie threw the bottle at the next man, catching him between the eyes, another fortunate strike.

Luck always ran out.

Bodie struck at the man with the gun, coming around and out of the protection of the sixth attacker without warning. The gun exploded, a bullet passing beneath Bodie's armpit and lodging harmlessly in the prison wall. Bodie used every ounce of his combat training to disarm the man quickly, but it just wasn't enough.

He grabbed and broke his assailant's wrist, twisted the gun, then felt a blow to the back of the neck that sent splinters of agony straight into his brain. He fell to one knee, feeling the blood flowing already, assuming he'd been hit by a length of pipe. Twisting, he saw the glint of a blade and just managed to avoid the thrust.

The blade withdrew, came in again fast. Bodie skipped away, deliberately slamming the man with the gun. The man overbalanced, went down on one knee. Bodie tumbled into him, hands jabbing cruelly several times a second. An eye went out, the throat cartilage broke. The gun fell to the dirt.

Bodie grabbed it and spun, but not quite fast enough. The knife skimmed his body, breaking the skin at the side of his ribs, slicing through the flesh.

Nothing punctured.

Win, win.

Realizing he had to focus on those assailants rearing up from behind, Bodie kicked the knife wielder in the sternum as hard as he could, gaining just a few precious seconds. Three quick shots then took three vicious lives. After that, he rolled back to the knife holder, twisted the man's wrist and broke it, managing to jerk the weapon free.

He came up holding the gun and the knife, his assailants reduced to three, plus one still clutching his damaged throat.

"Not your battle." Bodie waved the gun, chest heaving, panting hard. "Walk away now. I have no desire to kill anyone."

They saw the gun, heard the words. Tattoo Face hesitated; his lieutenants actually rocked back on their heels. Bodie pointed the gun to reinforce his words.

"Put it down," Tattoo Face said. "There are many pistols and rifles pointed at you right now. The only reason you live on is the men that paid for this want it public, and slow, very slow."

Bodie gritted his teeth. "So the man that threw me into this hellhole now wants you to torture me slowly and then kill me? What the hell did I do to him?"

"The man that put you here is not the people that want you dead," Tattoo said cryptically. "I will tell you that much."

Bodie resisted the urge to stop, pause, and investigate that comment. Instead, he fired into the dirt at their feet, figuring he should still have at least three bullets in the mag.

"Last warning."

The ground at his feet spat three times, three separate shots from three different guns.

"Back atcha."

Bodie aimed the barrel between Tattoo Face's eyes. "You go first, bro. Remember—you're here to torture and kill me. *I have nothing to lose.* You do. A bullet's the easy way out for Guy Bodie." He grinned more than a little madly.

"Point taken." His adversary backed down, holding both hands up, clearly rattled by the fact that Bodie would die easy rather than face down half a mag full of bullets. It proved the power of the iron hand that held sway over this place.

They moved away. Bodie held the gun on them as long as he could before collapsing, crawling off to the shade, and kneeling, doubled over, holding his bleeding side, shivering with pain. Somehow he still managed to watch the perimeter as he dealt with the cleanup, army training kicking in once again.

"We'll see you later," they had said.

It was scary to know that that would be the end of it, scary to wait. In the end, he'd saved himself to die a few hours later. In the end, he'd done what he had to do—stay alive as long as you can. Stay free until the very last instant. Stay breathing, just stay breathing.

Slowly, the sun began to set.

CHAPTER SEVEN

Bodie managed to stanch the bleeding, pour a new bottle of water over the wound, and clean it as best he could. Even still possessed enough good humor to ask directions to the nearest pharmacy. The good news was that the wound wouldn't kill him. The bad news was that it wouldn't have to.

The wolves were already massing.

Bodie located a new den. A small lee that lay at the junction of several narrow streets, with an unobstructed view, a brick wall at his back, and several escape routes. No doubt better places existed in here where a man might hide. Right now, he had no friends and no prospects.

A passing family saw him and quickly moved on, feet no longer dragging in the dirt. Such an unusual sight in prison that Bodie let his eyes follow them. But this was an unusual prison. A preacher walked by, looked hard into his eyes, and gently shook his head. No words were exchanged. A nearby guard gave him a look of resignation, and shifted his gun between hands.

The last cinema reel of his life consisted of those who passed by against the prison backdrop.

They came well after darkness fell. Bodie's watch read 22:30 hours. The moon was full, blazing a silver shimmer over what would be one of the last scenes of his life. They made no effort to come stealthily, instead shouting his name, smashing baseball bats against their hands, brandishing homemade shivs and a rather impressive machete. They came with so much anger, hatred, and intent to murder, Bodie wouldn't have been surprised to see the Grim Reaper creeping along behind them.

He rose, struggling, holding a hand against his side. The blood had ceased to flow hours ago, but the pain still came in waves. Training taught him to compartmentalize, but training had never included this scenario.

Interestingly, Bodie noted there were only four of them. This meant they were the cream of the crop—no thugs or bullies this time, only hardened, seasoned fighters. Professionals. If he was lucky, he'd take one down before the others obliterated him.

Don't make a stand. Survive.

Out of options, Bodie took it straight to them. The baseball bat was the easiest weapon to handle, so Bodie attacked the man head-on. The move didn't surprise his opponent, it was simply accepted. The bat came down in a short swing; Bodie ducked under, only to meet an upcoming fist. He twisted away, dug two hard jabs into a kidney, and then dived to the right. Left a winded opponent behind, but an opponent still very capable. Machete Man came in next, whirling his weapon like rotor blades, spinning sharpened silver death before Bodie's eyes.

Bodie rolled quickly, desperately, to the left, putting as much distance as he could between himself and the attackers. He raised the gun, hidden until now. They pounced at him, four men coming as one, but he wasn't distracted. The first and second bullets took Machete Man in the meat of his body, the third passed between attackers. He had no time to line up another shot. He ran, ignoring the pain as adrenaline fueled his steps. Pounding up a set of stairs that led to a house, he leapt off the far end, hit the dirt street, and changed direction. He jumped onto a fully loaded dumpster, grabbed a ladder, and used it to scramble up to the rooftops. His pursuers weren't shaken off, and were closing in.

Bodie sprinted across the first roof, uneven concrete beneath his feet, the full moon shimmering above, then leapt over a narrow gap to the second roof. Another dead run, and he gained a third, making his way toward the front gate. A swift glance back showed his three assailants only six meters behind, one of them lining up a knife. The throw came a second later, Bodie luckily able to switch course and jump over to another roof.

Unfortunately this one was made of wooden planks, and poorly constructed at that. The planks shifted as he hit, making him fall. He rolled, chinks in the floor below passing before his eyes. The impact of the trailing men came next, making the planks shift even more and, in two cases, shoot up like medieval trebuchets launching rocks. Bodie clung on as the timber he lay across rose, then slammed back down, battering every bone and nerve in his body. He scrambled up, used his hands to launch off, and ran headlong for the next opening between roofs. The boards shifted beneath his flying feet.

With no time to waste, he launched toward the next roof, twisted in midair, and fired off another bullet. This one took his closest pursuer in the arm, made him grunt and stagger and trip up the man behind.

Score for me. In the next instant, though, he realized, in all his planning, he'd misjudged the distance between roofs. His back struck the edge of the next building, sending blades of fire up and down his spine, but the momentum still wasn't enough to carry him over. The next second he was thudding onto the street.

Bodie was curled up but hit the dirt hard, every molecule of him jarred and bouncing and screaming. He landed on his side, the gun skidded away. The breath was smashed from his body. For a long moment he lay stunned, unable to move.

In that time his three attackers made their way to him, laughing now, none the worse for wear following the chase, ensuring the gun was safe, and then moving closer to his wracked body.

"Get up," one of them said.

Bodie looked up to see the man's face framed by the enormous round moon. The light made both of them squint.

"Well, that was fun," Bodie managed. "Would you like to do it again?"

"Up." The man kicked him in the ribs. The pain made Bodie's blood rise and sent his nerves back into overdrive.

"All right. All right. Hold yer horses, boys. I'm trying."

"Don't try anything." The man's English was good. Bodie guessed languages were an important commodity to an enforcer.

"Me? As if."

Bodie struggled to his knees. Blood seeped from the knife wound. Grazes stung his temple and his right arm. Impact bruises ran down his right outer thigh.

"Don't worry," he said. "Nothing broken. I think I'm okay."

Somewhat unsurprisingly since he'd skipped the chase, Tattoo Face sauntered up, fresh as the morning's sunrise and grinning ear to ear.

"Not much of a chase, my friend. I expected better."

Bodie guessed there had been more men tracking from below. "Not my fault they changed the gap between roofs. I'm complaining to the governor."

His pursuers gathered. Bodie didn't move, but stared up at Tattoo Face, capturing every iota of the man's attention.

"You can tell me now," he said. "Doesn't matter anymore. Who put me in here, and who ordered the hit?"

"In here?" The tattoos creased in mirth. "I guess that's no big secret, my friend. The man that put you in here is named Jack Pantera."

Bodie fought the rush of shock, and, truth be told, if he hadn't been already kneeling, he'd have been on his way down.

"Jack?" The word crawled painfully from his throat as if attached to barbed wire.

"Ah, you don't like that? Good."

The first blow was a knee to the face. Bodie couldn't have moved right then if he'd been injury-free. The pain didn't register, the hard ground was nothing. They dragged him back onto his knees, and Bodie wasn't sure he'd ever moved.

"Jack . . ."

Mentor, friend, counselor in more ways than one, Jack had molded Bodie. Integrated him into the dark underground world of relic smuggling where a man was never safe, and a deal could never be said to be complete until both parties were a country apart. Betrayal was the name of the very complex game.

Jack Pantera had transformed Bodie from a top-flight thief wanting to switch from a life of crime that targeted mostly innocent individuals, to a world-class procurer of artifacts who, at least physically and mentally, harmed nobody that didn't deserve it.

Another blow, and the blood was flowing freely from his nose and a split at the cheekbone. His ribs pounded. His body was a great slab of hurt.

"Pantera would never do this."

Tattoo Face stepped aside then, and three more men approached. Not Mexicans. Their tattoos were different, darker, harsher. On their faces, nothing was expressed except his own terrible death.

"These men were ordered to carry out your execution. Not me."

Bodie stared at them, instantly knowing they were not inmates, not of this continent. But who the hell were they? And why . . . why him?

Gonna die without knowing. Shit.

The new men came in close, hands made into hard fists, tattooed down to the knuckles. Bodie was transfixed, though the end of his life approached. The old adage slammed at his mind like an incessant jackhammer.

Survive. Survive. Survive.

I did well. But never lived up to my promise.

Bodie raised his face, defiant, gathering himself for a final onslaught. No way would he let them take him without a damn bloody last fight.

A shot rang out. Nothing like the handgun he'd used; this was new and military grade—a Heckler and Koch, if his ears weren't playing tricks. On the surface that didn't tell him a whole hell of a lot, but what he was certain of was that nobody chasing him around this prison had access to one. That left various groups from the SAS and Delta Force to HRT and GSG9. Either way, it was an interesting intervention.

More shots followed the first. Darting figures were everywhere along his peripheral vision. Then Tattoo Face collapsed midstride, a bullet shattering his chest. The attacking force took no chances, riddling everyone in the vicinity with bullets. Bodie finally got a look at them.

Clad in camo, with full-face masks, flak jackets, and bristling with weapons, they were about as intimidating as an attacking force could get. Special Forces teams were usually quite small, but this was ten strong, and had to have more support close by. They came in formation, firing constantly and carefully, spreading the Mexicans out and lacing the three unknown men with lead. Those who returned fire were killed. Bodie saw a handful of guards attempting to intervene and then saw them gunned down.

This new team meant business, all right.

They ran up to Bodie, guns down, lifted him under the armpits, and pulled him along between them with his feet barely dragging.

Still laying fire down at every head that popped up.

Bodie let the situation claim him. The pain was immense. The mental anguish was almost overwhelming. If this were his team, they would have let him know. So after ten days in hell, another crew had assaulted the prison to break him out.

What next?

CHAPTER EIGHT

Cassidy Coleman dried her long red hair with a towel. The shower had steamed up her room, obscuring all the windows, but she didn't have to check that she was alone because none of the security procedures she'd put in place had been tripped. Naked, she stood for a moment, clearing the glass of her second-floor window so she could stare out across the golden beach and shimmering Acapulco Bay, far across the Pacific, taking in the calmness and the breadth of it all, the natural wonder of the vista.

Although usually outgoing, loud, confident, she enjoyed the quiet moment before dressing, then grabbed her gear. They were ready for tonight; all they needed was to assemble and get going. Cross had suggested 9:00 a.m. in the lobby. The plan was set. They would hit the prison hard and retrieve Bodie. Finally, their critical inaction was at an end.

She exited the room with no intention to return, found the elevators, and made her way down. The lobby area was busy, conversation rolling in from every corner. Cross, Gunn, and Jemma were waiting for her in the far corner, the quietest place they could find and one from which they could keep an eye on the parking lot.

"All good?" She sauntered up to them, stopped, and planted her hands on her hips.

"Yeah." Cross was studying the vehicles outside, squinting hard.

"You forget your contact lenses, old man?"

Cross didn't even look around. "Go to hell."

"I just got here."

"I think we all need to move out," Jemma said. "Once we get close we have some setting up to do."

They hefted their backpacks, lowered their caps, and headed out into the sunny parking lot. A bellboy stared over, but made no move to follow. A large SUV crunched up to a free spot, reversing in. The skies were bright blue and the temperature already climbing as the team walked toward their van.

"Idyllic days," Jemma remarked.

"I prefer London," Gunn grumbled. "There's nowhere like the place you were born, and it's too bloody hot here."

"Yeah, you got that right," Cassidy said. "Nowhere like a fume-choked, overpopulated, underfunded hive of wealth, poverty, greed, and dog-eat-dog. I love it there."

Gunn glared. "Where were you born, Miss USA?"

"Look at me, fool." Cassidy lowered her voice. "Where d'you think I was born?"

"Hollywood," Cross said.

"Close enough."

Gunn made a neutral face. "I never actually knew that."

"Well, I never actually tell anyone."

"You get any movie roles?"

"A few. Bit parts, you know? Mostly after I learned to fight. Catwalk model turns to MMA, that kind of thing."

"Really?"

"Yeah, it was shit, and I was much younger."

"Forty?" Cross sent over a bold grin.

"Ooh, says the senior citizen over there."

"Age doesn't impede you, Cass. It's an experience that *enables* you."

"Yeah, yeah, whatever, Grandpa."

"I wouldn't mind seeing one of those movies," Gunn persisted.

"I bet." Cassidy laughed. "Maybe one day I'll reveal a title. Maybe. You gotta prove yourself to me first, Gunn."

The tech geek turned away. "So I understand. Being the only nonfighter in this group really pisses me off."

"Yeah, sucks, doesn't it? You gotta put yourself in harm's way to get real respect from soldiers, dude. Sitting behind a desk, no matter the results, just isn't gonna do it."

The van they'd hired was large, powerful, metallic gray, and comfortably held five people with an abundance of room in the back. They'd left it parked in a quiet corner. Cross flicked the remote at it and a double beep sounded. Lights flashed. Cassidy shrugged off her pack and prepared to stow it in the back. The soft, warm breeze and glowing sun rays caressed her shoulder for a moment.

Nice to have the sun on my back again. We've been to far too many places, crawling in and waiting for the darkness, risked too much, not to enjoy a moment like this.

The roar of an engine brought her instantly back to the present. She pulled the pack close, opening the zipper, and turned around.

A black van, similar to their own, swung in alongside them. Two men wearing sunglasses occupied the front. There was no telling what might emerge from the rear. It could be innocuous, but their team hadn't avoided capture and death for so long without taking immediate precautions. Cassidy put a hand inside her pack. Cross slipped to the rear of their vehicle, taking Gunn with him. Jemma was as streetwise as any of them, and followed Cassidy's lead.

The other van's side doors flung open, and legs emerged. Cassidy pulled out a brand-new Glock and fell to one knee. Jemma covered her exposed side with another weapon. The man who exited wore black trousers, an expensive jacket, and mirrored sunglasses. Then another identically dressed man hopped out.

Cross covered them from the rear as Cassidy moved quickly to the front. No words were passed, but then neither were any threatening movements. It was all very neutral. Cassidy had seen it before in the ring, when a fighter wanted to call a truce. What came next surprised them all, though—three soldiers dressed in camo, weaponless, fanning out to the sides of the first two men.

Cassidy glanced down the line at Cross and mouthed, "What the fu—"

Then Jemma squealed in joy.

Cassidy snapped back, finger tightening on the trigger, only to see Guy Bodie step out of the van. Her initial reaction was open-mouthed shock, her second one to put away her weapon.

Bodie just stared at them.

"Nice hotel," he said.

"We were coming to get you."

"How many days?"

"It wasn't that easy."

"Probably not. My own poolside margaritas weren't quite as nice as yours."

"Fuck's sake," Cassidy said. "Quit whining and get in here for a hug." She spread her arms wide.

Bodie looked like he wanted to embrace her, but hung back. Cassidy looked properly at him for the first time. Bruises, grazes, dried blood in several places. The man looked beyond weary. And yet he stayed with the people who had clearly rescued him.

What else is going on? More importantly—who are these guys?

No one moved, still cautious. Bodie sat himself down half inside the black van. They must have driven him straight here after the breakout. Cassidy decided the hell with it and started to walk forward, choosing to talk to Bodie.

At that moment the final pair of legs swung out, these belonging to a woman. She was tall with curly blond hair and an attractive and wise, lived-in face that offered up a worldly expression. Perhaps that was her standard expression. Who knew?

"Hey," she drawled in an American accent. "I guess you guys are *the team*." She emphasized it only slightly, and not in a malicious way.

"Cassidy Coleman." She walked in close, staring hard into the new woman's eyes, gauging the mettle there.

"I'm Special Agent Moneymaker. You can call me Heidi."

Cassidy shook her head slightly. "So your name's Heidi Moneymaker?"

"Since the day I was born."

"Wow. That's cool. I like it."

The two women sized each other up. Neither moved a muscle as the warm local breezes played through their hair. Both teams' members watched carefully, but with a relaxed attitude.

Bodie breathed shallowly, his aches making him groan. "The long and short of it is that Heidi and her special ops team broke me out of that prison just a few minutes before I would have died. I owe them my life."

Cross came over. "And who do you work for, Heidi?"

A tight smile came over her face. "America."

Cassidy blinked. "You're CIA! Are you kidding me? You mean to say that the fucking CIA broke master thief Guy fucking Bodie out of a Mexican prison? I don't fucking believe it."

Cross looked equally flabbergasted. "And the big question of the day is—why?"

CHAPTER NINE

"You need to come with us," Heidi told them. "I have a relic hunter story to tell you."

Bodie frowned. His rescuers hadn't spoken much on the way here, only expressing the urgency of their journey, feeding him water, food, and painkillers, and advising him to rest. Heidi was quick to assure that he was in no danger, and Bodie, always suspicious but wanting to believe in new friends, accepted her words.

Of course, he had hardly been in a position to protest. It took hours for the painkillers, food, and water to really make a difference, and by then they were nearing Acapulco. Nobody had spoken about his life, his job, the prison, or the attempts on his life. Heidi had explained who they were and their intent to rescue him, but nothing beyond that.

"No point explaining it twice," she told him.

He'd been hoping they were reuniting with his team. Now that they had, he felt elated to see them again, but didn't want to express his feelings too much. That wasn't his nature. Instead, he kept it inside, using it to regain his edge.

Heidi indicated that there was a safe house about three miles away, toward the older part of town, and asked Cross to follow them. Bodie stayed with the CIA agents instead of joining Cross and the others. Wouldn't hurt to keep his team wondering. He still had questions about the eleven-day lag between his abduction and their operation to find him.

Ten minutes, and they pulled up to a dirty curb. An agent pulled the door open and jumped out, then popped his head back in to give the all clear. Hands on weapons, the others followed. Heidi urged Bodie ahead. He fell in behind them, seeing his team lined up alongside their own van.

"You coming?" he asked, flashing a grin.

"Always." Cross would leave his side only in death.

"Cassidy?"

"Don't be a dick. Of course I'm coming."

"Jemma? Gunn?"

Gunn squinted over, uncomfortable without four walls and a computer desk around him. Jemma shrugged in a relaxed manner, happy to go with the flow.

Cassidy leaned in as they headed for a battered metal door. "Glad to see the teeth survived."

Bodie grinned, then put the light show away. "Can't lose my biggest asset."

"They're your biggest asset? Man, most guys would refer to something else entirely."

"Some people just aren't that honest." Bodie winked.

Heidi glanced over her shoulder. "Says the world's most infamous thief."

That shut them both up. Heidi waited for the metal door to rattle open, then showed them up a narrow flight of stairs, through two sets of dilapidated-looking but strong and closely supervised doors, and then a claustrophobic corridor where their shoulders rubbed each wall. Bodie knew it was all set up for security and defense, but was still glad to reach the inner sanctum—a sizable room replete with sofas, armchairs, drink machines, TV, and several working communications devices. The only window was smeared with dirt, no doubt deliberately, and the door to the kitchen stood ajar, a wondrous smell wafting through.

Bodie's taxed body and deprived taste buds exploded into life. "Oh God, what is that?"

"Homemade chili," Heidi said with a smile. "Who said the CIA can't party?"

"Funny thing is," Cross said quietly, "I never met a CIA agent that admitted they were a part of the agency."

"Ah well, that may be true," Heidi said. "But the reason for that is about to become very apparent."

Cross acknowledged her candidness with a bow of the head. Bodie made his way to the coffee machine, the window briefly, and then the comfiest-looking part of the sofa. Gingerly, he settled down.

Cassidy flopped herself beside him, shaking his bruised bones and slapping a bloodied knee. "How's it hanging?"

"Ow."

"Oh, that bad? So, you find out who screwed up our last job and sent you to jail?"

Bodie let out a deep breath. "I'm still trying to get my head around it."

Cross leaned forward. "Is that a yes?"

"Jack," Bodie said tonelessly. "Jack did it."

Now it was the entire team's turn to look stunned. Even Cassidy was taken aback; she knew how much Pantera meant to him, knew what they'd been through.

"But Jack . . . he treated you like a son."

Bodie shrugged. "Second time in my life I got orphaned, then."

Cross finally found breath. "But why? *Why?*"

"You can all ask him when you see him." Heidi stepped to the middle of the room, eyeballing each member of the team in turn. "But for now, I want you to listen to my relic hunter story."

Bodie studied his team as they rose, brewed drinks, and settled down. They owed the CIA agent this—at least *he* did—and they knew it.

"What's going on?" Heidi began. "That's the foremost question on your minds. We have an interesting scenario. An intriguing one. Guy Bodie has been a thorn in our side for years. International relic smuggler. Purveyor of ancient artifacts, stolen at great risk, but with expert planning and execution. Admired and hated by criminal and police organizations the world over. You are a rogue, a villain, a specialist, and a connoisseur, and your team isn't far behind you. Special teams from all walks of life study your jobs as works of art. And yet it took just one man to bring it crashing down. A man you all loved and trusted."

Bodie's eyes flashed. "Do carry on."

"I mean no disrespect." Heidi held up both hands, and her curls bobbed. She shifted so that she could see everybody at the same time, and Bodie caught himself watching her long legs a little too closely.

Jesus, Guy, I know you've been in prison a while, but get a grip.

But he guessed Heidi could handle herself. She was here. She'd found them and executed an operation before his own team was even close. That fact by itself demanded admiration.

"You guys have everything you need?" She looked around. Cross held up a steaming coffee mug and nodded. Cassidy settled back with water, long red hair draped over the back of a padded chair. Jemma and Gunn sat forward in expectation.

"What's going on?"

"All right. As explained, the CIA broke Bodie out for a reason. To follow a map, and so you and your team can help us discover lost relics. But I'll get to that soon. Apologies, Guy, but if we didn't need you, we'd have let you rot in there until you were dead. Some still think it's the best place for you." Heidi mimicked balancing weights. "And I'm holding them at bay. But we need results." She took a breath. "The Statue of Zeus," she said.

Bodie stared, waiting for more, but nothing came. "Is that supposed to mean something?"

"Well, does it?"

Gunn tapped his knees, imitating himself using a laptop—one of his more annoying habits. "If you mean *the* Statue of Zeus, then yes, we know what you mean."

Heidi nodded. "Good."

Cross looked over at Bodie and mouthed, "Do we?"

Bodie shrugged and mouthed back, "Roll with it."

Heidi glared at both of them. "*The* Statue of Zeus," she said, "was one of the Seven Wonders of the World. You're familiar with those, I guess?"

"The Hanging Gardens of Babylon." Cassidy nodded.

Cross snapped his fingers. "Pyramid of Giza, right? The only one still in existence."

"The Lighthouse at Alexandria?" Jemma added.

"I'm more interested in the seven wonders of the modern world," Bodie admitted. "Shakira. The V12 engine. Jean-Claude Van Damme—"

"Stop there," Heidi said disapprovingly. "We're on a timetable here, and I'd like you to respect that. The Statue of Zeus at Olympia was a colossal figure seated on a throne, created around 435 BC by Greek sculptor and artist Phidias at the sanctuary of Olympia, Greece. Around it was erected the Temple of Zeus. A sculpture of ivory plates and gold panels, it depicted Zeus himself seated on a throne festooned with precious stones and ebony. It was destroyed during the fifth century AD, and no copy has ever been found. It was said that a single glimpse of this statue would 'make a man forget all his earthly troubles.'"

"We could do with some of that now," Bodie said. "So what has breaking me out of a Mexican jail got to do with a two-and-a-half-thousand-year-old obliterated statue?"

"A bit of background. The statue was erected at Olympia, yes? Which was the original site of the Olympic Games. The statue was there near the beginning and during the ancient games. No single account out of hundreds agrees on how it was lost, and we're talking an immense piece of art, people. Old-school, here"—she nodded at Cross—"was right about the Giza pyramid being the only surviving ancient wonder."

At that, Cassidy laughed aloud; Gunn and Jemma sniggered. Bodie waved it down. "Cross doesn't like to be reminded that he's the oldest of us."

Cross glared. "Let her carry on."

Heidi, despite her urgency, looked slightly embarrassed. "Right, well, this brings us to a recent event, which I'm sure you're all familiar with. Except you, Bodie, since you were on vacation."

Cassidy guffawed at that, clearly warming to the CIA agent. "Kicking back with the boys."

Bodie stared at them both. "Eleven days," was all he said.

Jemma and Gunn both looked uncomfortable. "About that—" the dark-haired American began.

"No time," Heidi said. "Work out your issues later."

"What's the rush?" Cassidy was always the most fiery.

"Because several hours ago, the Archaeological Museum of Athens, one of the world's foremost museums, was destroyed in a presumed terrorist attack. People were killed. People were injured. That's why."

Bodie sat back, mouth suddenly dry. "Destroyed? My God. Is that why you broke me out?"

"No. But it *is* related, and it's no coincidence. It proves we're already behind."

A somber silence fell over the room. Bodie eventually said, "You mentioned the word 'presumed.'"

"I did. The world has been told, through news media, that a suicide bombing was carried out in Athens. The CIA, well, we believe that the entire event was meant to cover up a theft."

"They killed all those people, devastated all those families, to steal something?" Jemma said, her tone revealing utter disgust.

"The kind of people we're dealing with have no regard for life. No morals or regrets. No matter what is in their way—your husband, mother, even your child—they will sweep and smash and strike it away without thought, without any concern, an act that would actually ease their anxieties rather than exacerbate them."

"Which people?" Bodie asked.

"We'll get to that. Now do you see why we're in a hurry? The man that perpetrated this act is on the run with whatever he stole. He's running back to his master. And, in truth, we're absolutely terrified that he might do something like this again. Today. Tomorrow. Very soon." She looked around the room. "We need to catch this man and recover what he stole. Before they strike again."

CHAPTER TEN

Bodie listened hard, as Heidi Moneymaker explained more details.

"Information came to light a few weeks ago. Excavations at Olympia are, of course, ongoing, as they are at so many ancient sites across the world. An old map was found, nothing spectacular at first. But, on examination, this map was thought to reveal where the Statue of Zeus was taken after it was dismantled and stolen in the fifth century AD."

"So, not destroyed?" Gunn asked.

"That was always one of the theories. That it was stolen, transported away, and later razed in a great fire. The map, though early in its assessment, appears to support this theory. We kept apprised of the findings, as we are apt to do on many continents, in so many diverse situations."

"For the good of America," Cross muttered.

"Let's not get into that. Once the map took on a significant role in the search for a lost treasure, and more people became involved in its study, we took a sharper look. It was then that we understood what we were dealing with here. A map that, through the travels of the Statue of Zeus, would lead us straight to the door of the enemy who stole it and now shapes the world's greatest and most devastating events."

"You're talking about a switcheroo." Bodie squinted in thought. "Instead of following the map to the treasure, you're using it and the artifact to track down the secret HQ of . . ."

"The Illuminati," Heidi finished.

Bodie found he couldn't speak for a moment. Cassidy, never at a loss for words, blurted her reaction without thought. "Don't be so fucking stupid!"

Heidi smiled grimly, no doubt expecting this reaction. "Well, that's what they call themselves, even though they're not quite the organization a thousand conspiracy theories would have you believe. We'll come back around to it another time. Let's say that *somebody* stole one of the ancient wonders of the world for their own private viewing, someone immensely powerful, and that this map tells us where it is—and consequently where they are. Let's just say that. And I might add—they've already demolished a museum to cover up the theft."

"You're sure only the map was stolen? How can you be sure?"

"Our agents entered with the first responders. You want the truth? We already had an operation planned. Nothing on this scale, of course. But the United States wants that map."

"The group you mentioned," Cross said. "I thought these shadowy, all-powerful organizations were a myth. I mean, they don't really exist. It's all fiction, right?"

"Then you're fucking stupid," Heidi bit back. "And naïve beyond belief."

"Listen," Gunn put in. "Internet whiz kid here. Conspiracy-theory specialist. I've read it all, and I gotta say—if the CIA state that the Illuminati exist, then that's good enough for me." He paused, blinking rapidly. "On the other hand—the CIA do love their false flags."

Heidi inclined her head in his direction. "So the man that stole the map is currently taking a low-key route, returning to the man that sent him. We need to locate him and take back the map. Understood?"

"What do the locals think?" Bodie cut in. "The cops?"

"They're not involved."

"And by that you mean you can't tell them, because *you* want the map."

"You got it. Is that a problem?"

Bodie stared at Heidi, seeing all the arguments in her eyes, the pros and the cons of the CIA plan. He was a thief—victimless or not, expert or not, he still broke the law. The CIA broke him out of a Mexican prison. Without them, he'd be very dead right now. They could put him back there. They could clap his whole team in chains and drag them back to the United States. Drop them into a black site forever. The responsibility was his—as conveyed by Heidi's hard, unwavering gaze.

"I have to ask something," Gunn said, still tapping at his knees. "Why us? I mean, Jemma and I are understandable—strategy and tech support that rivals the best in the world at what we do: plan heists. Cross is a bit long in the tooth, but even with all the cataracts I guess he's still a pretty good thief. Cassidy? Good to look at and handy in a fight, but not a lot up top. And Bodie? Is it the teeth?"

"We're *thieves*," Gunn continued. "Don't you need SEALs or Rangers or something?"

"Well, Team SPEAR would be good, but they're MIA for now. Don't ask. And don't underestimate your own effectiveness. Ancient relics are incredibly valuable, and not necessarily in monetary value. Bad people have few actionable weaknesses, but one thing they seem to have in common is a deep desire to possess the unattainable. We need cunning, intelligence, street craft. We need experienced, resourceful witchery. We need military-standard muscle. We need a hard-assed team of fighters. Oh, and on top of that we want clear deniability, and, at the end, we're gonna need the best thieves on the planet."

"Really?"

"How does stealing one of the ancient wonders of the world grab you?"

Cassidy squirmed. "By the balls."

Gunn nodded. "Yeah, you got mine too. That does sound appealing."

Bodie didn't want to play, but saw the attraction. "You want our expertise to help track this man, the one that stole the map, then nab him without using your own agents. If we're caught, we're just a group of international relic smugglers. Chasing an ancient map. I get it. You want to bring down the Illuminati, recover the ancient wonder, and return to the US covered in glory. A bold plan, Miss Moneymaker. A bold plan. But tell me—what do we get out of it?"

"Ah, the typical question out of the mouth of a crook," Heidi said. "How about no more devastating events at the behest of a mob of old, all-powerful asshats? Fuck the ancient statue," she said. "How about a safer world?"

Bodie knew she meant it. There was more to Heidi Moneymaker than what they saw on the surface—much more. It was refreshing to find an agent who cared as much about strangers as she did her career, country, and orders. Not unheard of, of course—there were thousands of agents who played it straight and narrow. Problem was, in the global game, they were as rare as pearls.

"All right," he said. "You got me intrigued."

"And *your* balls?" She raised an eyebrow.

"Consider them well and truly grabbed. Where do we go from here?"

"The man we're chasing is known as a Hood. An elite member of an elite team of assassins that works directly for the Illuminati. Of the passengers on four buses and one train that left Athens directly after the explosion, only two had fake passports. The Greeks didn't know they were fake; they don't work as fast as us. One is a forty-five-year-old woman . . ."

"And the other?"

"A thirty-eight-year-old man that didn't exist until the age of fifteen. It's the Hood."

"Where?" Jemma asked.

"Larissa. The bus he was traveling on was stopped and searched. They released it eighteen minutes ago."

"Next stop?" Jemma's brain was already working through scenarios.

"Thessaloniki."

"Then we should get going. That's a long way from Acapulco. We can talk more and plan en route."

Heidi sighed as if she'd known this all along. "Jet's already running. Five minutes from here."

Bodie rose with the others, leaving their drinks and trappings of normality behind, heading into the unknown. He took a moment to wonder if this might be the turning point in his life, the junction where all futures were possible, and then joined the chase to the CIA jet.

One thing was certain—the future was looking up.

CHAPTER ELEVEN

Xavier Von Gothe kept Baltasar on the phone as long as was necessary, extracting every last morsel of information from the murderous acolyte. The man was a monster, for sure, but a dependable and necessary one.

"The museum at Athens was a required destruction," he assured Baltasar now. "They sealed their fate when they accepted the map. It does not matter that they did not know; it matters that we remain where we have been since the beginning."

"Invisible," Baltasar said.

"In the seat of power," Xavier corrected. "By any means."

"Yes, Master."

"I am exalted. I am the glorious one. My reign is all-conquering. Do you know what they will say about me in one hundred years, Baltasar?"

"No, Master."

"That I ruled with majesty, implacably, and with the organization's well-being at heart. Always Illuminati. Always first. You will be happy to know we consider the Athens event a complete success."

"That is good to hear, Master."

"So make your way back, Baltasar. And be invisible. The authorities are clueless, but even a stumble can sometimes lead to good fortune. You know we have other events planned in most cities and towns around the world. If you need our help, Baltasar, tell me. Staying quiet is not the answer. Not today."

"I understand that what I have in my possession is important, Master."

"Important? No, it is not important. It is a fundamental piece in history, *the* crucial requirement to our future. And to think it has lain hidden, unnoticed, in Olympia for so long." Xavier shuddered so badly that goose bumps rose along his arms. "Frightful. We have been vilified, outlawed, imprisoned, and worse, particularly by the Roman Catholic Church, but this is the worst news I have heard in decades. It scares me like none of these media-driven disasters ever could. Because *I know* that that map leads straight to our door."

Baltasar said nothing. Xavier sighed, sensing trouble. "You do not approve of Athens, my young acolyte?"

"I just worry that one of our own may have been inside, Master."

"Nonsense! That is ludicrous. The society would never hurt one of its own. Of course, the word went out to the chosen few. And only the herd suffered. Do you weep for the herd?"

"No, Master. They are there to be sacrificed for the greater good."

"And?"

"What they think and believe is not relevant. But they must always believe the opposite."

"Good." Xavier wrapped a black cloak around himself. "Their weakness and grief turn their eyes inward and away from us. Now tell me, where are you?"

"We have just resumed, Master. Thessaloniki is the next stop."

"Good. Call again only if the need is great."

Xavier ended the call, thinking hard. Baltasar was the best of the Hoods, the Illuminati's branch of superassassins and first-class agents, but even excellence was no gauge of loyalty. He was not carefully recruited, not even a member of the inner order, and by no means an Illuminated Minerval. And yet he *was* Xavier's choice, and thus one to be taken care of.

Xavier rang a bell to summon a maid, and ordered a pot of tea. He sat down behind a mahogany desk, the seat plush, black, and leather trimmed. In front of him, all he could see was the narrow strip of glass—a large window that looked over some rather impressive snow-tipped mountains. Lavish sofas sat to both sides of his desk along with low, expensive tables holding decanters of brandy at their centers.

The walls were ornamented by brass fittings and large portraits—every one a long-dead leader of a secret society that had been misunderstood and maligned since May 1, 1776. Their mission—to oppose religious influence over public life and abuses of state power, to combat superstition—was very likely as close to perfect as any society would ever get. Xavier thought their methods may have changed through the years, but the world needed a steady hand to guide it, to take it through wars and recessions that it never knew it needed to survive, to help take the good with the bad, to look beyond today's atrocity and see tomorrow's promise. *My path will not always be easy, nor without tragedy and the herd's loss, but I will ensure that I stick to it, and that they follow it.*

Events like the museum destruction were one of the keys to overcoming adversity, but in the right amount—staged only occasionally, they were more shocking and led to a better overall outcome for the organization. They would employ every trick in their arsenal to help guide the world toward the right path. The real reasons behind some of the most notorious and terrible global events were known only to the Illuminati leaders of that era.

Xavier stared out the window, then accepted his tea from the maid. She didn't speak, and he barely noticed her. His thoughts revolved around his ancestors and all the incredible trappings of preeminence and supremacy they had amassed.

From the object of the moment—the Statue of Zeus—to the Ark of the Covenant and all of the lost Fabergé eggs, from the bones of kings to the robes and rings of magicians, from mysterious superancient objects to future weapons capable of global destruction.

They had it all. And most of it was stored with the statue.

Complacent? Maybe. *Confident?* Utterly.

Xavier knew the discovery of the map might lead to their true, secret headquarters being exposed. Even their leadership, composed of politicians, masterminds, literary geniuses, influential millionaires, diplomats, and royalty, risked being revealed. A centuries-old world order was in the balance.

But plans, like a chain of explosions, had been set along the route of discovery. It would take a very dedicated group of individuals to get even halfway without failure or death. Xavier imagined few groups to exist, and his resources would get the better of them.

The game, as they said, was on. And there was no player who could beat Xavier.

CHAPTER TWELVE

Bodie took a seat in the jet and closed his eyes. Spending time in a Mexican prison sure took it out of you, and he hadn't had the time to recover properly. Physically and mentally drained, a little alone time was just what he needed.

Cassidy Coleman plonked herself right down beside him. "Y'know, Bodie, I said time and time again that I wanted to hit that place and break the door down. They said it was too risky, but in the end that's just what the frizzball did—and, hey, it worked!"

Bodie sighed. "Frizzball?"

"That CIA chick with the hair."

"Ah, Heidi. Well, I appreciate the sentiment, but I'm sure you all had my best interests at heart. And no harm done."

"No harm? You look worse than crap on toast."

"Aww, thanks. But Cassidy, I know you—impetuous, hard, physical, and always wanting to be the hero. You need somebody like Cross to temper your recklessness—"

Cross leaned over the aisle as the engines began to spool up. "Don't forget she's thirty now too."

Bodie smiled despite his pain. "Ah yes, the big three-oh. I'd forgotten."

"Yeah, and you'd best forget again. Any more of that shit and I'll personally dump you both back into that prison. Or worse."

"Well, I was about to say, next in our merry band of hunters is Cross. Career thief, slow, redneck, slooooow." Bodie grinned as Cross turned away in disgust. "Somewhat paradoxically, he needs you to keep from getting stale. You guys feel like a great mix. So between you and the backroom staff—Jemma and Gunn—I'd say we have a compact, useful, and effective team." He paused. "Bit slow on the uptake, though."

Jemma turned around in her seat. "Backroom staff?"

Cassidy shook her head. "Are you pitching us for a job?"

"I think we already have one. Is anyone else in shock about what they just heard?" Bodie asked.

"Wait," Jemma said with a little venom. "Backroom staff? Really? And you put me in the same sentence as Gunn?"

Bodie shrugged. "Been a while since I saw you in the field, Jemma. But I guess Gunn's never been out there."

"Gunn's a pussy," Jemma grumbled. "And lately, I'm often more useful as the overseer, back at base."

"All very true," Bodie said to Gunn's annoyance.

"So maybe I'm not backroom staff? And Gunn's still a pussy." She laughed.

Cassidy bounced in her seat, sensing prey and always happy to work on a new victim. "Take it easy, girl. Gunn's still not entirely sure what that means."

"Ahh."

Gunn clearly decided it was time to make a stand. "I think you will find my work is invaluable to the team." He ran a nervous hand through gelled hair. "Isn't it?"

Bodie guessed it was time to stop teasing Gunn. "Don't play into her hands, Sam. She's a predator; the only way to shut her down is to stand up to her. Cassidy—you happy with the new arrangements?"

The redhead shrugged. "Not worried either way so long as we're together and working hard. Jemma and Sam are the ones with morals."

"We all have our honor," Bodie said. "Ex-soldiers-cum-ex-criminals-cum . . . what? Government agents?" He laughed.

The jet sliced through the air, buffeted by high winds. Heidi used the seatbacks to climb her way along the aisle and get close to them. "Watch the TV," she said, "if you need any more persuasion."

Bodie sat in silence as a news report came on the TV positioned just below the bulkhead at the front of the plane: coverage of the Athens museum. The team sobered quickly. Devastation filled the screen, drifting smoke and shattered walls, ambulances and police cars strewn left and right, those structures still standing casting a sad shade over the whole scene.

"If the Illuminati did this," Jemma said, "their membership truly needs to expire."

"Yeah, in every way possible," Cassidy said. "And some that aren't."

Bodie waited in respect until the broadcast finished and then turned to Heidi. "Any news on this Hood we're tracking?"

"We should be able to intercept the bus somewhere around the final Greek stop. Of course, the whole op is unbelievably delicate. We're depending on you."

Bodie accepted the pressure without question. "We'll make it work."

"Remember, this Hood is the best of the best. Maybe even better than you. Do not underestimate him." She paused. "Or his bosses."

Cassidy choked on an olive. "Better than us? What you smoking, bitch?"

Heidi laughed, taking it in the spirit it was meant. "Just be careful and fight hard."

"Story of my life."

Gunn spoke up then. "We're not fighters. We're thieves."

His team stared at him, but none laughed. For the first time since he'd met Gunn, Bodie saw real surprise and acceptance dawn on the young man's face. Finally, he was starting to understand the kind of people he'd fallen in with.

Cross broke the silence. "I like to consider myself a man of many talents. Able to adapt to any situation."

"All the best thieves can and do," Bodie said. "I started young. Parents died whilst I was at a birthday party. Orphans adapt or die, and they do it very quickly. They learn to live with what they get, and forget what they once had. Except sometimes . . ." He closed his eyes. "Late at night."

For a moment the only sound was the rumbling jet.

Then Bodie went on. "Adapt to hatred. Adapt to prison. Adapt to real life again. Hatred. The cycle, it never stops. I—" He stopped himself, conscious he didn't want to reveal too much, and aware that Sam Gunn was also an orphan—a fact Bodie found hard to live with because the few other orphans he'd ever dealt with turned out to be selfish, untrustworthy, and downright repugnant. His friends didn't need to know what he'd been through since he lost his parents to a tragic event.

In their favor, though, the children of his foster families were far, far worse than all of the orphans he'd ever met.

"You'd better adapt now then," Heidi said. "We're about to land."

CHAPTER THIRTEEN

Switching quickly to a chopper, Bodie and the others shrugged into flak jackets, thick civilian clothes, and as much disguise as they were able. The mission was simple; the aesthetics of the operation were not. The bus, when they found it, was twisting through a Greek village, following a snaking path around grassy hills. The air was bright, the winds low—perfect to stay on top of the coach at a safe distance. Bodie may have been the first to think about weapons, but he certainly wasn't the first to speak out about them.

"Gun?" Cassidy held her hand out.

Heidi, crammed into the seat across from Cassidy, made an unhappy face. "It's a bad idea. You're operatives on foreign soil."

"Bullshit," Cassidy said. "We're thieves operating alone. That's our forte, yes?"

"A lot of civilians in a bus station."

"Yeah, and we wanna keep them safe."

"It's not you," Heidi said. "It's the Hood. And the event he may call in."

Cassidy wouldn't relent. "I understand. But we won't be as effective. We won't take him down as fast. We won't be sailing at full mast without a friggin' weapon."

Bodie tightened his seatbelt as the chopper veered downward. "She has a point."

Heidi relented with a sigh and handed them used Glocks. "No serial numbers. No provenance. These alone mark you as criminals."

"Don't worry. We won't be as obvious as you guys are, flying around in your chopper."

"It's local. And registered. The CIA is not stupid, Miss Coleman."

Cassidy opened her mouth, but Bodie jumped in fast, scared of what might leap out. "Bad news," he said. "The bus station is right there."

"Damn." Heidi stared out the window. "Change of plan. Land this thing and we're gonna have to comb the station. This is a scheduled fifteen-minute stop." She checked her watch. "We have time."

The helicopter descended fast. Bodie held on. The skids bounced, and then the door was open, flattened grass at their feet. They had landed in a field just a few minutes' jog from the bus station, on the blind side of the small building in order to prevent anyone noting their approach. Bodie, his team, Heidi, and one of the Special Forces soldiers jumped out. Bodie sensed a deep anxiety in the CIA agent and didn't question her accompanying them. They moved across the field, slowed at a large brick wall, then headed for the far side. This would take them into the station and among the passengers.

Heidi sent a glance. "Remember who we're looking for?"

The passport photo was fresh in Bodie's mind. He moved to Heidi's side and pretended they were a couple, sauntering around the wall and into the station. It was the best cover he could come up with at short notice, and to get close to the Hood, they would need it. What they might have been doing behind the wall crossed his mind, and Heidi's too, it seemed, for she inclined her head toward his shoulder. Even better cover.

Three buses sat in the station, divided by shelters. A melee of passengers swarmed the platforms, the road, and the sidewalks, passing in and out of the ticket areas and shops. A hubbub rose to the rafters. Finding anyone in here was going to be a challenge.

Bodie took hold of Heidi's waist and pulled her into the crowd. He met no resistance from her, and kept his hand there, enjoying the closeness and the human touch. It had been a while. His eyes studied every face they passed, every contour slipped under every baseball cap, and mentally removed every tightly lowered beanie hat. Heidi followed suit, scanning face after face, as the rest of their team moved over to the parked buses and the shops.

Eight minutes had passed already. Bodie knew finding the Hood was a tall order despite their skills. The crowds ebbed and flowed, doubled back, and simply wandered. He'd seen the same man with the same Pooh Bear baseball cap three times already.

"All these people," Heidi whispered. "I hope to God the Illuminati don't act."

Bodie felt the same with every fiber in his heart and soul. "They will only act if the Hood feels threatened," he said, "and has a chance to report in. We just can't give him that time."

"Agreed."

A wave of noise washed over them—a party of Greek mothers flowing by. Bodie saw Cassidy and Gunn walk down the side of a bus, checking windows; Cross and Jemma exited a gift shop and entered a small café. No signals were raised.

"This would be easier with comms," Bodie said as they walked. "Next time?"

"I hear you," Heidi said, then smiled. "But only because I'm right here. Yeah, you're right. Next time."

Bodie was pleased the CIA agent could manage a witticism or two. The prospect of the next few days and weeks would be even more gloomy if she'd proved to be a stick-in-the-mud.

A hundred faces had already passed him by, but the next face made him do a double take, for it was moving against the crowd.

Bodie allowed his eyes to relax, his gaze to drift past the Hood. If the man was that highly trained, it wouldn't do for Bodie to let his eyes linger too long on him. The Hood was taking a diagonal path toward a vending machine, backpack clutched in his right hand, and it was the unerring angled route he'd chosen, against all the random human tides, that made him stand out. Maybe he was used to people getting out of his way, maybe he didn't notice them, but either way Bodie made him and nudged Heidi's hip with his own.

"My two o'clock. Possible sighting."

Heidi slowed, glanced casually. Her sharp intake of breath verified his claim. They quickly modified their own path so they were on an interception course, but sauntered still, arm in arm. Bodie gauged the distance to his weapon. Heidi steered them a little further afield, scared the Hood might detect them. When Cassidy and Gunn reappeared around the back edge of a dirty bus, they dared not make any signal. It was Bodie's hope that Cassidy would see their purpose.

Not to be. She's too busy scolding Gunn over something.

Heidi saw it too, her face unimpressed. The Hood made his way to the vending machine and dug in his pocket for change. He bought a can of Diet Pepsi. Bodie and Heidi came up steadily behind, still a dozen steps away. The Hood secured his backpack over his shoulders, then paused and spun around.

He hurled the can directly into Bodie's face.

Bodie was surprised, but instantly glad it hadn't been a knife or even a brick. The Hood had made them and used the best weapon he could find on short notice. As Bodie staggered and tried to stop blood flowing from his nose, the Hood made a break for it, straight into a gaggle of passengers. To her credit, Heidi was straight after him, looking to give chase.

Bodie struggled to hold his nose and wondered how well trained she was.

The Hood threw passengers left and right, each one getting in another's way. Heidi tried to skirt them, but became entangled with an older man. The Hood burst out of the pack and ran toward the back of the buses.

Straight into Cassidy Coleman.

Bodie tried not to smile. Fortune had favored them. The Hood saw his mistake almost instantly as Cassidy squared up to him and Gunn fell in behind. The Hood hit Cassidy head-on, punching and kicking, but she managed to block each blow. Bodie forced himself into action.

If anyone else was watching, they were already in deep trouble.

The Hood disengaged from Cassidy, sizing the redhead up anew. Bodie had seen it happen dozens of times—men and women at the top of their game suddenly forced to reevaluate their prowess when confronting the American.

The Hood lunged forward again, forcing her back. Bodie ran harder, now joined by Heidi. Together, they approached the scene. Cassidy deflected and counterattacked, her blows striking with shocking force. The Hood, seeming bizarre in his T-shirt and jeans and sporting a backpack, tried to find a true opening. As he spun he saw Bodie's approach and broke off.

Cassidy went after him.

The Hood took three hard punches, went down, and then rolled. Somehow he managed to rise up, and even Cassidy paused, amazed. People were everywhere, shouting, screaming, pointing. Some now digging out their cell phones. Bodie thought that might spook the Hood more than anything given the secrecy in which his master's existence was held. The Hood backed away fast, quickly evaluating the scene. Turmoil filled his vision. Too many random outcomes and possibilities.

Bodie saw the Hood place a hand in his pocket, probably flicking a trigger that would send a message to his bosses. "No!"

The man never showed a flicker of emotion, no doubt or anger or fear, no remorse, just turned on his heel and ran. Full speed, head down, showing them only the soles of his feet. He was getting the hell out of there.

Bodie turned to stare at Heidi. "He called it in! Now what?"

"Are you sure?" Gunn asked. "I didn't see that."

"Pretty sure," Cassidy said. "Look at him go."

The CIA agent stared at him. "We don't belong here. We can't—"

"Can't what?" Jemma came running up. "Can't save these innocent people? Fuck that." She pulled out her gun, raised it into the air, and fired three quick shots.

Pandemonium filled the bus station.

CHAPTER FOURTEEN

Baltasar knew the event was coming. Something devastating. There was no stopping it. Minutes were a precious commodity, as he had no idea what chaos the masters would bring down. Not just his own master this time, but all of them. For his master worked alongside several others who handled Hoods of their own. It would happen quickly. It didn't matter which town, which city; as soon as they knew his route, they would have arranged something within close proximity of every point all the way to his home, and then potentially all the way to their true headquarters. He had never seen the Grand Lodge so intense, so focused. Because of them, nobody was safe in the world today.

Except him, it seemed.

Baltasar backed away from the tussle, forced to recognize the higher ideal of taking the map he'd stolen to his masters. The redhead with the muscles stared at him hungrily, causing a moment's confusion. It was rare to see an opponent still standing after a skirmish, let alone wanting more. Baltasar had not seen it since the training ground, and it made him slightly nostalgic.

A few more moments with her . . .

The network of old wounds that crisscrossed his body began to itch. Baltasar forced himself away, using every ounce of will, and then ran, remembering he was relatively blind now and had no idea how many his enemies numbered. He raced away from the bus station.

It was coming. Three minutes gone, and time was short.

The backpack bounced on his back; inside it, the map, a relic his master held in higher regard than every life on the planet.

Baltasar's peripheral vision caught the sudden onslaught of two more people—a young woman and an older man. Both looked in good shape and were wearing flak jackets underneath their clothing. That put them in league with the redhead and the others.

Baltasar saw no way past them, and no option to slow down. He truly had no idea as to the scope of the event that was coming. Directives said "get clear." For those on the ground, in the thick of it, directives were occasionally a little vague.

Baltasar met the black-haired woman head-on, dipped, and let her slide over his back. Still, she managed to drive a knee into his thigh, causing the muscle to bark in pain. Another interesting contest. The older man came next, stance betraying a belief that he could hold his own in this battle, but telling Baltasar he was no match. The Hood slammed an elbow at the face, then a jab to the chest, a spinning kick that sent his opponent crashing to the floor with a tremendous double bounce.

Baltasar didn't stop for even a second. The bus station ended up ahead—a retaining wall dividing the passenger area from delivery bays and other distribution areas. Baltasar slowed and looked back as he reached the wall, intent on quickly evaluating the threat.

The things he saw, despite his training, would live with him forever.

All this mayhem to cover one person's escape.

He saw a bus driven by a madman, grinning and animated at the wheel. He saw the speed at which it was going, the back tires skidding out of control, the entire vehicle leaning to the right. He saw the arc of its journey, and its destination. He saw travelers spot it and run and scream, heard shots being fired by the men and women who had accosted him, causing panic.

The careening bus struck the back end of one that was already parked, the fanatical driver standing up just before impact, arms in the air and pumping. He wore a suicide vest. The aftermath would paint him in only one way, and, although Baltasar had no idea who these people were, he did know that his masters regularly called on their handlers and spiritual leaders to apportion the blame. They were puppets, bent on achieving a twisted goal, with no idea they were being used by those truly in power.

Civilians ran, jumped, screamed, leapt out of the way. Those seated inside the parked bus didn't stand a chance; they never saw it coming. Sounds of terror filled the bus station. Many inside the shops and the café dived for cover. Baltasar saw four members of the team he'd fought and watched their actions.

The redhead and her geeky friend started sprinting as soon as they saw the bus, sensing the event. The geek was all for himself, head down, aiming for cover; the redhead shouted loudly as she went, herding individuals into her path. The other two—a woman with curly hair, and a tall, clean-shaven man with dubiously white teeth—grabbed as many people as they could, shouting for more to follow. They ran for shelter. The curly-haired woman fired her weapon into the air.

Whatever the reason, whatever the effect, it was a gesture too late. The bus struck its target and exploded. A fireball stormed the air, radiating outward as a massive explosion struck the bus station. Concrete shook and crumbled, windows shattered. A shock wave knocked running bodies to the ground, saving lives. Debris punched outward at a deadly rate—twisted metal and shrapnel, glass and plastic—a killer storm set alight by the deadly, blazing fire.

Baltasar embraced the mayhem. It was his shroud, his mantle. Something to hide behind and make use of. Now more than ever, he knew he would need all of his wits, guile, and considerable training.

He would not be able to use the bus or the train, except perhaps upon reaching Hungary, Austria, or even Germany. The route remained open, though, and he was ahead in every way. All they had managed to do so far was slow him down.

And look at what they had brought down upon themselves.

One tactic his masters used was to make a positive end result prove too costly for an interfering government. In any way possible. If his attackers back there were government funded, their wings were about to be clipped.

Baltasar fancied that they were something else, though. A diverse mix—like soldiers and hired mercenaries. Confident, tough, resourceful. Their presence would be worth mentioning to his master.

As soon as he got away from Thessaloniki.

CHAPTER FIFTEEN

Bodie understood one thing immediately: if he had thought the prison was the worst kind of hell, then he had been very, very wrong. Hell was right here, right now, for everyone affected by the incident and its aftermath.

Although he had lived an outgoing, streetwise, dangerous, and often violent life, nothing had prepared him for this. The sheer trauma caused by the moment of impact, the terrible shock—he would never forget one second of it. Upon picking himself up, he found a piece of metal shaped like a dagger just lying next to him. Ragged, deadly, it showed him the difference between those that got lucky and those that didn't. Injured civilians lay between him and the bus, most sitting up, some lying still and groaning. The area in which the explosion happened was a parking bay—fortunately not a place many people lingered. The only ones injured were those returning to the bus.

Flames billowed through the broken windows, so hot they warped the metal frames. Black smoke plumed toward the sky. What struck Bodie at first was the absence of noise, no screaming or yelling, no running. The nightmarish unreality of it all lay over the scene like a fine mesh, waiting to crack.

Through the chaos, Bodie saw Cross and Cassidy—the ex-military man and the conundrum—checking the wounded, shepherding to safety those who could stand and hobble, dragging those who couldn't. Bodie forced his body upright and then checked himself for damage.

A figure loomed next to him. He blinked. It was Heidi Moneymaker, regarding him with haunted eyes, a dripping gash across her forehead.

"All this . . ." she gasped. "For *him*. For the Hood. We . . . we failed."

Bodie reached down and unclasped the gun from her fingers. "Don't blame yourself. The people that did this are the worst kind of evil."

Heidi put a finger to her temple; it came away bloody. "Did I get hit?"

"Yeah, just a scratch." Bodie walked her over to the vending machine and, in a particularly surreal moment amid the chaos, paid for a bottle of water and used it to clean up her head. Jemma was on her knees, talking to a man with a shoulder wound, and Gunn was sitting with his back to a wall, dazed.

"It'll be fine." Bodie gently dabbed away.

Heidi grabbed his hand. "We have to go."

"We can't. They can't. *I* can't. We can't leave people like this."

Heidi's face creased with anguish. "The cops are on their way. They catch us and the Hood gets away. The Illuminati will never be found. We've never come this close before, and they'll make sure we never do again."

Bodie heard sirens and made a decision. Head still spinning, he moved into sight of the members of his team, signaling them. One by one, they ran over. Cassidy came last after helping a young woman sit up and bind a deep cut on her arm. The redhead was dotted with blood—none of it her own.

"Emergency services are almost here," he said. They could see flashing lights in the distance. "We should get clear. Jemma?"

"Wait," Cassidy said. "People need our help."

"Three minutes," Bodie said. "They'll be here."

"Not the point," Cross said. "If one person bleeds out because we—"

"If we don't go," Heidi said quietly, "the people that planned this attack will stay free to plan the next. And the next . . ." She spread her hands, her laceration still weeping blood. "We're behind already."

Bodie nodded. "She's right. Look, better people than us are coming to help them," he said. "We can do it a different way."

Reluctantly the team looked to Jemma. "Plans are pretty straightforward," she said. "If Heidi can get the chopper moved there"—she nodded to the field beyond the station—"we can make it and take off behind that ridge." Bodie saw a progressively rising crest to the right of the station. They would be a speck before anyone might catch sight of them.

"But," Heidi warned, "once clear, we have to lie low. If luck is against us, they'll be hunting us next. It may even be that the Illuminati use their influence to point the finger our way."

"We're almost out of Greece," Jemma pointed out, walking faster.

"You keep mentioning these Illuminati bastards." Cassidy spoke the word like it was a bad taste in her mouth. "I think you owe us a more detailed explanation. Who the hell are they?"

Heidi nodded, focused ahead. "I agree. Let's just get clear first."

She wiped her forehead with the back of her hand, and looked sadly at the devastation.

Bodie spoke quietly. "You're not to blame, Heidi."

The CIA agent nodded grimly. "Oh, I know that. I just look back there and wonder what I'd do if my own daughter had been involved. I . . . I . . ." She shook her head, unable to finish.

Bodie saw the complex emotions waging war on her face. A human disaster always wrenched the humanity of anybody who wasn't already dead inside. He placed an arm across her shoulders and helped her to the chopper. They didn't look back. The authorities had more than enough to concentrate on. Bodie considered their stand on keeping everything quiet, an American operation, but again decided the pros outweighed the cons.

"Any of you have kids?" Heidi asked suddenly as they approached the chopper.

The lack of an answer was answer enough.

"You never stop worrying," Heidi breathed. "Not even for a minute. Even . . . even when they refuse to speak to you."

Bodie knew the agent was feeling overwhelmed with the human suffering she'd witnessed during the callous attack. He helped her onto the chopper, and remembered Cassidy's comment about the Illuminati. It would help redirect her mind.

"Heidi," he said. "Tell us the worst of what we're up against."

"References to the Illuminati first appeared in the 1700s. We don't know why, since it's also been said the *first* member of the society was Adam. Their original goals were noble, worthy ones. To help oppose superstition and halt abuses of state power. But power itself can corrupt even the incorruptible, and it's believed the rotten apples soon infected the entire cart. Early roots were dropped in Bavaria, blamelessly, but it wasn't long before they, along with the Freemasons, were outlawed. Now, of course, they could continue only underground, and this act alone helped contribute to their change of ideals."

"You're saying the man that outlawed this new society actually made them a worse kind of enemy?" Gunn asked.

Heidi met his gaze. "I'm saying look much deeper than that. Read between the lines. Burrow among them like a snake, a venomous snake. What do you see?"

Bodie knew. "That somebody—deep inside the Illuminati—orchestrated events to make it happen. They planned for the society to be taken underground."

"Yeah. Once there, it gave them a new kind of freedom."

"No rules," Cross said, rolling an aching shoulder.

Cassidy glanced at the oldest member of the team. "You okay, Eli?"

No banter. No bickering. Bodie saw the anxiety and concern generated by the event on all their faces, knew it was reflected on his own.

"I'm good," Cross said.

Heidi continued as the chopper flew low over the treetops. "So the secret society was born. Legends grew. Some were true, others fragments of the truth. It all helped seal their notoriety. We do know that the Illuminati were responsible for many events that shaped our world today. The French Revolution. The outcome of the Battle of Waterloo. Even the assassination of JFK."

Bodie raised his eyebrows. "Shit, you're telling us that was for real?"

"Well, the last is unsubstantiated. But, judging by the other two events, it's viable. They have agents planted worldwide in governments, corporations, and the police force. If they want something to happen, it generally happens. They shape their own future, as they see fit to arrange it. They congregate in 'lodges' and aspire to higher 'degrees' of participation and even rank through different colored lodges. It is only the higher degrees that are privy to the innermost secrets and far-ranging plans. I would state categorically that those below a certain level have no clue as to the monster they nurture, encourage, and support."

"And the Hoods?"

"A whole different savage. The Hoods are loyal to the Illuminati to the point of death. They are, quite simply, unquestioning foot soldiers. They would bring a building down to kill one man. Kill thousands as a distraction. They would raze anything, anyone, at their masters' command."

"So they can't be reasoned with," Cassidy said seriously. "Good to know."

Heidi looked at her, equally honest. "Do not talk to them," she said. "Do not show them mercy. Kill them."

"Not a problem."

Heidi waited for the chopper to land. The team climbed out, and it departed. Their flying days were at an end, for a short while at least. They seated themselves around a clearing beside a dusty road, waiting for a car to arrive. Heidi continued her brief history.

"With Lodges, Grand Lodges, and Premier Grand Lodges, the Illuminati's structure became murky. No doubt yet another agreed intention. Grades were equally incomprehensible. The Nursery. The Scottish Knight. The Mage and the Priest. They sprang up outside Bavaria, around Germany and the United Kingdom. Their influence grew. And they survive to this day."

"Despite the conspiracy theories? The scorn? The disbelief engineered in people when they imagine the things they read in books may be real?"

"Tell me," Heidi said, "what was the greatest trick the Devil ever pulled off?"

"To convince people he wasn't real," Jemma said. "Obviously, that's fiction."

Heidi nodded. "Of course. But the message stands. The public gets fed all its Illuminati knowledge through Hollywood, the daily rag, and Internet conspiracy theorists. It's entertainment. Escapism. If they thought for one minute even half of it was real, there would be a rebellion."

"Hollywood's a part of it?"

"Imagine the most influential dens of wealth, power, and iniquity on the planet. It is inside all these that you will find the Illuminati and all their followers."

Cassidy rose as a black SUV approached, her hands hovering close to her weapon. "Back to the real world, and where to next? The Hood won't be using the bus anymore, or the train. My guess is he'll be finding a car. Just like we are."

"Agreed." Heidi squinted at the SUV. "Public transport is a big no-no for him now, and the map, of course, is everything he cares about. He will never stop."

Bodie made a move toward the parked vehicle and spoke to Heidi. "Have you guys had any contact from your men at Athens? Surely copies of the map were made."

Heidi made a face like she was sucking on a nettle. "You'd think. You really would. But archaeologists . . . they're an odd bunch. Secretive. Distant. Unsociable. A decent archaeologist wouldn't breathe unless he'd first assured himself it was authentic. They keep quiet, work hard, sharing their findings only among trusted friends until they can share it with anyone else. And, to be fair to them, their findings are judged, evaluated, and discussed the world over. They have to be sure."

"So, you're saying . . . what?" Bodie shrugged.

"You don't photocopy a relic, Bodie. But, early on in the examination, you might scan it and send a copy, by email, to your trusted friends. We're checking. Only problem is, the Hood checked before we did. And then he cleansed the museum's system."

"Crap. But he's on the run. Ineffective."

"The Hoods are an army. They have people everywhere. Now get in. We have a lot to do."

CHAPTER SIXTEEN

Xavier Von Gothe watched news coverage of the Thessaloniki bus station "terrorist" attack with deep satisfaction. Baltasar was free, untracked, and unscathed. All was well—the single hitch now the amount of time the journey was taking. Every moment was a pain in Xavier's side.

Such a delicate journey, with the most fragile of relics, surrounded by devastation.

The media speculations continued. Xavier tuned them out, preferring to fix his thinking on the truths that only he knew. A race was still a race, if conducted painstakingly. And this race was now well and truly begun. It reminded him of the ancient relic that had started this series of events—the Statue of Zeus that had once stood at Olympia and witnessed the early Olympic Games. Once one of the Seven Wonders of the World, it had come under Illuminati control in the 1800s. In truth, it was a recruitment tool—one of many used to entice wealthy men when one needed something unattainable to look upon.

Was there anything more unattainable than an ancient wonder long thought destroyed? Every man had his vices, but this . . .

May have undone us all, Xavier finished cynically.

But the rare moment of weakness passed quickly. Xavier took a moment to be surprised at himself. It was certainly past the time for another purification ritual. He wondered what fresh delight they may have down in the basement . . .

The phone rang. Xavier knew immediately who it was.

"Yes?"

"I am clear. The event has worked. All is well."

"I am aware, my acolyte. The bus and the train, however, are also now impossible. Your papers are in order?"

He was referring to Baltasar's ID in his own outdated way.

"Yes, Master. I have them right here."

"Then proceed by car." He knew he did not have to tell Baltasar this. The man was trained beyond the highest level. Everything he told his acolyte was mere reassurance, simply a way of *being there*.

"I am sorry for the delay."

Xavier smiled. "It cannot be helped."

"And the team following me?"

"We are searching our records. The moment we have something useful I will contact you."

"Thank you, Master."

The line went dead. Xavier replaced the receiver thoughtfully, reflecting on this new team and what might be their true objective. For certain, they were not Greeks. They appeared a mismatched group. But time would tell. His people were on it.

Of course, the appearance of unknown newcomers and the slow rate of transport now threw into light yet another of Xavier's problems.

He walked to the single picture window, and studied the far-off vistas. A snow flurry harassed the top of a distant mountain, such random fury unleashed with nothing to show for its efforts. The Illuminati he saw as the mountain; the herd—common civilians—as the wrathful snow.

Somebody at the Archaeological Museum of Athens had forwarded the map to four different people before they and the computer system were rinsed clean. That meant four other people required visiting, and their computer systems sanitized with extreme prejudice.

The Hoods had already been dispatched. He switched his attention from the snow scene to the enormous TV on the wall. He split the picture into four separate screens and watched each one in earnest.

The operation was nearing its end.

CHAPTER SEVENTEEN

In London, a man with thick hair and the kind of gaze that never stops shifting walked out of an overpriced coffee shop with a hot drink and a muffin balanced precariously on one hand. He loved his morning ritual—the fast, calorie-burning, fifteen-minute walk there and back, the cappuccino, and the blueberry feast. All this before returning to what he saw as a humdrum existence chained to an office desk, and party to only one-fifth of a large window that overlooked a busy road and a few straggly trees well past their sell-by date. People-watching passed time and offered a small diversion, but the desk, the lab, and the computer screen were George Stroup's lot in life.

A day rarely passed when he wasn't bored out of his skull, and today was one of those days. George took in the fresh air and the sights as he made the painful journey toward his working day. The cappuccino tasted sweet, the muffin soft and moist.

This was as good as it got.

Wondering if he should start considering a lifestyle change, George saw the entrance to his building and slowed down. The museum could wait. The artifacts could wait. The endless computer entries could wait. It occurred to George that some of the people he worked with might not even know he existed. Was that possible?

He sniggered softly to himself. Possible? More like a sure thing. Perhaps if he had a wife . . . a family . . . but that side of life had passed him by.

George paused beside a black trash can, finished off the coffee and the muffin in one last sweet mixture of ecstasy, and deposited the empty cup and wrapper inside. Said goodbye to happiness and freedom for the next eight hours, and looked up. The path was busy, the roads crammed. Diesel fumes curdled the air, and a big London sightseeing bus cut off a cyclist just as a delivery driver weaved through crawling traffic with inches to spare on either side. Business as usual, then. A thought struck George: he'd been meaning to take a look at the email that had come over from Athens a few days ago. Lethargy had prevented him—lethargy and a severe, untreatable case of "can't be arsed." That was the worst, and might have contributed to this year's substantial weight gain. Interestingly, the bigger he got, the less people noticed him, especially bosses.

That could be your work ethic.

George shrugged and made his way to his desk. The first thing he did was to turn his computer on; the second was to nod at the various colleagues who barely noticed him. Inwardly, he cursed them.

He was about to take a slow meander over to the water cooler when he noticed that the computer screen wasn't doing what it normally did. A horrifying collection of images filled it, pictures he'd never imagined let alone browsed for. At that moment something wrenched deep inside his gut, something fundamental, and without too much surprise or regret or even an iota of fear, he understood he was about to die.

That's odd. Why? These things happen. Bloody cappuccino.

The new guy . . . ?

These were the final thoughts of a man who would not be remembered.

In Paris, a middle-aged woman settled her overlarge spectacles onto the bridge of her nose and tried to read the ingredients in her microwavable croissant. It felt wrong, *it was wrong*. Who the hell microwaved a croissant, especially in Paris? She'd lived here eight years and had never considered such lunacy. She knew of three lovely bakeries within easy walking distance.

Why, then?

Well, from past experience of other microwave delicacies such as popcorn and corn on the cob, she knew it was simple, and stupidly easy. And today that was exactly what she needed.

Joy, she said to herself. *Get a fucking grip.*

Never again. She shoved the croissant inside the microwave, slammed the door, and set the timer. Walked over to the window and sipped her instant coffee. Bloody disgusting. In this direction, many miles distant, lay her homeland. The sweet, sharp hills and narrow, twisting lanes of the Lake District, in the UK. It had been a while. She missed the place, her parents, and her old boyfriend, George. Seven years since they last saw each other, they kept in touch now only through mutual work, and then infrequently. But George was on her mind of late—he had been copied in the email from Athens, two days before the terrorist attack.

Weird? No. Coincidence. Terrible, unreasoning coincidence. Joy considered the email that she'd received, the picture attachment showing the old map and the chance that it might show the whereabouts of one of the world's ancient wonders.

Shit, we have to be so careful. There's a career killer right there.

It wouldn't do to look stupid.

Joy wandered over to the computer and switched it on. Their mutual friend—a man who gladly referred to himself as "Niki for short"—emailed four people the map in confidence. Joy was pleased she had been included.

The microwave dinged. The freak was ready. She opened the fridge to grab margarine.

The click barely registered. The whirr was louder and made her frown. The explosion occurred right in her face, obliterating her from existence before traveling at incredible speed through the apartment, destroying everything in its path, and damaging the apartment next door. Windows blew out, walls collapsed. The computer was swept away by the fire, already cleansed, the Hood long gone through the darker watches of the night.

◆ ◆ ◆

In Milan, an old man sat at an old desk, staring at the screen of one of the oldest working computers in the museum. Like him, it was slow. Like him, it had developed odd issues with its inner workings. Like him, it should be retired.

He enjoyed his job. He loved the pace of the computer. He would rather tinker here than head home and be nagged by an unstoppable shrew. The first thing he noticed this morning was that the computer was sluggish, even by its own standards. The second thing he noticed was that the museum was oddly quiet today. He hoped that, after the incident in Greece, nothing else terrible had happened to the world, prayed not to see the staff clustered around a TV screen.

Not today.

Today was his birthday.

Sixty-eight and counting. The old man still had all his faculties, but most of them were diminished now. Thus, he didn't hear the creeping footsteps nor see the burgeoning shadow. He felt a lance of cold pierce his heart—a premonition—but assumed it was the by-product of a conversation with the shrew this morning. Such things never went well, and he tried to avoid them at all costs.

The first thing he knew was the hand across his mouth. The second, an agonizing pain through the ribcage. After that, the shadow fell across him further as gloved hands reached toward his keyboard.

He died wondering how a man who had lived such a long life, experienced sixty-eight years, had been fated to die at the hands of a silent killer. All that life, that understanding—for what? For this . . .

He fell off his chair, his fall cushioned by his killer, the Hood.

The job was already done and, like the other Hoods before him, this one checked to see if their target had forwarded the Athens email to any others. Damning in the extreme, the Athens email contained a copy of the map.

The old man was left, dying. It didn't matter now. Only the master's command mattered.

◆ ◆ ◆

In Warsaw, Gabrielle said goodbye to her family and headed out the door. A biting wind greeted her, and that was okay. She barely felt it, so consumed was she with the events of last night. Her cheating boyfriend had confessed his third one-night stand in two years. The next few hours were volcanic, fraught. The final few hours she spent with her mother and father, lamenting the end of one more failed relationship.

The walk to her work was short. Gabrielle couldn't remember taking the bus or crossing the busy road junctions. She ended up standing outside her place of work, looking up at the blank windows, wondering if there might be more to life than all this. A career in archaeology had sounded impressive, exciting. The truth wasn't quite in the same league as the thought.

The man came out of the museum, actually holding her computer. Gabrielle knew it was hers as she recognized the yellow happy face stuck on it next to a postcard sent from Athens by her friend Niki.

She opened her mouth to talk to what she assumed was an engineer. Had something happened during the night?

The silenced revolver filled her mouth, the taste metallic, hard, and revolting. She saw a glimpse of gloved hands pulling the trigger and then knew no more.

The killer didn't even break pace.

CHAPTER EIGHTEEN

Bodie evaluated the team at a rest stop. The cuts, bruises, and scrapes they'd already received since leaving Acapulco were surprising when compared to their usual job, but not in relation to this. He was more concerned that they were operating outside their expert skill set. Of course, they all had their strengths, and could mix it up with anyone in a wide range of circumstances, but they were all gifted at one thing in particular—planning and carrying out heists.

The rest stop consisted of a large, curved turnout wider than the main road, with several benches and a burger van. Trees sheltered the clearing from any sun that may threaten pasty tourists, but, Bodie thought with a slight shiver, there was no chance of that today. Sunlight had vanished with the earlier atrocity, and now the skies were a deep, leaden gray, promising only misery.

He perched on a bench opposite Heidi. The CIA agent was just getting put through to somebody via a satellite phone. Out of courtesy Bodie gestured that he would leave, but Heidi shook her head, asking him to stay. The gash on her forehead had finally stopped bleeding.

"Yes, sir," the blonde finally said. "The Hood escaped by car, we think. We're no further forward."

Bodie felt bad about that, but their trip to Thessaloniki had been based on an educated guess, and they'd been at a disadvantage since hopping out of the chopper.

Heidi listened for a while, then turned to Bodie. "They found which IP address belonged to the Athens archaeologist tasked with studying the map and are remotely checking the museum's server to see if he sent out any emails."

Bodie refrained from the pointless comment of legality. This was the CIA. "Didn't the Hood cleanse the system?"

"Yeah, but he can't turn back time. There's always a digital footprint, Bodie." Heidi turned a quick smile upon him. "Always."

What's that supposed to mean? Bodie frowned.

"The best, wiliest, and cruelest thing the American government ever did was convince the public that the Internet meant freedom," Gunn said from behind. "The entire world connected. Freedom like never before. The planet becomes a much smaller place. Freedom?" Gunn shook his head. "Nah. It's the opposite."

Heidi held up a finger to stop him. "Four?" She sounded surprised, then looked down at the table in regret. "Ah, I see."

"Heidi?" Bodie saw it wasn't good.

The blonde muted her phone for a moment. "The fuckers killed them all," she explained in a quiet voice. "Four emails were sent containing the map attachment. All four recipients are now dead. All unwitting, innocent people. Goddamn it."

Gunn plonked himself down beside Bodie. "As I was saying. Nobody's safe anymore."

Heidi ignored him. "They're checking now to see if the four recipients forwarded the emails to anyone else."

"In one way, I hope they did," Bodie said. "As it will give us something to work with. But on the other hand . . ." He paused as Heidi nodded and started listening to her superior again. He took the time to finish his evaluation of the team. Gunn, of course, was being his usual quiet, detached self, a quirk of his high-intellect makeup. Human emotion, especially shared, did not come easily for him. Cassidy was raring to go, desperate to hunt and bring down a bad guy—any bad guy, but the Hood would be preferable. Cross conserved energy by resting on a bench and demolishing a bacon sandwich. Jemma couldn't get the look of sadness off her face, moved and crushed by all that had happened at the bus station.

Bodie listened up as Heidi ended her call. He saw a complex mix of emotion on her face. "What?"

"One of the original recipients forwarded the map to somebody else." She shook her head. "We have to assume one of the Hoods extracted that information too."

"And the bad news?" Gunn asked blandly.

"That is the bad news," Heidi said. "The good news is that he sent it to an address in Istanbul."

Bodie stared for three seconds, then looked to his right. "Istanbul? Shit."

"Exactly." Heidi's face crinkled as she found Bodie on the same wavelength. "We're an hour away from this guy."

Bodie rose fast, then paused. "Awesome," he said. "We need—"

"Chopper's on its way back," Heidi said. "The boys back home are working on some kind of clearance."

Bodie looked surprised. "Above board?"

Heidi's eyes widened. "I'm not sure what that means."

Gunn chortled. "Never break cover," he said. "You should know that."

"And what about the Hood?" Bodie asked.

"He can wait," Heidi said. "One hour there, one hour back. We'll catch up."

Bodie wasted no time rounding up the team. "Okay people, we're making a little side trip. Istanbul."

Cassidy looked over. "What? You need a souvenir or something?"

"The map," Gunn explained. "An email was forwarded over there. We can get the map."

"Not to mention save a life," Heidi said pointedly. "Which is the big issue here."

"I thought the map . . ." Gunn began, then held up his hands. "Oh, never mind."

"Don't you have a team over there?" Cross asked after reflection.

"Sure do. They're heading over now, but we're the infil team. And the extraction team. We're point on this mission, with all the data, so, barring anything critical, we're going in first."

"They will have a Hood stationed in Istanbul," Cassidy said. "Of that you can be sure."

Heidi looked up as the chopper appeared above the treetops. "Then let's not waste any more time."

CHAPTER NINETEEN

Bodie's team and Heidi Moneymaker swept the clouds and the skies apart in their headlong helicopter dash to Istanbul. Nobody checked to see if their way had been cleared; nobody checked to see if their arrival was going to be valid. The life at stake and the map that might lead to taking down the Illuminati was the sole focus of everyone's attention.

A call came in from the Istanbul ground team. "We're outside the apartment," a gravelly voice drawled. "I see your archaeologist at the window right now. He looks fine. Drinking coffee, bare chested. I'd say he's relaxed."

"Alone?"

"Impossible to say at this time. I'll keep you informed."

Cassidy watched as Heidi pocketed the cell phone. "Coffee and a bare chest at this time of day? I'd say he has a lady in there." She glanced at Gunn. "Or a guy. No judgment."

Gunn spluttered. "Why the hell did you look at me?"

"Like I said: no judgment. I mean it."

Gunn looked ready to explode. Bodie wished Cassidy would stick to the mission. "Relax, people. Time is short." He included Heidi in his gaze. "I'm assuming we have no time to prep?"

Jemma sat up. Excited. "Get me a blueprint of the building and I'll work you out the perfect extraction plan. No hassle."

Heidi inclined her head. "I'm grateful, but we really don't have the time. In, out. Sixty seconds max."

Cassidy couldn't help herself, and stared directly into Gunn's eyes.

The geek looked like he wanted to throw something at her.

"Istanbul." Cross was seated near the window. "Wow."

Wide blue waters led to a great bridge and a sprawling city. The white buildings and orange roofs were striking, but then he saw the Hagia Sophia, the fifteen-hundred-year-old building considered to have changed the history of architecture, the incredible dome standing out like nothing Bodie had ever seen before. Staring hard, he knew he'd never be able to take it all in even if he had a week, but then the chopper was swooping down, heading fast toward a discreet helipad.

"Public area." Heidi shrugged. "Only problem will be customs. You ready?"

They were. Their own passports were civilian and had initially brought them to Mexico and then the European continent. Heidi's had been supplied by the CIA.

Thankfully, the customs check was exhaustive but professional. The team was soon beyond and trying to flag down a taxi. Cassidy solved it by rustling up two Uber rides, and they set off, following Heidi's directions.

"Eight minutes," she told them quietly.

Get ready.

Bodie knew Heidi would do the talking. His team would provide support and reconnaissance, while the team already on the ground would be perimeter and weapons. The cars pulled up, and the team got out. Quickly, they made their way to the man they had spoken to an hour earlier.

"Any change?" Heidi asked.

"Not a darn thing." The CIA operative was dressed as a local, looked like a local, and sat smoking at an outdoor café, a half-drunk specialty tea before him. "Nobody in or out. I guess we're a go."

Heidi waited until he'd checked with his colleague—currently lying prone on the roof holding binoculars—and received the same answer.

"Good," she said. "Follow me."

Bodie did as he was told, ignoring the stares from Cassidy and Cross, who were still getting used to the CIA agent leading their team. They crossed a road, waiting for traffic, walked through a dust cloud, and entered the building. Inside, it was small and dingy. Bodie smelled spices, urine, and bleach. The stairs were empty, and Heidi led them up to the second floor.

Raised her hand and knocked at the wooden door. Eight seconds passed before it was pulled open and a bare-chested young man confronted them.

"Günaydin," he said with half a smile.

Heidi stepped back nonthreateningly. "Hi, do you speak English?"

"That depends," the man said, smile widening. "Are you the cops?"

Cassidy laughed, stepping alongside Heidi. "Pretty much the opposite, dude. You sound English to me. Any chance we can—"

Bodie practically jumped out of his skin when Heidi received a text message. She read it aloud: Hood in apartment right now.

"Fuck!" she shouted. "He's stealing the laptop."

The man looked shocked and then scared. Heidi pushed him to the side before rushing in. Cassidy was at her heels and then Bodie, trying not to be impressed by Heidi's fearlessness. The apartment was small, with a window, a balcony, and one door that led to a bedroom. A desk sat in one corner, over which now hovered a man clothed as a civilian, but was clearly anything but.

He looked up, face hard as an ancient redwood. Not even the ghost of an expression crossed those pitiless features, but the promise of death and savagery was evident.

"Put that down." Heidi motioned at the laptop he held in one hand.

Cassidy ranged to the right, Bodie to the left. Nobody expected this to go down without one hell of a fight. Nobody was disappointed.

The Hood could not release the laptop, which hampered everything he did, but he still came at them with speed and fury. He swung it straight at Heidi's head as she closed the gap. She blocked. The Hood spun and used her own momentum to send her tumbling. Cassidy waded in hard as Heidi's blond curls connected with the far wall.

The Hood cracked the laptop into her to no avail, then kicked, spun, and kicked again. Cassidy took the blows for what they were—mere distraction as he eased his way toward the balcony. Bodie stepped forward, trying to block the way, but the Hood reacted instantly and leapt.

"Ground team," Heidi was shouting into her phone. "Move in."

The Hood reached the window, jackknifed through, and landed catlike on the balcony. Bodie was a few seconds behind. The Hood jammed the laptop into his waistband, jumped onto the narrow railing, and then leapt upward, in full flight. Bodie climbed out of the window, looked up, and saw the figure already six feet ahead, scaling the building.

"Sheeyit."

But Bodie had skills of his own. A man didn't become the world's most infamous VIP thief by being inferior on his feet. Using the handrail, he caught hold of a pattern of stones that decorated the building's frontage and used them to pull himself up. Cassidy was at his back, undaunted, and then Heidi, who shaded her eyes to look up.

"I'll meet you on the roof."

She vanished. Bodie propelled his body up fast, bouncing nimbly from handhold to foothold. The rocks were rough and regular, ideal for the quick ascent. The Hood showed him how to do it, though, now eight feet ahead and converging on the roofline.

"Taking risks like that," Bodie said to himself, "it's gonna be the death of you."

Bodie progressed, sensing Cassidy hot on his heels. The redhead would be shouting soon, you could guarantee it. Back in the room she hadn't been able to help secure the Hood, and she'd be as frustrated as a shark in Sea World, stuck behind the glass while the meat buffet strolled by. A lowering sun burned down on them, still hot, especially when you were inches from death. Sweat poured from Bodie's brow, his grip precarious. Once, Cassidy brushed the soles of his feet, grumbling.

Then the roof, and he had to slow once more, worried that the Hood might be waiting. But a glance over the top showed the Hood already sprinting across the level rectangle, laptop clutched in his left hand. Bodie heaved himself over the edge, rolled, and rose. Cassidy was quicker, gaining the lead. The redhead tore after the Hood, and Bodie saw Heidi smash through a door to their right.

"Where?" she cried.

"There!" He pointed.

The Hood was airborne now, leaping across the gap between roofs. Cassidy followed him, closing the distance, Bodie and Heidi trying to keep up. Another roof and then another yawning space, this one wider than the last. Bodie made it with room to spare, checked on Heidi, and saw her clear the gap even better than he. Again, he was impressed, then not sure if his feeling was complimentary to her or quite the opposite. Complex.

And why the hell does it matter?

The next roof was blazing white and cluttered with all manner of trash. The Hood slowed, forced to pick his way through more than one sharp hazard. Cassidy gained at first, then got her foot caught in a wooden crate and had to stop to shake it off.

Bodie passed on the inside, chuckling.

"Fuck off, asshole," he heard her mutter.

Ahead, the Hood leapt across another roof, landed, and rolled twice.

Behind, Cross was keeping up with them. Bodie heard a shout, "Why is she dancing?," followed by Cassidy's profane reaction.

The gap was huge. Bodie ran hard and took off for just a moment before coming down and scraping his knees and elbows. He rolled, rose, didn't give chase until he saw Heidi land at his side. The Hood was still on this roof—a large rectangle—and, perhaps now seeing the futility of the chase, investigating a smoking chimney that jutted out at his feet. Bodie saw what was to come, but had no chance of stopping it. The Hood was still a good ten feet away.

The laptop went down the chimney, falling two floors to the fire below, probably belonging to one of Istanbul's many restaurants. Bodie attacked the man as he spun, smashed a fist against the temple and another to the jaw. The Hood reeled, stepped back. Bodie fought harder. The Hood blocked and danced aside, making space. The face was bloodied and strained, but still lacked any sign of real emotion.

"Who do you work for?" Bodie panted as he fought. "Where are they? Why do you want the bloody map?"

The Hood dropped to one knee, delivering a punch to Bodie's lower groin that dropped him right on the spot. The pain resonated throughout his body, making him retch, even making him lose the power of speech.

Heidi stepped up, closely backed by Cross. The latter was panting hard, while the former was the first to strike. The Hood blocked and counterattacked, making Heidi cry out in pain and fall back. Cross leapt in without thought.

The Hood brushed him off, sending him lurching toward the edge of the roof. Cross managed to catch himself and looked back at the Hood.

"What the hell are you, boy?"

Cassidy reached the fight. "So you *do* have a pair?"

Bodie could only groan and watch through narrowed eyes. Cassidy engaged the Hood from the front, taking all his attention; then Cross came in from behind—a mistake to let the older man remain there, and Heidi was back in from the Hood's right. Jemma came up as Bodie struggled to his feet, hands clasped between his legs, still heaving. Gunn was four steps behind her.

"Nowhere to go." Jemma took out her Glock, aiming it at the Hood. Bodie was confident she wouldn't use it—too much risk all around—but the vicious Hood didn't know that. Cassidy landed a blow at that moment; Cross kicked him in the spine from behind and lost his own footing, ending up prone. Then Heidi struck too, and the ground team finally joined them, Glocks at the ready.

The Hood cast around for a way out, started to run at Cross, but received a flying kick from Cassidy that sent him tumbling right at the edge of the roof. Heidi caught him, pushed him back with a withering glance at the redhead.

"Now we talk," she said. "Or I let the old actress here have you."

Cassidy flexed her knuckles. "Thirty, hon. It's not old. It's pretty damn perfect."

"Aren't we all." Bodie stepped in to help pull Cross to his feet. "Lose your footing, pal?"

"I won't be trying that again."

"Me neither." Bodie grimaced at a sharp pain below the waist.

"Well, look at it this way. Better the nutsack than the teeth, eh?"

Bodie wasn't sure he agreed, and poor old Cross was struggling and trying not to show it. He left the forty-three-year-old to recover and advanced on the Hood.

"What are your orders, ya fucking weirdo?"

"Maybe leave this to me." Heidi held out a hand to stop him. "You remember the big picture? What these people are capable of?"

Bodie backed off. Heidi then turned and delivered four crushing blows to the Hood. The man staggered as everyone winced. The face ran with blood; one arm was broken. Bodie stared at Cassidy in disbelief and Gunn cleared his throat.

"Hey? Is that . . . I mean, bloody hell. Is that really necessary?"

Heidi caught her breath, holding the Hood upright so that he could not sag to the floor. She delivered another intense blow, this time to his solar plexus, then held him in place. "Are you stupid?" she asked. "Do you not remember Athens? The bus station? You saw that and then you ask me if this is 'necessary'?"

Bodie saw that the archaeologist who owned the laptop had followed them and was now loitering at the rear of the group. He motioned to Gunn. "Look after that guy for us, Sam. He could be invaluable."

Gunn looked only too pleased to do so.

Heidi shook the Hood hard. "I want to know everything," she said. "About the map. Your master. Your *life*. Upbringing. Training. If you won't tell us, it will only go downhill from here."

"He won't talk," Cross said. "He's an elite assassin. You'll never get him to say a word."

Cassidy bit her lip. "I have to agree with the ol' boy here. I'm just a failed actress, MMA queen, and underground street fighter. This guy's harder than hardcore." Then her expression changed. "Unless they offered me coconut ice cream. Hey, Hood, you like coconut ice cream?"

The Hood only gasped, now hanging weakly. Bodie knew it was a ruse. "Don't trust—" he began, and then their enemy exploded into action.

He kicked out, driving Heidi away. He danced back, forcing some room, and cast wild glances left and right.

"Nowhere to go," Bodie said. "You can't outrun us—"

But the Hood did run. He ran to the edge of the roof and dived off, plummeting two stories to the street below.

Heidi shook her head. "Shit. No Hood. No laptop. Shit, shit, shit."

Bodie expressed it somewhat differently. "Bollocks."

The entire team then turned to the young archaeologist. Heidi managed a strained smile.

"Hey," she said. "Hey, what's your name?"

CHAPTER TWENTY

They made their way quickly, and with local expertise, back to the helipad and the waiting chopper. As they waited on the tarmac to board, Cassidy leaned in to Bodie's right ear.

"So the CIA agent's the hardest member of our team. Who'd have thought it?"

Bodie gritted his teeth. "It's an eye-opener," he said. "And not necessarily a good one." He then added, "In the long run."

"You're thinking after mission?"

"Always," he said, then shook it off. "But now we have Jeff. Jeff the archaeologist."

"Yeah. I seriously hope he's better than Gunn." She shook her head.

"Oh, give the kid a break. He's more than useful in his own way and you know it."

"I'd prefer someone older."

"Nearer thirty?"

"That age does not bother me," Cassidy said, her tight-lipped comment betraying the truth.

"All right, then. Let's see if Jeff can help."

They boarded the chopper, the new flight path aiming to take them straight back to Greece. Calculations revealed that the Hood they were chasing might have already left the country, depending on how long it had taken him to procure a car, but the reality was they were laboring in the chase now, struggling to catch up.

Jeff crowded in beside Gunn and Jemma, the chopper's interior hot and crowded. Heidi had already given him the brief history of events, backed it up with proof, and backed that up with news coverage of the death of the woman who had forwarded Jeff the original email. That woman had been Jeff's teacher in Oxford, a woman he highly respected. Jeff took it all in, but barely responded.

Heidi didn't want to bombard him with further atrocities. "The map," she said. "It's why we sought you. It's why they sought you. It's why your teacher and her colleagues were killed. What can you tell us about it?"

Jeff gave them a look that revealed his fear, his youth, and his awkwardness all in one go. Cassidy patted him on the knee.

"Don't worry, bud. We're far more dangerous than the guy who attacked you."

"Ah, okay, well . . ." He didn't look reassured. "Miss Brady liked to push me. Saw something in me, I guess. I like to travel, though"—he nodded back the way they'd come—"anywhere there's history, I guess."

"Stop guessing," Heidi said quickly. "I want to hear your damn story before we run out of gas."

Again Jeff looked scared. "Oh, okay. Miss Brady was always sending me something to tax my brain. I think she valued a second or third opinion, or whatever. She sent a map, recently discovered at the Olympia dig site, alleging to show the whereabouts of the Statue of Zeus." He paused. "One of the seven ancient wonders?"

"Yeah, yeah, go on." Heidi waved at him.

"I don't remember it that well—"

Heidi whipped her head around. "What? Do not say that. I don't believe you. You hear me? A young archaeologist gets a message from his revered teacher claiming to believe and know of the route to and existence of an ancient wonder? You'd have been stuck on that like maple syrup on bacon. Right now, boy, you are the only link we have to that map. Our quarry is out there, we don't know where. So believe me—you will remember. *Everything.*"

Jeff gulped theatrically. Bodie leaned over to whisper in Cassidy's ear. "Please don't squeeze his knee again. The guy'll leap through the window."

"It was an old map," Jeff tried again. "I believe it showed the journey of the statue after it was disassembled in the fifth century. From one place to another and where it rests now. All taken with a pinch of salt, of course."

Bodie pursed his lips. "Why's that?"

"Well, because the statue was destroyed around the fifth century AD. There were no copies, no imitations, only images on coins."

"Who destroyed it? Why?" Cassidy wondered.

Gunn cleared his throat as if to speak, but Jeff beat the Internet geek to the punch. "Well, if I remember rightly, it all started with Caligula. The mad Roman emperor? He decreed that all statues of the gods especially revered by the masses should be brought to Rome, their heads removed, and replaced with his own."

Heidi blinked and turned around. "You're kidding, right?"

"No. History sure has placed some megafools on the throne."

"And repeats itself to this day," Cross grumbled. "Go on."

"Well, Caligula was assassinated before that could happen. But when Theodosius banned pagan cults and closed the temples, the statue and Olympia became abandoned. Nobody really knows what happened to the statue after that—lost to history—but the map posited a believable theory."

"Which was?" Gunn asked, flicking around his cell phone.

"That the statue was dismantled and then shipped to Constantinople. This fits because it actually matches one of the original theories."

"Damn," Cassidy said, deadpan. "We've just come from Constantinople."

"Yeah, but it's not there anymore. The old theory was that the statue perished in the great fire of AD 475. The map suggested that it didn't . . ." Jeff paused.

"You mentioned there were no representations of the statue?" Heidi pressed. "Isn't that odd? How do we know it even existed?"

"Well, through the writings of ancient scholars. The engravings on old coins. And we have recently discovered the workshop of Phidias, the man that built the statue, at the very site it was erected. The tools, gold and ivory fragments, and terracotta mold were dated back to the statue's time. The molds were used to create sheets of glass that formed the statue's robes, after which they were gilded."

"So right now," Heidi said, "you can travel to Olympia and see the very workshop and tools and items this Phidias used to create one of the seven ancient wonders of the world?"

Jeff nodded.

"I didn't know that. How incredible."

"Better than gawping at a pyramid, I'd say."

"Any of the other ancient wonders still around?" Bodie asked.

"Who really knows? The Colossus of Rhodes, the Lighthouse at Alexandria, the Mausoleum at Halicarnassus, the Temple of Artemis were all destroyed. It's possible that the Hanging Gardens of Babylon never existed. The wonders essentially came into being because traveling Greeks saw great sights around the world and wanted to list them. It is believed that all seven could have existed at the same time, over a period of sixty years, before the Colossus was destroyed by an earthquake in 226 BC. Earthquakes and fire took most of them, but that was said of the Statue of Zeus."

"So, of the seven, the only ones without a true image are the statue and the garden," Heidi said. "But we digress. The map?"

"How long have you got?" Jeff asked.

Heidi rounded on him. "The longer you take, the more people will die. Do you really want that on your conscience, Jeffo?"

"Of course not. It's just . . . just a bit much is all."

"Take a minute," Bodie said and turned to Heidi. "Where are we with locating that Hood?"

The CIA agent took a deep breath. "Nowhere. We've lost him and the map and any chance we had of finding them. For that—we got Jeffster here. He'd better be worth it."

Now Bodie turned to Jeff with a grin. "You hear that, mate? This is your chance to shine, my friend. Better make it good."

The chopper came in to land, and the entire team transferred to a big SUV. Heidi directed Cross to drive north, purely because the original route of the Hood's train put it on a northern path, twisting through Hungary and, potentially, Austria. The A/C kicked in fast, and Bodie passed around some snacks.

Jeff took a long gulp of water. "All right," he said. "This is everything I know."

CHAPTER
TWENTY-ONE

"I have to say," Jeff began, "that the one thing that made me suspicious, disbelieving, was the one thing that doesn't seem to have occurred to you. I mean, how the hell did this map, showing the path of this ancient wonder from the sixth century to the present day, end up buried back in Olympia, at the statue's starting point?" He widened his eyes. "How did that happen?"

Bodie thought about it. "Actually, that's a good point."

"I'll let you ponder the map's travels and get back to it soon. Miss Brady always taught me to expand on the background first, so I spent a whole lot of time researching the statue, the history that surrounds it, Olympia and the Olympics, and finally the four waypoints shown on the map."

"Waypoints?" Heidi asked. "You mean places where they stopped with the statue?"

"Exactly. Four waypoints, all interesting. The map itself is a map of Europe, with many footnotes. The footnotes are numbered. But it gives us only tidbits at best, and in all honesty I can't remember everything."

Bodie stared at the long, winding road ahead, the horizon disappearing into a haze. They were a long way from the Acapulco job, and even farther from the prison he'd almost died in. The CIA was to thank for saving him there, but this job didn't suit him. So far, they had chased one new clue after another, chased a man across a country, always one step behind and reacting instead of acting. At least three members of his team functioned beyond skillfully only when there was a plan. The other two—Cassidy and himself—could pretty much adapt to anything.

That left three members struggling to catch up.

"Tell us what you know," he said and then looked to Heidi. "And then we craft a plan. Yes? It's what we do. You wanted us, you wanted the best, then *use* us. Use our skills. Our expertise. Use us the right way."

Heidi nodded.

Jeff went on. "It's generally agreed that, one way or another, the statue disappeared in the early fifth century. Through footnotes, the map reveals that, initially, it was dismantled and taken by the Romans. But they didn't enjoy it for long." He paused. "Clearly the footnotes are designed to be read in conjunction with the waypoints, but it will save us time to think ahead."

"Us?" Cassidy repeated. "You part of the team now, Jeffrey?"

"It's Jeff. And I want justice just as much as you."

Bodie waved for him to continue. The SUV bounced over a pothole, and Cross received a reprimand from Cassidy.

"So, the Romans? Well, Rome was sacked by the Goths in 410 AD. They ran riot for four days, committing all manner of atrocities. One of those outrages was to steal the Statue of Zeus, probably delighting in taking plunder from the plunderers. So the Goths took the statue with them, one prize among many, and again it became lost to history."

"But not really?" Jemma asked.

"Well, this was actually the time when all knowledge of the statue faded away. Deliberately, I suppose. Engineered by the man that acquired it."

"Famous, no doubt," Jemma said.

Jeff nodded. "Yes. The Goths may have settled in Spain and Portugal, but they played key roles in a new empire, a little later. The statue was spirited away and taken to the kingdom of the Franks. It came under new ownership, great ownership. It came to Charlemagne."

"The king of France?"

"Well, yes. Charlemagne was the king of France, king of the Lombards, and emperor of the Romans." Jeff coughed. "All at the same time."

"Whoa," Cross said. "Sounds like a dude."

"He was a dude. And obviously his name became legend. Linked to every organization, every conspiracy, every rumor there has ever been. But there was no doubting his greatness. He was the first man to unite Western Europe since the Roman Empire. Thereafter, all Holy Roman empires considered themselves descendants of Charlemagne's empire. Charlemagne also took Bavaria, and spent some time there."

"And the statue?" Heidi pressed.

"Yes. Charlemagne had many homes across his kingdom. I guess you could call him a living legend of the time, and most of the world's collusions and intrigues involved him in some way. Truth be told, I'm not an expert on Charlemagne, but I do know a little of his history."

"Me too," Gunn spoke up, cell phone still in hand. "The man that ensured the survival of Christianity in the West."

Heidi twisted around in her seat. "All right, guys. We get that he was great. What next?"

"No," Jeff said. "The reason I articulated about Charlemagne was to show how *important* he was. The Goths gave the statue to Charlemagne. It then stayed in his family for over one thousand years. That's how important he was."

Heidi nodded, but remained tight-lipped.

"The footnotes point to Charlemagne, and then nothing for untold decades. After that, there was something about Liege in 1869, though I honestly can't remember the details. But the waypoints offer four clues.

We have to find one to get the other. Obviously, I do remember them, as I read and reread them a hundred times."

Bodie had been listening carefully, and now turned to Heidi. "How does this fit with your theory?" he asked.

"Theory?" Jeff asked.

Cassidy shifted. "Well, Frizzbomb here thinks the location of the statue will lead us to—"

"It's just a theory," Heidi interrupted. "And Jeff's a civilian. Let's keep it professional."

Bodie saw they were entering a large town. The road dipped and a row of houses came over the horizon, sprawling as far as he could see. He thought about all that Jeff had told them.

"For me," he said, "the footnotes mean nothing. Not yet anyway. What we need are hard facts that tell us first, where the statue is now, and second, where that bloody Hood might be going."

Heidi agreed. "Yeah, keep it succinct from now on, Jeff. Waypoints, waypoints, waypoints."

Jeff shrugged. "Of course, but there is only one to start. As I said— one leads us to the next. If I knew the whole story I might be able to help more."

"Ah, so you *do* wanna be on our team?" Cassidy asked with a smile.

"Well, I don't see anyone else figuring out how the map came to be found at Olympia in 2017, thousands of years after the statue was moved."

Gunn waved his cell phone in the air, somewhat ineffectually. Jemma looked frustrated. "C'mon guys," she said. "We have no plan, and a team without a plan is just in chaos. We have a lot of information here, but nothing to act on."

Cross slowed as they entered the town, negotiating the narrow streets. Bodie saw parked cars and people meandering among them, the place a hive of activity. "Gonna slow us down," he said.

"On our road to nowhere?" Jemma said.

"She has a point," Jeff said.

Everyone looked at Jeff. "Do you get to comment?" Cassidy asked.

"I think so," he said. "Especially when I have the first waypoint on the map. And also because I know what the map actually is."

Heidi frowned. Bodie stared harder into the young archaeologist's eyes. "What does that mean, mate?"

"The map," Jeff said in a stage whisper, "is one man's account—one archaeologist's account—of how he set out to find the statue in the early 1900s. And of how an exiled and disillusioned member of the Illuminati helped him."

Jeff's ear-to-ear grin said it all.

Cassidy laughed as Heidi rolled her eyes.

"For fuck's sake. Does everyone know about these guys?"

CHAPTER
TWENTY-TWO

"Where is the first waypoint?" Heidi asked.

Jeff closed his eyes, remembering the words. "We returned something new to Spartacus, and 1776."

Heidi blinked. "That's it?"

"Yeah, is that not helpful?"

Heidi narrowed her eyes this time. "It better be if you value your ass, bud."

Jeff gulped and realized he'd overstepped the mark. Bodie tried to hide his own amusement.

Gunn saw a chance to make himself useful. "I could start a search. Maybe combine the—"

"Don't worry," Jeff said. "I already did it."

"Kirk Douglas was great in *Spartacus*," Cassidy said wistfully.

"Shit, you're older than you look," Jeff said. "But this has nothing to do with the movie."

The SUV ground to a halt, faced with an obstruction ahead. Cross cursed at the large white van that had crossed their path, shooting out of a side street.

"What in the hell," he muttered. "Guy's got a death wish."

The van revved loudly as it inched past. Cross waited, drumming the wheel with two fingers. Bodie watched it carefully, giving the high, rusty side his full attention. Cassidy checked the rear. For a moment everything looked harmless.

Then, outside on the sidewalk, Bodie saw the man they had chased through the Thessaloniki bus station. "There!" he cried. "Shit, I'm getting out. Keep it running, Cross."

"Got it."

Bodie cracked the back door open. The Hood, passing along the sidewalk and still carrying his backpack, looked over and smiled.

"No, it's a—"

Somehow the enemy had tracked their route. The Hood leapt at Bodie, expecting surprise, but Bodie was made of far harder stuff than that. Moving forward, he met the Hood and exchanged blows.

What are the chances? Why would the Hood wait here?

The answer soon became obvious.

Cassidy and Jemma piled out of the car, racing to Bodie's aid. Heidi threw open the passenger-side door. Cassidy yelled out a further warning.

"More! To the left!"

Three more Hoods of varying heights came around the large white van, which now completely blocked their way. Cross made to remove his seatbelt, but Heidi cried out, "Stay there. We may need you!"

The older man complied with unease. Bodie glared into the Hood's hard, ungiving eyes. There would be no talk. No compassion. And just like his colleague from Istanbul, if he saw no way out he would certainly try to kill himself. The man was skilled, possibly more than Bodie. He landed blows where Bodie could not, but the wily thief knew tricks the smallest Hood hadn't even heard of.

Using a nearby newsstand he flicked magazines at the Hood, threw bottled water and soda at him. The Hood struggled to adapt at first, unsure where the next attack was coming from or even what it might be, but then blitzed through the onslaught, butting heads with Bodie and pummeling his chest with iron fists.

Bodie fell back, breathing hard. The Hood was so skillful, but then fighting was all he knew. Seemingly unhampered by the backpack, he bruised and battered Bodie, and forced him back onto the road.

Then everything happened at once, the wide-ranging battle coming together. Cassidy launched an attack at the tallest aggressor just as the other three Hoods joined. Jemma jumped in, putting herself in front of their attack, competent, not at their level, but willing to protect her friends.

Cross sat inside the car, engine running. The white van finally moved out of the way, giving him a clear road. Cross blasted on the horn to let the team know. Pedestrians lined the street, some running, others huddling for protection or to take photos. A market stall ahead was disgorging even more people as they came over to find out what the commotion was all about.

Bodie spun as a car, undeterred by the melee, drove past about thirty miles per hour, clipping Cross's side mirror and continuing on.

"Madness." Cross glanced from man to woman, from skirmish to skirmish. "This is utter friggin' madness."

Cassidy fought toe to toe with the main Hood, forcing him back. Cassidy was no tip of the knife, no perfectly trained fighter, indoctrinated from a young age as the Hoods had been. Everything she'd learned was either in a steel cage or on the meanest street. Combine that with rough-and-ready MMA training and you got Cassidy Coleman—she could use every weapon from the tip of her finger to batons and a sword, and though many had tried, she'd never been beaten.

Somebody's out there, she once told Bodie. *Somewhere. Maybe one day I'll meet them.*

She'd said it like she looked forward to it.

Blood ran from above the Hood's right eyebrow and left cheek. To the left Jemma blocked one Hood and tripped another, falling herself but halting their attack. Gunn launched himself atop another, using his weight to stall the man rather than any kind of fighting expertise, which he totally lacked. Bodie felt a small surge of pride for the geek.

Gunn soon received an elbow to the nose, which he rolled away from, groaning. Bodie took it back. The kid was a fucking pussy after all.

Jemma grappled with the guy she'd tripped, holding on to him and taking him out of the fight. Bodie met the medium-sized Hood she'd blocked, coming at him before he'd fully recovered. Three swift blows and the Hood was gasping.

Then Heidi came around the side of their car.

"All right," she said. "The fucking gloves are off. Who wants to get shot first?"

In her right hand she held a trusty Glock.

The melee continued unabated, blood splashing boots and concrete and curdling in the dirt.

And then, the first shot rang out.

CHAPTER TWENTY-THREE

The Hood atop Gunn screamed and arched away, blood pouring from a new wound at the top of his thigh. Scrambling through the dust and dirt that covered the street, he crawled away. Gunn rose slowly. Heidi aimed the gun at the rest of the Hoods.

"Give up."

The main Hood simply sidestepped so that Cassidy was in between him and the barrel, still fighting. It must have become apparent to them that their ambush wasn't going to work. Maybe their prey had put up more resistance than they'd expected. Maybe their plan was too hastily concocted. The Hood battling Jemma broke away, ran to his fallen colleague, and smashed a foot onto the man's throat. Bodie couldn't help but stare in shock.

The man fighting him gave him a one-two across the face. Bodie went down.

Heidi spun and fired another shot, this one taking Bodie's Hood down, instantly dead. Now only two Hoods remained.

The tallest Hood jumped at Cassidy, landing both feet perfectly in the center of her chest. She was propelled backward, kept her balance, but by then the Hood had turned tail and was running hard, sprinting up the street.

The last Hood darted off too, choosing a different direction. It was Heidi who shouted out a decision first, but Bodie would have made the same choice. "Follow the one we know! He has . . ."

She didn't finish, didn't have to. They ran hard in pursuit, Cross tracking them in the SUV. Heidi shouted that she'd radioed the chopper back; they needed to employ every resource to catch the Hood this time and get a definitive look at the relic he carried.

Down the street, cutting through the crowd, turning right at the first market stall, they followed his pounding legs, keeping the blue jeans and new white T-shirt in sight, the black cap that he might discard, the general body frame and way he held himself. One thing they could watch—his backpack—was highly unlikely to be removed.

But the Hood was unbelievably quick. Cassidy tracked him closely, while Bodie panted at her back and Heidi followed him. Jemma and Gunn were left behind, jumping into the car and following as best they could through the milling crowd.

The Hood twisted right, followed another busy street, then negotiated a tight alley. Cassidy pushed hard, even gaining a little. Bodie fell back, unable to match the speed of Cassidy, Heidi, or the Hood.

A glance back from Heidi. "Waiting for a bus?"

Bodie waved her on. "Stitch."

Heidi grinned, pulling ahead. Bodie again wished for a comms setup, then thought for now it was probably a blessing. Some wiseass would no doubt crack a joke about his "snail's pace." Still, he was close enough to see the Hood race recklessly across a wide road, narrowly missing a bright-yellow car, and then dash into another alley. Washing hung across the street, and the walls were uneven, stones jutting out at knee and head height. Dangerous, but Bodie saw the Hood was intent on something else.

Grabbing hold of a piece of stone, the Hood hefted himself up into the air, then launched with one foot, grabbing another at head height. Quickly, he propelled himself up the side of the building. Cassidy stopped below, tested a length of drain pipe, and then planted her feet against the side of the building. She followed, bouncing higher and higher. Heidi split toward the front door, slamming it hard with her shoulder and disappearing inside. Bodie elected to follow her rather than Cassidy.

He'd scaled walls that way before, but thought stairs might be more appropriate today.

Heidi was above him, climbing over the top risers and then coming around a switchback. The staircase went all the way up—three stories— making Bodie hope to hell there was a roof-access door at the top.

The Hood went this way for a reason, the same reason as the one in Istanbul. If trapped, he could take a dive off the roof. In many ways they were still several steps behind, and nobody had mentioned what might happen if he called in another event like the Thessaloniki bus station.

Hopefully, the ambush meant he hadn't had time. That thought gave Bodie hope. Heidi reached the top of the staircase, Bodie gasping a few steps behind. His chest was on fire. He rested, head down, with his hand atop the banister rail as she approached a suspect door at the end of the corridor. Gun ready, she kicked it hard. The lock flew off, the hinges twisted. Daylight flooded the narrow hall. Heidi bounded through and Bodie followed.

The roof opened out ahead, blue skies to every horizon, broken only by tattered clouds. Bodie saw the Hood on his knees, only just having completed his climb.

Of course I knew the steps would be quicker. Knew it all the time.

The Hood looked up; their eyes met. Heidi pointed the gun.

"I will shoot you in the goddamn leg!"

The man with the map was trapped. His dilemma—he couldn't kill himself without destroying the map first. Bodie looked suspiciously around for chimneys, but lightning wouldn't strike twice. There were none. The Hood backed away slowly as Cassidy finished scaling the building, pulling herself over the edge with a graceful spring. She landed on two feet, careful not to block Heidi's firing line.

"Stop," Heidi said.

The Hood put his hands in the air, but kept moving. Cassidy shrugged her shoulders. "I'm happy to break something if you like. Knees. Toes. Teeth. Not a problem."

The Hood regarded her, perhaps considering speaking for the first time, but then said nothing. His eyes were fixed above Bodie's head.

Heidi closed the gap. Bodie stayed close. The four of them became a tense knot. The Hood backed up as far as he was able, the three-story vertical drop at his back. "Why don't you start by handing over the backpack?" Bodie said.

Heidi waved the gun. "Actually, just get on your knees, hands behind your back. I'd prefer you did that rather than try to play Superman."

"Why is that a problem?" Cassidy squinted. "The prick can jump for all I care."

Heidi flexed her fingers around the trigger. "We're here to save lives, not extinguish them. Besides, he might have valuable information."

The sound of the chopper reached Bodie's ears. That would be their way out of here, and a means of transporting the Hood to somewhere unknown. Not a bad plan, under the circumstances.

"Call Cross," Heidi told him. "Have him head north and meet us outside town. I'll send him the coordinates."

Bodie backed away. The chopper got louder. The Hood continued to stare at the skies as if they might offer some kind of salvation.

As if . . .

Bodie swiveled on the spot and then reeled. Never had he seen what he saw now. "Heidi," he said. *"Heidi!"*

She turned. She saw the wide blue skies and their chopper, only half a mile distant, but behind that, hanging in the air like deadly black predators, came a dozen more attack choppers, closing in fast and mercilessly.

Heidi turned to the Hood. "Call them off. There's a town full of civilians down there."

"You should let me go." The voice was as gravel-laden as the face was stern.

"I will. Just call them off."

"You put the gun away and step back. Call your helicopter off."

Heidi watched the approaching choppers, shared an anxious glance with Bodie, and then put her weapon away. The Hood stepped between them, close enough to touch. Bodie wondered if the CIA would weigh the cost of a town against the map's retrieval. Behind closed doors, would they do that if they could? But this situation was too fluid to make any kind of call, too crazy to make any difficult decision.

They let the Hood pass. Bodie heard Heidi make the call and watched for their own chopper to veer away.

It didn't.

Heidi stared at the oncoming wall of death.

"Shit, this is gonna be bad."

CHAPTER
TWENTY-FOUR

Bodie saw the gunman—one of the Special Forces guys that had rescued him—lean out of their chopper and take aim. The Hood ran for shelter. Bullets stitched the rooftop, chasing his heels. Bodie thought quickly and turned to Heidi.

"Might as well take him down."

"I don't want to be a party to this," she said. "First *they* send choppers and now *we* won't stand down. The innocent—they suffer. Not the men that pass down those orders."

"We keep it up here," Bodie said. "We can do that."

More gunfire rang out. Screams rose from the streets below. The Hood was hidden behind a wall, keeping close watch on them. Bodie knew the next decision was a big one.

He would help Heidi, then. He was still a civilian and could do what had to be done without compromising her ethics, allowing her to be saved by a thief.

Bodie strode toward the Hood, Cassidy at his side. Their chopper was maneuvering for a better shot, almost overhead now and buffeting the air so loudly it was hard to think. Bodie heard a hiss and then a devastating explosion followed by Heidi's scream.

"It's coming down on top of you!"

Their chopper was hit and losing altitude, the engine note dropping, stalling, the entire mass tilting and freefalling toward the roof. Both soldiers managed to jump out and land safely. The pilot had no time to react. Bodie and Cassidy rolled to the side of the roof, teetering over the edge, but out of the way of the initial impact. The chopper crashed with a sound like the collapse of a mountain. Debris bounded and sprayed and darted everywhere like mini cannonballs and lethal blades.

Cassidy curled into a ball. Bodie made an effort to cover her, saw a rotor blade scythe past his own head and bury itself meters deep in a wall opposite, then caught the redhead as she carelessly fell over the edge of the building. He grabbed her arm, pulled her to safety.

Cassidy looked up. "What?"

"You didn't realize you fell off the building?"

A pile of rubble undulated toward them like a wave. Bodie and Cassidy scrambled out of the way, heels struck as metal and concrete tumbled over the edge. By now, as he looked up, Bodie could see the attack choppers assembling overhead and a thick rope tumbling down from one.

The Hood was alert, watching for his chance.

Heidi removed her firearm, the Gatling-gun crescendo of multiple weapons churning up the roof all around her. The only reason they missed was the shifting pile of machine debris that still constituted the downed chopper, and the leaping flames that covered its wreckage.

The Hood ran, chasing the slowly shifting rope. Cassidy was closest and fittest and took off like an unleashed hellhound. Snarling, bloodied, she chased the Hood down, risking it all and coming at him with everything she had. At the last moment, as they came together, he leapt and caught hold of the rope. The chopper was already moving and the swing took him away from her. Cassidy leapt past, hit the ground, rolled, and turned on one knee, scowling with purpose. The rope swung faster, gaining momentum, the Hood climbing so fast he defied gravity, already halfway up to the chopper's doors.

Cassidy ran again. The other choppers started to drift away, but tracked her and Heidi in case weapons were used. No more shots were fired. This was a hastily planned evacuation, then, rather than an event. A favor called in. A reluctant service perhaps by somebody that wanted to be owed something. That would explain the choppers without markings and their unwillingness to cause havoc.

Bodie watched Cassidy. She mounted the wreckage, using it as a springboard to launch her body through the air and catch hold of the rope. The chopper was rising now, veering away, taking her with it. Cassidy clung on, dragged wildly by the rope, swinging across the rooftop. The Hood reached the doors and was hauled inside. Cassidy hung on tight, swept in a wide arc, her feet three meters above the roof. At the same time the other choppers started to move away, heading back the way they came. A man leaned out from one of the choppers and aimed a weapon down. The shot missed Cassidy by a wide margin. He tried again, but then Heidi whipped her Glock up and sent a bullet clanging off the metal beside his head. The man flinched and vanished back inside.

Bodie sprinted for the base of the rope. If he could steady it at least, maybe Cassidy could climb up or down or wherever she planned to go. By now, though, the chopper was in full voice, powered to the max. It swooped up and away, Cassidy still in tow, and then the rope was cut from the chopper as it flew.

The rope collapsed. Its momentum made the bottom flick upward. Cassidy let go in midair, propelled off the roof, across the gap between buildings, and landed hard onto the next roof. Rolling, she kept her arms and legs together, stopping about midway, bruised and battered but still alive.

Weakly, she raised a hand.

Heidi came up to Bodie's shoulder. "The asshole escaped. For now."

"For now?" Bodie echoed. "He has helicopters, now. He's gone."

Heidi shook her head. "No. Helos are traceable. They're big. Brash. Noisy. Everything our friend and the Illuminati don't want. This makes me think they're not a part of the secret society, but hired perhaps, so their owner will not wish them compromised. They won't want to attract any more attention."

"So you're saying the Illuminati conscripted them, and they'll—what? Drop him off?" Bodie kept a careful eye on Cassidy as the redhead pulled herself upright. All seemed in good working order.

"One thing I can't knock you for," Heidi said. "Trying. Man, you guys got a lot of heart, I'll give you that."

"Want to know our secret?" Bodie smiled at Cassidy and knew instinctively that Cross would be waiting in the street below, Jemma and Gunn probably on their way up.

Heidi nodded and returned the smile.

"We belong. Together. Our team has a sense of belonging, of togetherness."

"Even Gunn?"

Bodie shook his head with a touch of sadness. "Yeah, even that asshole. Even bloody Gunn."

CHAPTER TWENTY-FIVE

Reunited with Cross, Jemma, and Gunn, the team took their original seats and rested as the older man drove them north out of the city. Jeff was buckled into his seat right where he'd been when they left him.

"'Kin 'ell, Jeffo," Cassidy said. "Move much?"

"I'm not a fighter," the young archaeologist said.

"That makes two of you." Bodie nodded at Gunn. "But Gunn did jump in when needed."

"To receive help in life you have to show willing," Cross said from the front seat.

"Ancient proverb of the day." Cassidy grinned with mischief. "But true."

"You okay, Miss Movie Star?" Cross looked at her in the rearview. "Any more cuts like that and Hollywood will be saving you for the slasher flicks."

"A past life." Cassidy waved it away. "And probably one better not spoken of in front of the CIA."

"Apologies, that's my bad."

Heidi looked hurt. "Am I not a member of the team? Not proven myself yet?"

"No," Cassidy said.

"Well . . ." Bodie tried.

Cassidy rolled her eyes. "He's always like this. Pretty chick comes along, bats her . . . frizzbomb, and he's all Lady Gaga."

"My frizzbomb?"

"Yeah. What do you call it?"

"We're digressing here," Bodie said. "The Hood is out there, wherever he's going, and still with the map"—he turned to Jeff—"and you're our next best thing, so make yourself useful. What did you say was the first waypoint?"

Jeff sipped at a can of Pepsi Max. "We returned something new to Spartacus, and 1776."

"Ah, yes, the movie reference. Any ideas?"

"It's not a movie reference. It's actually an easy first clue if you know your Illuminati history. 1776 is the year they were founded."

Jemma shook her dark hair. "No. Someone said *Adam* was the first Illuminati."

"Well, yes, the ancients may have had a similar form of secret society, where events were manipulated for the sake of a greater power that believed it had the right to rule over all. Perhaps the Illuminati used it as their role model, but officially they began in 1776."

"Officially?" Heidi asked. "Now I'm stumped. I thought they were secret. Shadows behind the scenes, manipulating the puppets."

"They are now, but I think that you are testing me. You, Agent Moneymaker, are on their trail, so you must know their history."

"Ah, ya got me. Go on, kid."

"The Bavarian Illuminati were the first of their kind, the first of their order. Formed by a man named Adam Weishaupt. Weishaupt was deeply nonclerical, made that way by Jesuits who frustrated and discredited any manner of work that they regarded as liberal or protestant. Weishaupt resolved to spread the word of enlightenment through a secret society, but considered the Freemasons of the time too expensive and actually too narrow-minded. So they formed the Perfectibilists and decided on the Owl of Minerva as their emblem."

"Perfecti-what?" Cassidy asked.

"Yes, yes, that's what Weishaupt thought after a time. He contemplated naming them the Bee Order and then decided upon *Illuminatenorden*, or Order of Illuminati."

"In 1776?" Bodie confirmed.

"Yes. And each member of the Order used a code name."

"You're kidding. For real?" Bodie never would have imagined the TV sometimes got it right. "Let me guess . . ."

"Weishaupt's code name was Spartacus."

"Right," Bodie said. "So you're saying the first waypoint is to return to Spartacus in 1776. Then that's gonna lead us to the next." He put his head down in thought. "We need to return to the place where this Weishaupt guy created the Illuminati in 1776. Yes?"

"Or his house?" Jemma said. "'Return something new to Spartacus' could mean to where he lived."

Heidi pursed her lips. "I guess."

"I don't," Jeff said. "This whole thing is about the Illuminati, yes? Their base, their statue, their hoodlums. Their bosses. It won't be where Weishaupt lived. It will be where he created the larger Order."

"And where was that?" Cassidy asked.

Gunn put a hand up, intent to join the conversation. "Bavaria," he said.

"Well done," Jeff said a little condescendingly. "We start there. The statue will be somewhere else, of course, but that's our first waypoint. You ask why? Because, if anywhere at all, that's where the Illuminati will still be operating."

"The place they were founded. The longest roots. Makes sense," Heidi said.

"And you think that's where the Hood's headed?" Jemma asked.

"That also makes sense. The route you told me of so far points that way. Of course, he could literally be stopping off at any town, in any country, but Bavaria is where it all began. And Bavaria is where they still exist."

"Do we know where he created the Order?" Heidi asked. "Because, seriously, I don't."

"I have an idea," Jeff said. "But let's get to Bavaria first."

Bodie was already unfolding a map. Gunn was flicking it around on his iPad. "Bulgaria. Romania. Hungary. Austria," they read out. "It's a long, long way."

"Good," Heidi said. "It will give us a chance to catch up to the Hood."

"Can you call more people?" Bodie asked.

"With this operation? Maybe. But we're gonna need actionable intel. The American government doesn't sneeze these days without incontestable proof and reassurance that it's getting its back nicely scratched. We'll see."

Cross put his foot down as the town ended and the countryside began. "Sit back and rest, guys," he said. "You deserve it."

"Except for you," Cassidy said pointedly to Gunn. "You can slip my boots off and rub my feet."

The geek sulked. "I jumped on that guy's back. I helped. I tried. It's not my fault I can't fight like you."

"At the moment you're pretty redundant," Cassidy said. "Jeff here's doing your job. Y'know, if this were a book or a movie, I'd be a little scared the creator was gonna kill you off."

"Not everything's a friggin' movie, Cassidy. I grew up an orphan, half on the street. I paid my dues."

"And so did I. So did we all, to be honest. Bodie was orphaned, went to jail, and became a better thief. He wouldn't hurt anyone after he saw what his earlier crimes did to people. Cross is old, slow, loses his glasses, and takes his time. And that was during his prime. Jemma's quiet, able to ponder a dozen things at once, but she paid the price for it in her youth. Bullies, hooligans, others that would take advantage. Me? I won't lie. I didn't do so bad. But I was never loved, never wanted. I knew I'd have to go my own way by the time I was in double figures. Grew up fast, studied fighting, made a few bit parts early on. I was homeless before I was a cage fighter. Did you know that?"

Gunn shook his head, eyes rapt, taking it all in. It wasn't often Cassidy was so forthcoming, so when she was, the group often learned more than they should.

"Then street fighting. No rules. And I was top of the game. Then Guy came along"—she shrugged—"and here we are. Point is . . ." She glared at Gunn. "Man the fuck up."

The team chuckled, even Heidi joining in. The road wound out before and behind them, and they sat back, comfortable in each other's company, wondering where they would end up next.

CHAPTER TWENTY-SIX

Xavier Von Gothe saw everything. In most instances he kept his own counsel, weighed the options and the information, and issued the orders that would condemn some to death while freeing others that may have been persecuted justly or unjustly. All for the good of the Order. Some matters, though, required input from others, especially when, in the future, he might need somebody to blame.

For that reason his second-in-command, a man known by the code name Typhon, joined him now on an ultrasecure video conferencing line from the UK. Typhon's first comment always revolved around the weather.

"Cold and wet?" Xavier replied. "Yes, well, it is here too. But a different kind of cold and wet."

"Snowy mountains? Warm sunshine? I would hardly call that cold and wet." Typhon chuckled.

"That depends on how and where you live. Some of us choose contentment. Others . . . don't."

"And many don't get the chance to choose."

"The herd? Of course not. The herd moves where we want it to move."

Xavier had a feeling Typhon was complaining, but truly didn't care. Not a man prone to slothful chitchat, he pressed on.

"I wonder, Typhon. I wonder what your thoughts are regarding this map." He left it there and would judge Typhon on the strength of the reply.

"My initial thoughts center on how it came into being."

"Exactly. As do mine. Of course I prefer to deal with the genuine article and get it tested, but it appeared to be old. A hundred years or more. It is written in the old style."

"A malcontent? Somebody the Order expelled?"

"Very possibly. But it feels almost like an account of exploration rather than a revelation. Don't you think?"

A nod from the head on the other side of the world. Xavier saw only mahogany paneling around Typhon and glanced to the left where his own picture window revealed lofty mountain heights. The differences were telling.

"Investigation is required," Xavier said firmly. "And possible retribution. I don't care if it's two hundred or five hundred years old— the traitor that did this will pay, and his name will be trampled to dust when his current bloodline is wiped from the face of the earth."

"Of course." It went without saying.

"Baltasar is coming, but he is being pursued. The normal mode of transport is compromised. The fervor is rising every day, every hour. It is good that he has now left Greece, but I fear there is more to come."

"An unusual scenario," Typhon said with genuine surprise.

"Yes, agreed. We are investigating the appearance of these new players, and, rest assured, when we find their superiors and their weak points, we will crush them."

"And the other map recipients?"

"All taken care of bar one. He has joined this new team, or so I believe."

"Ah."

Xavier watched Typhon. That one exclamation said it all. Though short, it contained shock, fear, and . . . greed. Typhon saw the last man still being alive as a big mistake, that was clear. Xavier tended to agree, but wouldn't air it even with his second-in-command.

"Perhaps a mass tonight?" Typhon suggested. "Say, eight your time? We will offer something up at this end too."

"The Great Dragon will be assuaged," Xavier agreed. "At least for a short time."

"And our contacts will do the rest."

"That is why they exist," Xavier said assuredly, not able to see any other reason. "We know where Baltasar is. And we know the following team are currently chasing in a helicopter. An event is being set."

"It is? How are—"

Xavier cut him off, saying goodbye. Everyone always wanted to know more of the events and how they were planned. Everyone wanted more secrets. Didn't they know that the more secrets they knew, the more expendable they were? Fools. Hypocrites. Liars. Xavier was under no illusion as to the men and women that made up the Order of Illuminati.

But, in mentioning the appeasement of the Great Dragon, Typhon had raised a good point, and it was important to respect it. Not just for Typhon, but for the entire Order.

Tonight, there would be a mass. Not a brief, hasty ceremony, but a full-on, dutiful ritual of adoration, meditation, thanksgiving, and sacrifice. Tonight, they would humble themselves.

For tomorrow, they would again be gods.

CHAPTER TWENTY-SEVEN

Bodie relaxed as they drove across Hungary. The Hood was somewhere ahead, maybe an hour, maybe half a day, but Heidi had called in all the ground assets she could and was trying to utilize a localized satellite. Only time could tell, and they could do little more than drive north.

Bodie took the downtime to reflect. Though he was thirty-three, his life had already been overcrowded with highs and lows. Parental loss could hardly be understood by an eight-year-old boy, but his life had certainly taken an acute and inexorable change.

Heidi sat beside him in the car, took in his pensive face, and seemed to know just the right question to ask. "So," the American agent said, "why'd you become a thief?"

"It wasn't planned." He shrugged, not wanting to appear standoffish. Deep down, Bodie craved friendship simply because he'd lacked it through the early years, but found it hard to socialize and make friends. "A lonely boy's cry for help? Self-harm? A way into a new life? I've considered them all, but I really don't know."

"Maybe you enjoyed it."

"Maybe I did. But I didn't enjoy the prison time. Nor did I enjoy it when the judge made me watch the effect my burglary had on one family. You feel isolated, you know? When you're on a job. I did, at least. Emotionless, detached. Free." He gazed ahead. "Those people in court—they were devastated. Broken. It changed me."

"I heard." Heidi nodded. "I read your sheet. Victimless crimes, wasn't it?"

"Yeah, something like that."

"Proves you have a heart, at least."

"Relics were the way to go."

"And that's where you met Jack Pantera?"

Bodie couldn't stop the anger. "Yeah, and that reckoning's coming. It's coming hard."

"Any idea why he would betray you that way? Maybe it's because you started your own team."

Bodie shook his head. "I can't see it. Jack was fine with everything. Nothing he ever said or did painted him as the kind of guy that would double-cross you. Nothing. And those people who tried to kill me in prison? They weren't locals; they were some kind of Western organized gang."

"Don't worry," Cassidy spoke up. "We'll ask him when we see him. As I wring his scrawny throat."

"He was your teacher? Your mentor?"

Bodie nodded. "My only friend for a long time. I didn't trust anyone," he said. "Before Jack there was only deceit and betrayal, parents and siblings who either didn't care or only ever used me to get something. Then Jack came along, offered an olive branch, and gave me a friend." He sat back, folding into himself. "I *want* to trust people," he said. "But I don't even trust myself sometimes."

"I get that." Heidi slumped too. "My daughter, Jessica, often won't take my call. When she does, I can't trust myself not to question and argue with her . . . so I keep it calm, emotionless." She sighed. "It doesn't work. Maybe for some, but not for someone driven like me."

The car slowed as a bridge appeared ahead, four lanes across a hundred-foot span and a dank river below. Cross moved into the left lane, passing the slower traffic.

"You are a good thief, Bodie," Heidi acknowledged. "With a good team. It's a shame your whole damn operation is illegal."

The Londoner smiled for the first time in a while. "Yeah, yeah, tell me about it. But you say you're driven? You believe that you're helping your daughter and ex-husband, keeping them safe, but they don't see it that way. Am I right?"

"Exactly."

"And you're no better off than any of us."

"And amen," Cross said. "My wife hated the army life. Never understood why I had this urge to risk everything to save strangers, from across shores, but not our marriage." He shrugged. "Go figure."

"But this life." Heidi looked around. "Doesn't it ever make you feel *lonely*?"

Bodie shook his head. "We have a saying. *Family is a sense of belonging.* Those you choose to be your family don't have to share your blood."

"How about you?" Cassidy asked. "Ever feel lonely?"

Heidi looked away. Bodie sent Cassidy a warning look and received a shrug in return. Cross negotiated the traffic. It was the sporadic bright flash in the sky that sent Bodie's eyes upward. "What is that?"

Heidi heard the suspicion in his voice. "What now?"

He studied the small white object outlined against the blue sky, obscured by the drifting clouds. At this range it could be an insect, an elaborate kite, a . . .

"Get your foot on that gas pedal," Heidi said urgently. "It's a drone."

Bodie squinted as it came closer, swooping down toward the bridge. "Whoa, it's big."

"Yeah, it's big," Heidi said. "It's a fucking military Predator, or similar. Big payload."

Cassidy looked up through the window. "My guess is that's not good?"

"Not if you don't wanna turn that hair a deeper shade of red, babes."

Cassidy turned away from the drone to a matter more pressing. "Babes?"

"Sorry. It's the male chauvinist coming out in me." Heidi slapped Cross so hard on the shoulder the whole car shuddered. "Get a goddamn move on, Miss Daisy!"

They were halfway across the bridge, still threading through traffic. Bodie knew Cross to be a careful driver, not overly fond of speed and power, and hard enough to shake from his set ways.

"Eli," he said. "We should get clear."

The warning was obvious. The drone and those operating it would have no compunctions about collateral damage. Cross aimed the car toward a wide space, lightly pressing the accelerator.

"Jump on it, man!" Heidi cried. "They're gonna fire."

"Yeah, and swerve a bit," Cassidy said. "No point giving them a bull's-eye."

Cross breathed deeply, clearly out of his comfort zone. He twisted the wheel to the right, moving the car slightly. The drone drifted nearer, its miniengine loud now, spitting at the air like an enormous dragonfly. Gunn was shrinking away and Jemma looking to Bodie for guidance.

"Cross," he said. "You'd better learn to drive right now or we're dead."

Cassidy leaned over the seat. "No pressure, though."

Cross slammed his foot on the gas pedal—and Bodie cringed as he imagined him closing his eyes as he did so—just as the drone unleashed a part of its payload. The missile streaked through the short distance, colliding with the concrete and exploding. Fire raged in their wake, the flames washing over the rear of the SUV. Bodie, switching positions to stare out the back, saw other cars slamming brakes and swerving to avoid the blast. Mercifully, all made it.

Their own vehicle sped ahead now, making the most of a clear stretch of road. Cross kept his foot hard down, knuckles sheer white against the wheel, teeth grinding.

"'Kin 'ell." Cassidy turned to Bodie. "I've never seen the old man concentrate so hard."

"Leave him be," Bodie said. "You okay, Eli?"

"Be better if I could find my glasses."

Bodie cringed. *Fuck.* So Cross was driving at speed, ill at ease, the world a constant blur. Would this make Cross a better driver, or worse? An argument could be made both ways.

"You see that big, fuzzy mound ahead?" Cassidy said. "That's a mountain. The bridge runs into the heart of it. Miss, and we're fish food. Oh, and dodge left *now!*"

The second missile smashed the ground apart at their left wheel. Cars on the opposite side of the road took shrapnel and swerved to a halt. Fire washed over the front of the car this time, its heat making those inside bow their heads and close their eyes.

Cross took his foot off for a second. The car slowed. The drone adjusted overhead and came in even closer.

"Can't you shoot it?" Cross blustered. "Why aren't you shooting at it?"

Heidi wrenched her weapon from her waistband, scrambled across Bodie and jabbed at the electric window. Bodie leaned back, trying to remove his own gun. Cassidy glanced at the crazy shuffle the two were doing in the back seat.

"Erm?"

"Wanna shut up and get your gun out?"

"I guess."

Cassidy found her own handgun and lowered the window. She fired at the same time as Heidi, their bullets barely missing the drone as it hovered in the air. The machine backed off, its next missile delayed as the operators evaded several more shots from the car. Bodie finally pulled his own gun free, and tried to get in on the action.

The drone flew higher and farther away. Cross made the car veer to and fro, approaching a coach from behind and focusing on getting by as fast as he could. The drone tracked him, swerving sharply toward the mountain to get ahead of the coach.

"Punch it, punch it," Heidi shouted as she leaned even farther out of the window, her hair ruffled by the wind. Cassidy was hanging out of the same side of the car, nearer to the front, her red hair whipping back toward Heidi. Bodie tried to join them.

Cross pushed the pedal to the floor, hit the limiter. He didn't change direction, not wanting the coach to bear the brunt of any attack meant for them, but he did veer even farther toward the central divide. In the end, it proved to be a good move as a rocket smashed and smeared all over the upraised concrete, debris shooting everywhere. The three shooters ducked back inside the car so fast they landed in a heap.

Then fought to get back up.

Cross swung the vehicle past the coach and back into their lane. The drop to the side loomed big, straight down to the flat black surface of the river.

"It's not that far," Jemma was saying. "We could survive that."

Gunn glared at her, almost frothing at the mouth. "Are you kidding?"

"What? You worried it'll mess with your hair gel?"

Gunn looked away, refusing to continue the argument. They were nearing the end of the bridge now and approaching a tunnel cut into the mountain. As Bodie, Cassidy, and Heidi reached the open windows, they got one more chance to fire at the swooping drone.

The car bounced into a pothole, throwing their aims off. Bullets went high, but Heidi's cut through the air just a few millimeters low of the drone. Then they were inside the mountain tunnel, their eyes struggling to adjust, the road and walls lit by high-powered lamps.

Cross found he had to slow now as they came up behind a camper van. The road was a single lane in here, and no divide meant it was doubly dangerous.

Bodie stared through the rear window. "It's coming."

"It followed us inside?" Cross exclaimed. "Son of a bitch."

"And now," Heidi said as the speeding drone raced up to their back window, "we have nowhere to go."

CHAPTER TWENTY-EIGHT

The drone flew close. So close that Bodie could clearly see its weapons and unblinking camera's eye, its odd wings and markings. They could hear its high-pitched shriek.

"Do something!" Gunn shouted.

"All right," Cassidy replied. "Just let me get out my drone repellent."

The drone backed off a little.

The tunnel stretched long, dark, and very narrow.

"It's gonna fire," Jemma said, wincing.

Cross jammed the brakes on. The drone flew in hard, almost colliding with the back of the car, but swerving up sharply at the last moment. Cross set off as fast as he could again, putting some distance between them and the readjusting drone. Bodie almost clapped in amazement.

"'Kin 'ell, Cross," Cassidy said, "you hero."

"Good move." Heidi coughed. "Unexpected, though. Maybe give us a heads up next time."

"I think he just thought, 'What would David Hasselhoff do?'" Cassidy cackled.

Bodie motioned for Cross to keep his eyes on the road as the ex-military man turned around to retort. The drone dropped from the side this time, easing its way around the back. A car traveling in the opposite direction missed it by mere inches, causing Gunn to curse their lack of luck.

"Get down." Cassidy lined the drone up through her sights.

Everyone scrambled down, hearing the no-nonsense tone in her voice. Bodie pressed hard into the leather seats and jammed his fingers into his ears. Cassidy fired four shots in succession, while Cross bellowed in pain from the loud noises.

"You could have fuckin' warned me!"

"Ah, well, touché."

The rear windows shattered, the bullets flying true. They smashed the drone aside, destroying its body and wings, and sending it crashing into vaulted walls. As it fell away, the car left the tunnel and sunshine flooded the interior.

"Nice," Bodie said, slipping his head up over the back seat and gauging the terrain.

"We should get off this road," Heidi said. "If they found us once, they'll find us again."

"And a new car," Gunn said. "Fast."

"Not that many roads in Hungary," Cross said. "But there's a town not too far ahead. Maybe we can replan there?"

"Good thinking," Heidi said. "Make it fast. We need to get out of sight."

"I'm doing the best I can."

"Says Miss Daisy." Cassidy flicked at the shattered glass that littered the back seat. "Bit of a mess."

Heidi stared at her. "Don't know whether to be pissed off or thankful," she said, also brushing at the glass.

"Ow," Bodie said. "You just flipped a piece of glass at my arse."

Heidi sniggered. "Your *arse?*"

"Yeah, my arse. Is that a problem?"

"No, Mr. Darcy, it's all good."

Bodie noticed the only one not smirking was Cross, who was concentrating on navigating the windy route. Even Gunn was smiling. "It does sound a bit hoity-toity," the geek said.

"From *you?* Shit. Now I know I'm off-kilter. So I guess it should be 'ass' then?"

"Not ass," Cassidy corrected. "It's aassssss. Draw it out. Sounds ruder."

"I can't say it the way you do."

"Well, try. The—"

"Quiet!" Cross shouted. "We just barely escaped a rabid drone attack and you guys're having a schoolyard debate. Get the goddamn maps out and find us a safe place in this town."

"Already on it." Gunn was flicking through his cell phone, as was Jeff. "But we don't get our maps *out*, mate. We use an app to get them *up*."

"Whatever."

Bodie shuffled closer toward the window as Heidi picked out glass close to his legs. The CIA agent was a conundrum, on the one hand able to destroy his life and imprison his friends, but on the other a highly capable and trustworthy ally. He saw the road ahead starting to wind down toward a medium-sized town and nudged Gunn with an outstretched knee.

"You there with the location yet?"

"The signal's crap," he said, holding the phone at various angles.

Cross grunted from the front. "And that's why your app's bullshit, brother. You wouldn't get that from a paper map."

Bodie thought the man had a point, but didn't want to tax Gunn any further. Being the untested geek in a team of hardened combatants was difficult enough. The town sprawled below, filling a valley and running up into the lower mountains. They started to descend more sharply as the skies clouded over and a light drizzle began to fall.

"You think they're still tracking us?" Jemma asked.

"Doesn't matter." Heidi explained something Bodie already knew. "This is the only road we can use. Hoods could be here already."

Cross slowed. Gunn shouted out a location, a parking area next to a tired old building. Google Maps told him it was large, busy, and hard to find. They might be able to lose themselves awhile there and come out looking somewhat different.

"Eight minutes." Cross watched dubiously as Jemma leaned through to jab the coordinates into the navigation system. "That thing reliable?"

Gunn shrugged as the others all smiled. "Actually, it depends who manufactured it. As I'm sure most drivers will relate to."

Bodie watched through the side window, sharp droplets of rain drifting in through the shattered rear window. They asked Cross to turn up the heat and waited for the parking lot. At last, it appeared up ahead. Cross found a space from which they could watch the surrounding area, and they settled back, weary, stressed, worried.

Heidi took a big breath. "Situation report? We've lost our Hood, the one with the map. Gotta assume he's hours ahead of us, probably still in Hungary. *If* the Illuminati are sticking to their low-key policy."

"I think they will," Bodie said. "They're immensely arrogant, it seems."

"Yeah," Cross said. "Almost as if when they make a decision they expect it will work, regardless."

"They've had it that way for hundreds if not thousands of years," Heidi said. "Depending which story you believe."

"All right." Bodie didn't look away from the busy parking area and surrounding streets. "So how do we vanish and catch up?"

Cassidy shifted a little, her job to scrutinize the windows of surrounding buildings. "New car. Balls out. Sound good?"

Gunn tapped his screen. "I can find a rental place."

Bodie smiled at the kid's naivety. "We're already here, Sam."

"But . . . some poor guy's gonna lose his ride."

"He'll be compensated later, quietly. It's happened before."

Bodie wondered if that was strictly true. He guessed it depended on the morals of the agent in charge, but had no real reason to question Heidi's.

"I'm seeing three candidates," Cross said. "There, there, and there." He pointed in the general direction of the vehicles. "All common. All battered. All dull colors. Perfect for what we need."

"I'm seeing movement," Cassidy said. "Right there." She nodded at the seemingly abandoned building to their right. At the edge of the parking area, it rose four stories and consisted of a dirty white façade and many broken windows.

"Third window in, third floor. You see it?"

Bodie had his hand on the door handle, ready to move. "Actually, I don't see anything. Are you sure?"

"You don't get to live this long and look this pretty by second-guessing. Move."

They pushed open the doors, jumped out of the car. At that very moment a streak issued from the window Cassidy had identified—a thin white streak that dissipated as it went.

"RPG!" Bodie cried.

They dived. They rolled. They scrambled clear, looking desperately for cover—a nearby bench, a badly parked BMW, a litter bin. Bodie half ran, half scrabbled clear of the impact zone. The missile flashed toward its target. In those few seconds Bodie could only hope everyone had their wits about them—even Jeff, who had been seated on the other side of the SUV. Bodie saw it coming, saw its speed and power and the spitting fire it trailed, and was thankful Cross had chosen a quieter, more spacious part of the parking lot to stop in.

The explosion happened fast, the fire and wreckage shredding the air. Bodie didn't stop rolling. The power from the blast shook his bones.

Screams erupted from close by. People ran from the chaos. Bodie pulled out his Glock and fired four quick shots into the suspect window.

Nothing moved. He crouched behind a Jeep with big tires and looked back.

Cassidy was dragging Jeff along, just disappearing behind a red Prius. The rest were kneeling or crawling except for Eli Cross, who was flat out on the ground, unmoving.

Bodie felt a lurch deep in his heart. The older man of their team, the ex-military redneck, the careful, forty-plus, world-class thief that kept them all rational and together had not fared well in the missile attack.

Furious, scared, he rose and fired the rest of his mag into the empty window.

CHAPTER TWENTY-NINE

The chase was on, the battle lines drawn. There was nothing a Hood wouldn't do, nothing his masters would not do. Their vehicle burned and raged with flames; two civilians lay hurt and groaning, luckily none worse than that. Eli Cross was down and unmoving, and Heidi was the first to make it to his side.

Bodie changed the mag, kept an eye on the main window and all the other windows around it.

Shit, we still don't have comms.

It would have been good to be able to communicate fast and efficiently.

Behind him, Cassidy ran to Heidi's side, and the two women bent over Cross, checking on the man's condition.

Gunn, Jemma, and Jeff looked around the side of a broken car. Their SUV was a ragged mess, smoking. Bodie watched the abandoned building like a hawk, torn between wanting to rush inside and track the Hood down, and the need to run to Cross's side. As he studied every blank space in the building's façade, every deep recess, a shout rang out.

"He's okay!" Heidi sounded extremely relieved.

"Yeah," Cassidy shouted, also reassured. "Just needed a nap."

Bodie closed his eyes for half a second, the anxiety sloughing away. In another moment Heidi was at his shoulder.

"Anything?"

"Nope. I'm guessing he took off."

"Yeah, me too. This chaos will enable us to slip away, though."

Bodie regarded her, surprised but then understanding. Nobody was badly hurt. The Hood, if it was *their* Hood, was close. Matters could be worse.

"That car?" He nodded at a nearby old Audi with many seats.

"That car." Heidi nodded. "Round up the crew."

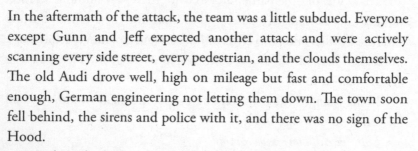

In the aftermath of the attack, the team was a little subdued. Everyone except Gunn and Jeff expected another attack and were actively scanning every side street, every pedestrian, and the clouds themselves. The old Audi drove well, high on mileage but fast and comfortable enough, German engineering not letting them down. The town soon fell behind, the sirens and police with it, and there was no sign of the Hood.

And yet he had to be somewhere ahead, driving the same road, passing the same signs as they were doing now. As the hours passed, it became clear there would be no imminent attack, but the team remained on high alert.

"That waypoint?" Heidi said as they rolled along the highway. "Say it again."

Jeff had been dozing, but now wiped his mouth self-consciously and sat up. "We returned something new to Spartacus and 1776."

"And you're *sure* that means Bavaria. We're pinning a whole lot on your guesswork."

"I honestly can't think of anything else it might mean."

Heidi stared at him. "Well, that's more sensible than it sounds. At least you've tried."

"I have."

Cassidy patted Jeff's knee. "Don't worry, man. As soon as she thinks you're useless, she won't throw you out of the car." A pause. "That'll be me."

Jeff's smile was an unmistakable rictus of fear. Heidi didn't break eye contact. "Of course, Bavaria's not just Neuschwanstein Castle, as many think. It's a big place."

Jeff gulped. "I'll get right on that."

Bodie saw his team on edge, out of their comfort zone. Jemma had nothing to plan; Gunn had nothing to steal. Cassidy had nothing to punch or distract. Gunn was letting Jeff read up on Bavaria. As for him? What did he feel?

An odd sensation. A warmth toward the CIA agent, which was totally unfounded and totally unlike him. Yes, given his past, he quietly craved friendship, but people had to jump through an awful lot of hoops to gain it—many jobs and many years and many life-threatening situations.

Heidi had gone a long way to gaining it already.

Outside of their comfort zone, the whole team had struggled more than a little. Even Bodie, who excelled at anything remotely connected to "secret acquirements," or the act of thievery where no clues were left behind, where the target might not even notice the theft for months. So far, they had chased and fought and chased again. Who knew what they might meet in Bavaria? Of course, they were the expendable team—easily shunned and blamed by the US government.

It didn't feel right. Bodie knew he should be on high alert, beyond high, but the events of the past few weeks had knocked his radar out of kilter. A smooth and relatively easy job turned on its head through the betrayal of his old mentor, the time in prison, the surprise rescue by the CIA, the shocking news that the Illuminati were a real threat, and the terrible revelations of what they did to maintain their mantle of secrecy. Then, the quest for an ancient wonder thought to have perished centuries ago.

They passed through Hungary, entered Austria, and headed for Vienna. It was there where Heidi had organized the local CIA outpost to have an unmarked and fully outfitted vehicle ready for them. It would transport them to Germany and their final leg to Bavaria. The issue now was not to arrive before the Hood, it was to find the next waypoint clue before the Illuminati. For only that would lead them on.

A sign flashed by: VIENNA—10 KILOMETERS.

"How's it coming, Jeff?" Heidi asked.

"Sorry, it's coming along okay. Getting bogged down in their idea of a 'one world government' and attempts to start and use the Napoleonic Wars as a means to force the Congress of Vienna, which brought about the League of Nations—their attempt to engineer this world government. Russia held out, though, as you remember, and the League of Nations wasn't formed. Close call there."

"That's so terrible," Jemma said. "And terrifying."

"But it's by no means the worst," Jeff said. "They also worked out a blueprint for three world wars that would end with one world government by the end of the twentieth century. Yep, we're now in the twenty-first, but the first two wars have been proven consistent with documents found, and the *third* war was designed to be fought between political Zionists and leaders of the Muslim world. It would drain the international community so badly they would have to form a single world government. Does any of that sound familiar?"

Bodie knew it did. "And they planned this before the First World War?"

Jeff nodded. "Their strategies failed short term, so they went long."

"Jeff," Heidi said with a hint of warning.

"Ah, yes. Adam Weishaupt founded the Order of Illuminati in Ingolstadt on May 1, 1776. It's not known if he indoctrinated members of an already existing group, but it *is* known that he pulled from the Freemasons. Interestingly, at an early age he rebelled against the Jesuit religion and later began a large library collection dedicated to the education of scholars. He read every ancient manuscript he could get hold of and also became interested in the occult. He became obsessed with the Pyramid of Giza, convinced that it was an ancient temple of initiation."

"Why is that interesting?" Cassidy asked.

"Because it is one of the ancient wonders, and also appears on the American dollar bill, along with countless other Illuminati symbols. Even the ranks of the Illuminati were fashioned in the shape of a pyramid—leader to seconds to lesser initiates. He once wrote, 'Sin is only that which is hurtful, and if the profit is greater than the damage it becomes a virtue.'" Jeff shrugged. "He's saying if violence is the answer, the way to further the Order's goals, then it must be done."

"Quite open from the beginning, then," Jemma pointed out.

"Called 'the profoundest conspirator that ever existed,' Weishaupt ended up fleeing Ingolstadt, scared for his life, and fled to Gotha, where he couldn't help but continue his manipulations. Of course, Weishaupt and thus the Illuminati are often accused of devil worship too, which leads us back to the major symbol of their hold over America—the dollar bill."

"I heard this before," Cross said. "Thirteen this and thirteen that, right? The all-seeing eye of the Great Architect—Lucifer?"

"That's not the prize, though, my friend. Not by a long way."

They all stared at Jeff, even Cross, who was driving.

"So," Heidi said. "What is?"

"There is a date inscribed into the base of the pyramid of every dollar bill." Jeff smiled. "MDCCLXXVI."

"And that is . . . ?"

"1776," he said. "The very date the Illuminati were formed."

Bodie blinked. "That's some coincidence."

"Or not." Jeff smiled wider. "When you see everything else. The eye. The thirteen stars. The thirteen letters. Thirteen arrows. Thirteen leaves. Thirteen layers of brick. It goes on."

Vienna surrounded them, busy streets and graceful, old buildings, tourists and coffee shops, and the world's best bakeries. Bodie saw none of it, focusing on Jeff.

"The best trick Lucifer ever did was to convince the public that he didn't exist," Jeff said. "And, recently, through Hollywood and fiction, the Illuminati have done exactly the same."

Bodie thought about it. Jeff was making sense, in a roundabout way. Still, the archaeologist hadn't answered Heidi's principal question.

"The next waypoint," he said. "Where will it be?"

"Where Adam Weishaupt spent most of his time. Either the University of Ingolstadt, or Gotha. Look, as I said before, the map isn't fully rounded off. It points to all of the old archaeologist's investigations. Looking for the statue, guided by the Illuminati member that was expelled, he started with Bavaria. He says the name Spartacus, which leads me to believe it's not Gotha, because Weishaupt formed the Order in Ingolstadt. I'm leaning toward the university."

Heidi tapped Cross on the shoulder and pointed toward a side street. "Down there. We'll change cars and get straight back on the road. If we want to reach the first waypoint fast, we can't afford luxuries."

Bodie saw the absolute sense of driving instead of flying, of keeping it low profile instead of high risk. Once, though, just once, he wished low profile meant high luxury.

"Don't worry." Heidi saw his face. "Bavaria isn't that far away now."

Cassidy looked pale. "Can we eat? I need food, woman. Real food."

"Yeah, sure, there's a burger stand across from the safe house."

Cassidy went even paler. "Are you kidding? Do I look like a girl that stands in line at a burger van?"

"Hard to say. I'm that girl. Is that a problem?"

Gunn laughed. "Cassidy is high society. Big maintenance. She thinks McDonald's is a farm."

"You think that?" Cassidy turned on Gunn. "Then you don't know me at all."

The car slowed. Men in suits appeared outside a recessed door. Heidi reached for the handle. "Let's move."

CHAPTER THIRTY

It seemed that one of the most notorious serial killers in Munich's history had been active again. The man the press had dubbed the Day Stalker usually took his victims, kept them for twenty-four hours, and then made sure the grisly remains were found by way of a phone call, having dumped the body and vanished without anyone ever seeing. The police secretly referred to him as the Vanisher—since no matter how many living, breathing humans were around, no matter how many windows overlooked the scene, nobody ever saw the Day Stalker come, and nobody ever saw him leave.

Fear surrounded him like the blackest tornado: impenetrable, furious, deadly. To attempt to discover the Day Stalker's true identity meant you would become the next victim.

Urban legend? Clever myth?

Well, Xavier Von Gothe mused, *perhaps a good mix of both.*

The Illuminati drew from the deep well of humanity that inhabited Munich whenever it suited their needs, killing them, using them, manipulating them like pawns. Why shouldn't they? The herd existed only to be ruled, led mostly by emotion, and fear was just one of those healthy options. Xavier made sure the victims were chosen at random, his best Hoods on the case, and the legend of the Day Stalker grew and grew.

Xavier held up a black candle and placed it upon an altar. He lit the wick, and watched it catch fire. The flame was hypnotic, an external reflection of his soul. The chamber all around him echoed a quiet chant, the darker, vaulted reaches above taking the whispers and feeding them back tenfold. A crescendo began to build, still quiet for now. Xavier took the candle, careful to hold it away from the folds of his hood, and turned away from the altar.

"Join me as I conduct this service in Your honor."

He spoke to the candle, to the air, to the night sky that hung high above, beyond the chamber. He spoke to that which they could not see, but worshipped with absolute conviction.

"Join me as I conduct this service in Your honor."

Another seven times he spoke the chant, starting the ritual. To the left and right, arrayed in a half circle, their bodies covered by cloak and hood, were his Illuminati brothers and just a few chosen acolytes. Soon, they all held candles, the fire catching the glint and glare of their eyes.

Xavier fell silent after the chant, and bowed his head. Sconces were lit around the room, offering only a faint illumination as was appropriate. The dim glow picked out the Order of Illuminati present, not the entire group by any means, not even the highest-ranking members, but the leaders of this particular lodge, and Xavier himself.

"Light Bringer," Xavier said softly. "Storm Bringer. Death Dealer and Great Dragon, we are thankful for You and we invoke You!"

A murmur of agreement from all present.

"Prince of Darkness. Lord of the Bottomless Pit. We invoke You!"

Another murmur.

Xavier lost himself in the ritual, consumed by his belief, knowing that everything he did and all he had was on the whim of the Great Lord, and he was but a lowly servant. The fervor rose within the chamber, the religious passions inflamed. A brief meditation followed and then a guttural chanting arose, their deity's name repeated in as many guises and languages as they could speak.

Xavier turned after it was done, and the low, animalistic urges rose within him.

A broad altar stood before him, three steps high, and upon the altar lay a body, naked, strapped down, rendered incapable of speech. Today it was male, average age, height, and build. Nothing remarkable. Nothing that would cause any ripples.

The body was clean, recently washed. Even now, it wriggled, pulled at its bonds as if imagining it might pull free. Xavier stared at it without compassion, without concern, wondering why such a fortunate creature would not want to be sacrificed to a greater, higher purpose. The pleasure was all his.

Others should be so lucky.

Xavier placed his candle at the head of the altar. One by one, the other Minervals—members of the higher Order of Illuminati—came forward, mounted the steps to the altar, and reverently placed their candles around the glistening body. Each Minerval bowed and spoke a prayer. Each nodded at Xavier. The writhing creature was ignored. The bulging eyes were regarded with dispassion, the pleading face overlooked.

All these years it had lived. All its hopes and dreams, leading to this very moment.

Xavier knew it didn't have the intellect to see how incredibly fortunate it was. He moved slowly to the center of the altar, held up two hands, the robe falling down his arms to reveal two pale, hairy hands and wrists, the left covered with ritualistic tattoos. The gathering spoke a slow, unknown language, taking their time, an invocation specific to the Illuminati order and kept secret for untold years. Only the initiated, the highest of the highest, would ever know it even existed.

A consecrated Host was then unveiled and placed at the back of the chamber. It required but a few seconds for Xavier to utter the Latin expression *"Ave, Satanas!"*

Welcome, Satan.

A gleaming, razor-edged knife lay out of sight upon yet another small dais at the foot of the main altar. Xavier reached down for it now, took hold of the broad, ribbed handle, and lifted it above his head, point first.

The tied creature began to writhe once more, finding some extra purpose in his struggle. Xavier allowed him to feast his terrified eyes upon the weapon that would exalt and elevate his soul and sanctify this sacrament. Its great blade flashed, bright and roiling with fire in the dimmed chamber. It was the center of all things, the dark and holy vessel for the Great Dragon called Azazel, Belial, Samael, and Leviathan. It held a mesmerizing presence, the fire and the darkness inherent, the life it could spare and the death it could deal as clear as the heavy, burgeoning specter that now filled the chamber, hanging and multiplying and weighing like blood, gold, and power on the hearts and souls of all those present.

Xavier could feel it; more than that, he could draw it in. Revel in it. Nourish his worthless, blasted soul in the spirit of the ultimate deity that they worshipped.

Between them, the believers, the crazy, and the intensely passionate conjured up that which they desired, a religious fever sweeping them away.

Xavier tasted their desires, but reveled in the blade. He turned it one way and another, let the fire catch and the darkness wither, then angled it another way. He lowered it slowly until his hands rested on the man's stomach.

"Out of love and thankfulness for you," he said.

The gathering chanted the words back to him.

"Amen!"

Xavier raised the blade, cracked a smile just for the man on the altar, to let him know before he died that there was a real—a *deeper*—truth here, before turning it and plunging the vessel of Satan to the hilt into the man's heart.

Not a sound was uttered. Not a limb moved. The blade stayed within, Xavier now with his eyes closed and a deep, satisfying ecstasy overcoming him, the vessel, the ritual, and the sacrifice all together for just thirteen seconds.

Then, Xavier removed the blade and placed it reverently back upon the dais. He ignored the still creature and turned to his brethren.

"Thank you, brothers. We are remade and will prosper again. The Great Dragon will guide us."

"The Great Dragon will guide us," they chanted back.

Xavier left the chamber quickly, eager to contact Baltasar and hear about the progress of the map—the one thing that could bring their inverted black heaven crashing down.

CHAPTER
THIRTY-ONE

Bodie gave Gunn and Jeff plenty of time to investigate the Bavarian Illuminati, the University of Ingolstadt, and Adam Weishaupt as the car wound through Austria and then entered Germany. With Munich coming over the horizon, Bodie knew they were finally getting close to where the Illuminati began.

"You think the Hood's already there?" Cross asked.

"If he's heading for this lodge, yeah," Jeff said. "There are small lodges all around Bavaria, some genuine and some not."

"If the bastard's going where we're going," Cassidy said, "we'd best prepare for a welcoming committee."

"Well, it's not going to be the university," Gunn said. "Or at least not Weishaupt's university. That closed in 1800."

Heidi thought it through as the others stared. "So what did our archaeologist visit in the early 1900s?"

"Good question," Gunn said. "Exactly my thought. But the building is still there, and receives visitors. Not only through the Illuminati connection, but because it was where Mary Shelley had Victor Frankenstein attend university."

Cassidy stared. "Weishaupt's university?"

Gunn nodded. "Yep."

"Obviously it's now no more," Jeff pointed out. "With some deep digging I found out that the Hohe Schule building was used by the first Bavarian state university—and that is Weishaupt's. It is now the Museum of Medical History."

Bodie nodded. "Superb. We'll go there. Hopefully the Hood will be miles away at their great lodge thing."

Cassidy raised a brow. "Great lodge thing?"

"Well, whatever these crazy asses call it. I don't know."

"Me neither. But good use of the word 'ass' there. You're learning."

The road around Munich took another hour, and then they were nearing Ingolstadt. Cross tapped in the coordinates for the museum and smiled at the result.

"Fourteen minutes," he said. "Better tool up, people."

Bodie reached for a black pack. Heidi did the same on the other side of the vehicle. The CIA car was equipped with all manner of items, everything from energy bars to machine guns. The group took their share of weapons, stores, a couple of satellite phones, and a varied pick of other paraphernalia. Bodie remembered the comms this time, making sure everyone planted a receiver in their ear and a mic in their lapel.

"Smooth and sweet," he said. "Just how I like it."

Cassidy looked over. "Haven't heard you say that for a bit, dude. Used to be your catchphrase, more or less."

"Yeah." Bodie shrugged. "I haven't been feeling quite myself since Jack friggin' Pantera threw me into a Mexican prison."

"Plus," Cross put in as he studied the road ahead, "Agent Moneymaker here has taken us way outside our comfort zone."

"Find yourself by testing yourself," Heidi said. "Isn't that what they say?"

"I think I know what I am," Cassidy said wistfully. "Don't exactly try to hide it."

"Yeah, rap sheets don't lie," Gunn said with a twist of acid to his voice.

"As a matter of fact," Heidi said, "they do. Mostly because they're very clinical. But, hey, why does that matter? Y'all are government agents now."

Bodie smiled at the sudden twang, not the new label. "We ready?"

"Four minutes." Cross was squinting through the windshield, searching out the correct building.

"Glasses?" Jemma held them out.

Cross took them reluctantly, pushed them over his nose. "Make my skin itch."

"No, that'd be the three-day growth," Cassidy said, then looked closer. "Urgh. *Gray* growth."

"Go boil yourself, Movie Star."

The team readied, unsure of what they had to do. Bodie likened it to reconnoitering a job and said as much to the team.

"Case the place. Check it out. Look for everything and miss nothing. Guys, we're the best in the business at this. Jeff cracked the first waypoint—we're here—now it's up to us to crack the second."

"Treat it like a job?" Cross shrugged agreeably. "Sounds good to me, boss."

Heidi slapped the proverbial damper on their sudden enthusiasm. "And don't forget to look out for Hoods," she said. "And bombs. Toxic gas. You know, everything our misguided friends might think of."

Cross parked the car and they jumped out, stretching legs, backs, and intellectual muscles. The Museum of Medical History was an old building, with a white-and-pale-yellow-painted exterior, the entrance marked by a series of baroque arches and symmetrical wings that returned in a C-shape. The gardens were well proportioned and well tended, with green and lush grass, bushes, and trees. The whole setting was pleasant, evoking little thought of Illuminati conspiracy, secrets, or even Victor Frankenstein. As he stood taking it all in, Bodie was reminded that they were following an old map and some odd clues they called waypoints, reading footnotes and treading in some 1900s archaeologist's irresolute footsteps all on the say-so of a particularly unusual CIA agent.

Could be worse, his brain told him. *Could still be in prison.*

Could be dead?

Bodie didn't feel out of his depth. He felt more like he'd been uprooted from contentment and placed in adversity. All the skills were still present, the knowledge, the spontaneous flair; he just had to learn to adapt and use them differently.

Cassidy was flexing her muscles and trying to conceal her weapons at the same time. "Take our time? Don't miss anything? Yeah, we know the score, Bodie. You ready?"

"And comms." Bodie tapped his ear. "Don't forget we're hooked up now."

"Not for long, I hope. Don't wanna be listening to Gunn when he has his 'special' time."

The computer specialist stopped preening for just a second to give her the finger. Bodie took the sign to mean everyone was ready. Together, they marched into the museum, paid for tickets, and took a moment to let their eyes adjust to the dim interior. Heidi wandered into a corner and tested the comms.

"Nobody's following us. Have to assume the switch back in Vienna worked. It's a certainty, though, that as soon as the Hood's finished his report and handed over the map, the Illuminati will be here in force. Now, get going."

The team paired off. Bodie took Jemma, the two walking through a door of paneled oak with a map of the museum in their hands.

We returned something new to Spartacus and 1776.

Applying the clue here, he knew, was the hardest task of all. *Literally,* he thought, *it means the very place Weishaupt created his new world order.*

They found a guide and asked. The question, Bodie figured, was genuine, honest, and probably voiced frequently. The guide—a long-haired man with thick spectacles—nodded with a sense of boredom.

"Toward the back. Name on the door. Don't be performing any rituals."

The English was broken, but coherent. The guide sniggered at his own joke, but gave Bodie a parting glare. The thief chose to ignore it and walked slowly to the indicated location, taking in the interior of the room. A few paintings and ornaments decorated the walls, some gilt and brass furnishings added luster. If the office didn't pan out, they'd have to check out every picture, every nook and cranny.

"It would help if we knew what we were looking for," Jemma said, tying her long hair into a bun.

"Start at the back and work forward," Bodie said. "At least we're here legally."

"I don't normally start in the field," she said.

"A good education, then. The trick is *not* to have a quick scan or even a leisurely one. The trick is to look and look again, then move away for a while, return, and study carefully. Use every moment wisely. Don't force it. Let it soak into you like a fine bottle of rum. Absorb the ambience and your surroundings until it all makes sense."

"And when will that be?"

"You'll know."

Bodie suggested that they should examine Weishaupt's office. Murmurs of agreement were returned, and Heidi again pronounced an all clear. They still had time. Jemma finally paused outside a half-open door, pointing at a plaque.

"I guess we're allowed inside."

"That's the general idea in a museum, love."

The room was relatively small. It was sumptuous, though, a regalia of plush fittings, chairs and drapes, the centerpiece a heavy, deluxe desk, the floor covered by lavish carpets, and the walls richly paneled, adorned by masterful paintings.

"Don't forget," Bodie said. "An archaeologist left something here. It won't be obvious, it won't be easy to spot."

His words proved prophetic, so much in fact that Jemma told him off for saying them. Three other couples entered the room as they searched, tourists killing time. Bodie followed a ritual—get a feel for the place, remember the placement. Forget and come back. Sit down. Think. Study. Something like this could not be rushed. Jemma searched carefully, opening up the desk and rifling drawers, searching under the chair and its coverings. Their study yielded nothing.

Jeff entered the room with his partner, Cassidy. Bodie stared at the newcomer with interest.

"Ah, an archaeologist. What would *you* do, Jeffo?"

Jeff settled himself, looking pensive. "I'd take it all with me," he said. "Archaeologists prefer to have their relics close enough to study at all times. But if I knew I was making a map? If I knew my quest would lead me from place to place?" He probed the room carefully. Bodie watched him, then watched Jemma watching him. Cassidy prowled over to the only window to scan the day outside. Cross joined her.

Jeff moaned. "It's staring us in the face."

Bodie jumped up, heart thudding. "Where?"

"No. I mean it's staring us in the face. I don't know what it is, but I bet it is."

Bodie pretended to reach for his gun. At that moment the door opened to admit Heidi and Gunn.

"We good?" the CIA agent asked.

"We're sick and tired," Cassidy said. "And can't find anything."

"Jeff's bloody useless," Bodie said.

"And what? You were gonna shoot him?"

"It crossed my mind."

"Everything is the same," Jeff mused. "It's the same because the museum *wants* it to look the same. But we have different paintings and photographs from different periods here. Weishaupt. King Ludwig from 1826. A photo of the founding building of the motor company Auto Union, which later became Audi, also in Ingolstadt. A portrait of Charles de Gaulle, who was detained in a Bavarian fortress as a prisoner of war. Different times, same look."

Bodie studied the pictures, the paintings. "All right, I see your point. But dude, what's your bloody point?"

"Spartacus and 1776, that's here where we are right now. But, as for the rest of the clue—we *returned something new* . . . ?" Jeff paused, choosing his words carefully. "I think we have to look at the archaeologist himself. This was clearly a highly secret mission, this journey of his. A revenge mission too. He couldn't risk anything. So what did he do? He left with the next clue and then *donated* something to this room later. Something new."

Bodie scrunched up his face in thought. His natural, nourished inclination to mistrust told him Jeff was reaching, probably mistaken. But his deep-set, conflicting need to hold on to some kind of belief pushed him in the opposite direction.

"Jeff," he said, "let's go find that guide."

They trooped out of the room. Heidi went ahead with Gunn, the two of them turning more and more restless and worried. Bodie helped Jeff find the museum guide and hovered while Jeff asked the key question.

"Can you tell me if anything was donated to the Weishaupt room in the early 1900s?" he asked.

The guide looked surprised, but willing to help. "Happy to look," he said in English again. "Break up the day."

Twenty minutes later and Jeff had the information. He and Bodie left the guide and returned to Cassidy, Cross, and Jemma, who were loitering close to Weishaupt's office.

Jeff grinned at the redhead. "We've got it."

CHAPTER
THIRTY-TWO

Back inside the room, Jeff went immediately to one of the side walls. There, amid a cluster of six-by-fours, hung a golden-framed depiction of Adam Weishaupt standing, poker-faced, outside the very building they now occupied.

Cassidy stared at it. "Crap, Jeffo. It's shit. Just this guy standing outside this building. Spartacus in 1776, right?"

"But it isn't *just* that," Jeff said, squinting. "Look closer. There's an anomaly."

Bodie crowded in too, leaving Jemma to watch the room. A closer look at the picture revealed a small amount of writing—the name of the university across the top of the building.

"Except it's the wrong name," Jeff said happily. "Whatever this building is and was called, whatever it has been through the centuries, I can categorically assure you it was never called the Grand Lodge of All England."

"And this was donated by our friendly archaeologist?" Cassidy asked.

"I can't confirm that for a certainty. The records, if they exist, will be obscured. He didn't want anyone tracking him down. But yes, it was 'something new' around the time he visited. And the only new item to be donated specifically to this room since 1887."

Bodie read the line without emotion. "The Grand Lodge of All England. So we're to believe that's the next waypoint?"

"I think so," Jeff said. "And a rather unique way of hiding it, I think."

"Still," Jemma said, "not easy to take at face value considering all that's at risk."

"There's nothing else," Jeff said with a touch of exasperation. "How long have we been here? Hours. Nothing else in this room is out of place, nor is it wrong or donated at the right time. The odds are good."

"Kid's right." Bodie decided. "And we can't hang around here forever. If we leave now, the Hoods will never know we were here."

The team started to move. Jeff hung back a little and Jemma tried to tug him along.

"You're thieves," Jeff said. "Are you really gonna leave this here for the Illuminati to find?"

Bodie opened the door. "They might not figure it out," he said. "And I'd take a special kind of pleasure in seeing it hang there for the next hundred years. Also, it hardly matters to them. *They* know where the statue is. Thievery, my friend, is sometimes only the art of deception. They may think we've done something to that room and miss the vital clue in all their frustration." He grinned. "Perfect."

Outside the room, they traversed the narrow corridor and made their way around to the front of the museum. Heidi and Gunn were nowhere in sight, but the path outside was clear, and the parking area was only two minutes away. Armed with their new knowledge, the team made their way outside.

Heidi broke cover first, emerging from a patch of dense foliage and waving her arms urgently, running straight for them.

Bodie stopped, staring.

Cross came next, ducking out from behind a low hedge and crab-walking his way over.

"Hoods," Heidi breathed. "All over the cars. Looking for us, I guess."

"How do you know they're Hoods?" Cassidy asked, trying to see over the hedges and to the parking lot.

"I'm guessing," Heidi admitted. "They're in plain clothes, but they're armed. They number over a dozen and they're checking plates and vehicles. It's just a matter of time before they come inside."

"Shit," Bodie said, looking around. "Just Hoods? Or do we have any hierarchy out there?"

The CIA agent bobbed her head. "I see what you're thinking, but I can't say. Didn't see anyone apart from young, confident, capable men with weapons exposed."

Cassidy stared, then blinked. "And you want to run away? 'Kin 'ell, girl. Sounds like Hollywood all over again."

"Guns, girl. Their guns."

"Ah."

"We need another way out," Bodie said. "The Hoods clearly don't know we're in here. All we need is . . ."

He spun, heading back toward the door.

The team stared after him. "What?"

He beckoned for them to follow, not raising his voice. If the Hoods were checking the parking area, they would be turning their attention toward the museum next. He estimated they had a minute, no more.

"Where are we going?" Heidi demanded, running at his shoulder.

Bodie entered the museum again, slowed and walked briskly to the right. The door to the interior stood open, tourists milling about.

"Guy?" Cassidy asked.

He didn't stop, just walked straight through, not wanting to take the time to explain. Every second was precious. Without turning around he said, "Cross. Check our rear."

"Already on it, boss. No sign of 'em yet."

Good, that gives us . . .

"Shit, here they come."

Bollocks.

Bodie sped up to a fast walk, turned a corner, and spied the museum guide. "Hey," he said. "Hey, there must be another way out of here, right?"

The guide stared through his thick lenses, eyes blinking and magnified. "Than the exit? Umm, no."

Heidi had already caught on. "Don't give us that. There must be another way."

"Well, yes, we have fire exits," the guide said. "Alarmed, of course. And leading back to the front, which"—he made a point of staring over their shoulders—"I assume you wish to avoid?"

The man didn't look scared, just bored. Bodie felt the seconds counting down. The Hoods would be approaching the entrance.

"CIA it," he said to Heidi.

The agent knew what he meant, took out her badge, and shoved it into the guide's face. "We need your help."

An intrigued expression crossed his face. "This day gets better and better," he said. "But the information is accurate. You can't get away from the museum without circling around to the front. Unless you can climb an eight-foot-high chain-link fence with ease."

Bodie refrained from revealing that was exactly what his team was trained to do. Jeff would struggle, and perhaps Heidi.

"This is a museum, once an old university," he said. "Don't tell me you don't have a basement. And to be fair, we know who Adam Weishaupt was, the secrets he kept. I'd be surprised if there wasn't a private way out of here."

The guide looked from Heidi's badge to Bodie and then down the corridor toward the front entrance. He would surely know a CIA identification meant nothing here, but he was also blessed with a good quantity of common sense, which helped him gauge the situation with an open honesty.

"We're in trouble, yes?"

Bodie nodded. "Everyone. If they find us."

The guide made a swift decision and led them away, toward the rear of the building. They passed Weishaupt's room and entered the one next door. Once inside, the guide closed the door, and turned to face them.

"It was found over a hundred years ago, but it has no value. Just a dusty old tunnel, so the museum forgot about it. Guides and guards need to know for obvious reasons, but"—he shrugged—"no one else."

Cassidy stared at the oak paneling. "Where?"

"Here."

The guide motioned at a heavy bookcase. Cassidy was the first to it, getting a good grip and shuffling the bottom edges away from the wall. Bodie squeezed into the back and helped push it clear.

"Gonna be a bit obvious when they check the room," Cross said critically, eyeing the angled bookcase.

"Well, sorry," Cassidy said. "I left my secret-passage-bookcase-tugging-hook at home."

Gunn shook his head. "Bit daft of you."

"Move," Bodie said. "Priority is to get out of the museum. We'll worry about pursuit later."

"I can cover the passage," the guide said. "It is my job, after all."

Heidi looked worried. "I don't want to leave you with them. Believe me when I say they're evil little bastards."

"They wouldn't kill everyone in the museum," the guide said with huge naivety.

Heidi clammed up. Bodie shoved Cross, Jeff, Jemma, and Gunn into the passage. "Your biggest asset here is your inexperience," he said. "Use it. You never saw us."

They filed into the narrow passage, leaving the guide to ease the bookcase back into place. Bodie closed the door behind them by the beam of Heidi's small flashlight. Cross was already leading the way.

"No talking," Bodie said. "In case it travels or the walls are thin."

They moved steadily, carefully, not unused to creeping around in the dark through secret byways. There were times in the past when Bodie had done more tunnel creeping than your average rat. Cross took it steady, either by design or necessity, but it didn't matter. There was only one way. And that way led down.

Handholds helped steady them. Cross soon raised a hand, which Bodie saw in the shifting beam of the flashlight. A sense of constricted space came over them as they paused, the walls a snug fit to their shoulders and the ceiling inches above their heads. The passage was rough-hewn, merely a fast means of moving about unseen.

For Bodie and his team it felt like home.

Cross found the handle and twisted, opening the door. They filed out to find themselves inside a dark and dusty basement, three meters high and approximately ten wide. Cobwebs covered every corner and hung from the ceiling. On the floor lay half a dozen chests and cases, all closed, all untouched for many years.

Heidi paused. "You think these chests may be connected to Weishaupt? The Illuminati? If they are—"

"No time for that." Bodie hurried her along. "We don't know where we'll come out yet."

"Just wait a moment," Heidi said a bit indignantly. "I'm in charge—"

"Not the point," Cassidy said. "Different mission. Send someone else."

Bodie had been taught time and time again to stick exclusively with the operation you had planned. Diversions led to mistakes and capture.

"And to be fair," Cross said, his voice echoing a little in the space, "you induced us into this op for a reason. For our expertise."

"Induced?" Cassidy repeated. "Are we pregnant?"

"Goaded. Exhorted. Forced."

Heidi let it go. "C'mon, forced? Really?"

Cross reached the other side and another door. This one creaked open, years-old dust and debris falling from the hinges and the edges. Cross stepped back, coughing as Jeff looked concerned. Cassidy patted his back.

"Want me to go in front, Granddad?"

"I'm . . . good," Cross hacked.

Another passage, this one leading up at an angle that strained their calf muscles. Jemma made a comment about the Illuminati being fit and lean, and Cross seconded it. Soon, though, they reached another door, and everyone smelled the change in the air.

Fresh on the other side.

Cross cracked it open, held it steady. The team crowded at his back, drawing weapons and taking a moment to adjust to the glimmer of daylight that shone through. Cross then allowed the door to open farther and they saw they were inside a mound of earth, a mossy overhang hiding the entrance.

"Still inside the museum grounds?" Jemma asked.

"Just outside," Cross said. "I see no fence through the overhang."

"No Hoods?"

"We'll see, go slow," Bodie said.

"There were an awful lot back there," Gunn said. "And since the original Hood came here, it must be an important place."

Heidi nodded, crouching down beside Bodie. "Yeah, probably a second or third in the ranking. We want the big HQ, otherwise it's all for nothing."

"Snake. Head. Chop." Cassidy mimed the action.

"Shush now," Cross whispered, moving ahead.

Cassidy sent him a glare, not liking the order, but said nothing, clearly seeing his point. Bodie watched as Cross surveyed the terrain and then turned back.

"All good," he said. "The museum's behind this big mound. We appear to be in some kind of wasteland. Any thoughts on transport?"

"If we get away without being seen at all," Heidi said, "that puts us a step ahead. Do that first, and then we'll see about getting across to England."

Bodie took the news without much pleasure. It had been a long time since he'd visited the home country. The last he heard, there was a warrant out for his arrest. For all their arrests. "Any idea where we're going?" he asked.

CHAPTER THIRTY-THREE

If the CIA knew anything at all, it was how to slip someone into a country quietly by plane. A fact for which Bodie was extremely thankful as they plowed through the night clouds on their way to England. Transport out of Bavaria had been tricky at first, but once the team had trekked far enough away from the museum and verified they hadn't been seen, a chopper picked them up and took them to the airport. Heidi was overjoyed they had made it clear.

One step ahead now.

The Illuminati had rarely been outdone by an opponent, Bodie imagined. Speed, purpose, and some skill had engineered this lead; now they had to take full advantage.

"So, England," Cassidy said from a single seat in front of Bodie. "What's it like?"

The Londoner pursed his lips. "Hard to say. Depends where you go, I guess. London's got most of the hustle, the glamour, the action, which would suit you. Then further north, lots of countryside and trees, which would suit Gunn—"

The computer tech lifted a middle finger. "I only hug blondes."

Cassidy pounced on that like a shark chasing a wounded dolphin. "Can't say I've ever seen a blond goat."

Bodie continued, ignoring the banter. "North east and we have a few seaside resorts. Scarborough, Bridlington, and Whitley Bay, that kind of thing. A nice area for the older folk to retire and enjoy the views." He sent a surreptitious glance over at the snoring Cross. Even Gunn laughed shortly.

"Libraries," Bodie said. "Plenty of those."

Jemma made a face at that one. "I wondered how low you'd go."

"Nothing wrong with a library, Blunt," Cassidy said. "But you're not gonna find a boyfriend there."

Jemma tried not to squirm. "I don't know what—"

"Sure you do." Cassidy turned to stare out the window. "You're a hot chick over thirty with no meaningful relationships under your belt. Life's getting away from you."

Jemma wasn't sure how to respond, but finally said, "And how old are you now, Cass?"

"Ah, that's just petty. You know I'm right."

Bodie shifted in his seat and made a point of looking over toward Jeff and Heidi up front.

"Any luck?"

"The Grand Lodge of All England?" Jeff asked. "Yeah, it exists. Since the 1700s. It's a 'Mother Lodge,' used to create new lodges and procure new members. Activity there has been infrequent through the centuries, but tends to spark up again every so often, perhaps when the Order needs new blood? Just a guess."

"And why did our old archaeologist send us first to Bavaria, and now to here?" Jemma asked.

"The map is his guide," Jeff explained. "It also forms a diary of his travels, his quest to find the Statue of Zeus. Obviously he's following the clues laid down by the disgruntled Illuminati member he found and clues in history itself. Like Charlemagne, like Olympia. The map isn't fully rounded. Yes, it's disorganized, but he probably didn't have time to write it up properly. Or chance," he added. "Maybe he didn't have a chance to do it. Anyway, we have waypoints and footnotes, that's it."

"One thing's for sure, though," Bodie said. "We're on the right track. The Illuminati know it, but the picture we found in Bavaria proves it without any doubt."

Heidi looked across at him. "My word not good enough?"

Bodie laughed. Cassidy chirped up. "Of course it is. We luuuurve the CIA."

Heidi sighed. "Have I not been good to you?"

Bodie heard the humor in her voice and laughed again. "Well, you did help me *Prison Break*–style and almost get us killed a couple of times. I guess you can stay."

"Why, thanks."

Heidi checked her computer. "All right, guys, here it is. We're an hour out. Once we arrive I'm gonna have to leave you. Something else big has come up, which I can't avoid." She gave them a tired, chagrined stare. "CIA politics say I have to take care of it. So this is where you prove your worth. This is where you shine."

Bodie was surprised to hear she was leaving them alone, but had been initially surprised when she tagged along with the team. At the end of the day, though, they were just one of many assets.

"You're trusting us?" Gunn asked naively.

Heidi tried her best not to embarrass the lad. "We'll know where you are at all times."

"Don't worry," Bodie said. "After what we've seen—after seeing what the Illuminati can do—we're all in."

Everyone nodded. Heidi looked satisfied. "Locate the next waypoint," she said. "Easy as that."

"Where *are* we going?" Bodie asked.

"The Grand Lodge of All England," Jeff said, "is in Yorkshire. Specifically, in York."

Gunn looked up. "Really? My auntie lives in York."

"So you know the place?"

"No. Not really."

"Okaaay, great input. And a shame. Because the Internet is a wonderful place most of the time, but it has no location for the lodge."

Bodie ripped open a packet of nuts. "Of course it doesn't. What do you have?"

"Lodge activity goes back to and beyond 926, when King Athelstan convened a great council there, around the time of the Vikings. York, of course, has a well-known Viking history, which it embraces, right up to the present day. I find the other interesting aspect about all this revolves around the York Legend." He paused for a drink.

"Which is?" Cassidy prompted impatiently.

"It's rather long-winded," Jeff admitted, "but points to facts and proof that York was the birthplace of English masonry, allowing the York lodges to claim precedence over all other lodges."

"Whoa." Bodie blinked. "So York is the birthplace of the English Freemasons as well as a convening point for the English Illuminati?"

"For a time," Jeff said. "Yes."

"Shit, they kept that quiet."

Jeff shrugged. "More like they didn't shout out about it like they do Vikings. They let it lie quietly. There were—or are—lodges attached to the York Minster and to the Merchants Hall. Saint Saviourgate, and a pub in that area. And Stonegate. We have to assume one of these lodges is our objective."

"That's too many," Cassidy said, then added with her usual directness, "Anyone we can target?"

"Straight for the jugular, eh?" Heidi nodded. "I like it."

"Well, the Lord Mayor of York was president back in the eighteenth century," Jeff said, still scanning the documents he'd found. "But no telling if that tradition changed. Wait, there's a fair bit about Drake here."

Gunn looked up. "Drake? Why do I recognize that name?"

"Everyone knows that name," Jeff muttered. "He's exclusively associated with England."

"Okay then." Gunn plucked at his hair, using the airplane window as a mirror.

"Francis Drake," Jeff said, "the antiquarian, not the sailor, gave proof that the York Lodge dated back beyond 600." He paused. "I wonder if we can date any of the buildings in the identified areas. Anyway, Drake was Grand Master. Ah, wait. It tells of the lodge at number 259 Stonegate as ceasing in 1767, so that one's out. There's talk of worship at a church in Coney Street and feasts at the Guildhall."

Gunn spoke up. "York Minster dates back to the seventh century," he said. "In a rudimentary state. A church built in a hurry, then later a stone building, both of which fell into disrepair. Fires and rebuilds plague it right through the twelfth century, and in the thirteenth it began to take shape right into the fifteenth. I doubt the Minster's our place."

"Agreed," Bodie said. "The Illuminati would have wanted a quiet area, clear of controversy, something that would go unnoticed."

"York was founded as Eboracum in 71 AD," Gunn said. "By the Romans. It was the capital of the province of Britannia and of the kingdoms of Northumbria and Jorvik. Occupied by a tribe named the *Brigantes*, later hounded by the Roman Ninth Legion. They started building York Castle at that time, the focal point of which now lies under the foundations of York Minster. Okay, on to more pertinent matters. Stone buildings were ordered by King Edwin of Northumbria around 630, so we can assume several were built around our target time. Now listen to this." Gunn's voice went high with excitement. "Alcuin of York came to a cathedral school of York . . . a teacher and scholar . . . first at Saint Peter's School founded in 627 AD . . . Alcuin was also known as Charlemagne's leading advisor. There's our link to the statue. Of course in the eighth and ninth centuries, York was captured by the Vikings and came under their rule, notably a guy called Eric Bloodaxe. I guess, if the statue came here, it was removed before that."

"Olympia to Rome to France to Bavaria to York," Cross muttered, waking up. "This wonder of the world is more traveled than I am."

"Granddad's awake," Cassidy said. "Better put the coffee on."

"I have some of York's oldest streets, but the Shambles, called England's most medieval street, only dates back to the fourteenth century. We have to dig deeper."

The jet crossed the English Channel and started to head up country. Bodie didn't ask how Heidi and the CIA guaranteed secrecy. He knew they'd never tell, and anything they said in that regard couldn't be completely trusted. It seemed only minutes had passed before the plane started descending.

"Time to shine," Heidi said. "We're counting on you now."

CHAPTER
THIRTY-FOUR

Confident that they weren't being pursued, and that no horrific event was in store, Bodie's team exited the plane and said goodbye to Heidi Moneymaker. The CIA agent closed the door, and the jet immediately taxied away, taillight blinking in the cold dawn.

Bodie spied the waiting car. The York city walls were a ten-to-twenty-minute drive away, depending on the density of traffic.

"Where the hell are we?" Cross asked, taking his time shrugging into a jacket and zipping fasteners.

"Elvington Airfield." Bodie shrugged.

"So we know where we're going?" Cassidy asked, walking off toward the warm car.

"Not a clue." Jeff went with her.

"How about a library?" Jemma suggested with an ironic smile that echoed their earlier banter. "Quiet and resourceful."

"Good call," Bodie said.

Twenty minutes later the team was climbing the stairs and entering a large, hushed room with long rectangular desks placed around the interior. The exterior and rear were a collection of bookshelves, the front occupied by a desk and more bookshelves. The team filed through in silence to the farthest table with a large shelf at their back and a window to keep watch out of. Jeff unzipped his laptop bag as Gunn pulled out an iPad.

Cassidy sat back, barely refraining from putting her boots up on the table. "Fuck," she said.

Jemma looked over. "That's not appropriate for a library."

"You're joking, right? It's one of the best places to do it."

"Yeah, yeah."

"Seriously," Cassidy said. "You and me are gonna have to have a night out on the town. Live a little."

"With you? That sounds scary."

"It is. That's part of the fun."

Gunn looked up. "You don't *have* to be a party girl to have fun."

"Says the Goat Whisperer," Cassidy grunted.

The tech team became absorbed by their work, using history and contacts they'd built up through the years. University connections became useful for Jeff, especially when he connected with a man in York and told him about the murder of Jeff's mentor and teacher. The man had known her also. After that, the man became a remote member of the team and chose a few others, though they were told little detail.

Slowly, through Gunn and Jeff, a network of help was built.

Bodie always knew the maxim *It's not what you know, it's who you know* was among the most significant slivers of advice ever offered. He used it to full effect now. Gunn was in his element with the networking, and Jeff was wholly gripped and totally committed. In the end it was a painstaking matter of narrowing down the known location with old records and archives, establishing when each area was built. The simple fact was that their initial thoughts were wrong—nothing could be found that was built in the seventh century. What they did find, however, was an area of York built around the time that the Grand Lodge of All England was recharged with a new energy. The time it defied London and attracted the most notable members.

The area centered on Saint Saviourgate.

It took many hours, many trips in turn to the lower-floor coffee shop, many sighs of boredom, and many false leads before they narrowed it down to a particular street with a building fashioned in a particular style.

It had wrought-iron railings and a nondescript exterior. A front yard that, though gated off, could be viewed from all the front windows, top and bottom. A rear garden that couldn't be accessed through the front yard but only through the house, and again, easily surveilled.

Bodie's team looked at each other, waiting for their leader to make a decision.

"Now we go in for a closer look," Bodie said. "Check their tech. Finally, this is what we *do*, people. This is what we do."

"You planning a break in?" Cross asked.

"Yeah, the best one yet. We have to break into the Illuminati lodge, find the waypoint, and then get out without them ever knowing we were there."

"Security's gonna be intense," Cross said.

Bodie smiled. "Damn, I really do hope so."

◆ ◆ ◆

As darkness slowly started to fall, the team decided they didn't want to waste any more time. This was a night job, a fluid job, and speed was of the essence. Jeff informed them the house off Saint Saviourgate was a good ten-minute walk from their current location, which was perfect.

Together, they left the library and stepped into the frost-dusted city of York. Bootham Bar sat near them, its intact castle walls stretching left and right. The entrance to the city was one large arch slightly wider than a car and two paths, one to each side. Bodie led the way with Jeff, guided by a cell phone and Google Maps. Ahead, they saw the impressive Minster, an awe-inspiring construction that never seemed free of scaffolding, stretching up until Bodie had to tilt his head backward to take it all in. Tourists milled around the area and filled the streets in between, checking out souvenir wagons and ice-cream vans, sampling the nectar in the pub, or walking to hotels. Bodie and Jeff threaded through carefully, with the rest of the team following.

Heading out of the city center, they found Colliergate, which had fewer crowds, and smaller shops, which were probably more attractive to the locals.

"Here." Jeff pointed ahead. "Saint Saviourgate. The lodge is up there along a little branch-off. You ready?"

Bodie looked around, saw expressionless, open faces and knew they were all good. Nobody was paying them any attention. The team was already in the zone. They turned up Saint Saviourgate, entering the narrow one-way street with houses to both sides, their facades practically touching the curbside. The roofs were high, yielding a rather claustrophobic feel to the entire area, the lowering sun completely blocked out. Bodie saw only a strip of darkening gray above and shadows lengthening along every window.

Presently, they came to the even narrower side road. Luckily it wasn't a dead end, so they wouldn't look too suspicious traversing it. They split up, one team heading for the front while the other wandered around the back. Both teams would circumvent the place and meet up to compare notes.

Bodie walked the front with Jeff and Cassidy, feeling a little at sea without Heidi and then feeling ridiculous and restless because of that. Tuning that out, he concentrated on what was before him—the approaching Grand Lodge.

Unassuming, unified entirely to the architecture all around, the building was nevertheless three houses wide and railed off, set back from the street as if everything else might have been built around it and at a slightly later date. The wrought-iron fence and gates were mostly decorative, unfeasible when it came to keeping out any kind of serious infiltration. Bodie ignored them.

He knew exactly what to look for.

The alarm keypad to the side of the door, its glass face and the manufacturer. The window locks, invisible to the average civilian, but clear to most average thieves. The CCTV cameras, again noting their makers and types. These windows were obscured, so he was unable to tell if there was a security office inside. The simple fact that the building was three houses wide and consisted of so many rooms told them it would require every ounce of skill to negotiate.

Cassidy looked gloomy. "Not much around here to distract or intimidate."

Bodie nodded, preoccupied. "I'm sure we'll find something."

"At least Jemma's gonna be happy. This will take a hell of a plan."

Bodie continued, observing the security. The sensors attached to the brick walls, the infrared beams that crossed the gate, the bars attached to the inside of random windows, the single man smoking a cigarette outside, who may or may not be a security guard.

And it was quite possible, of course, that all the houses overlooking the lodge had been purchased by the Illuminati.

Did I say possible? Bodie deliberated. *Of course, I meant probable.*

Passing the house, they made their way slowly down a side street, encountering Cross, Jemma, and Gunn coming in the other direction, and scoped out the rear. It didn't take long. Bodie estimated the wall at twelve feet high, topped by crushed glass. When they crossed to the other side of the road, he was able to view the very tops of the highest windows, the same uniform appearance as the front.

They met up at the junction of a busier street. Cross walked over to a bench and eased himself into it.

"Aching bones?" Cassidy asked.

"All the bruises," he said. "So far."

"Well, there's gonna be a few more to add to that collection," Jemma said. Bodie knew she was already formulating a plan.

"There's a body of influence that says hit them where they're strongest. They'll never expect it. There's another that states go for the weak spot because, by definition, it's the easiest. Gunn, I need the specs for all that security, ASAP."

"On it." Gunn was already visiting various websites and bringing up manufacturers' information along with hacks on how to render it obsolete.

"Cross, how are you at climbing three stories with a rope?"

"Do it in my sleep."

"Bodie, our problem may be equipment."

"Let's hear it first, Jemma. Then we'll worry about the gear."

"All right then. This is what we're gonna do."

CHAPTER THIRTY-FIVE

Jemma laid out the plan. Cross offered his experience and skill sets as a way of smoothing the rough edges, and Gunn added the tech skills for neutralizing any security devices. Cassidy was ready with the muscle. Bodie was project overseer, considering everything and missing nothing.

This was how they worked.

"Let's not forget the archaeologist somehow got a clue inside here. It's not a museum, so not easy to introduce even a paper clip. Any clues?"

"I have an idea how he did it," Bodie said. "But first let's get inside. Gunn, you good?"

The tech had all the equipment he needed. "Laptop's perfect, boss. The man in the shop set it up nice."

"Processing power?"

"Could be faster. I'll make do."

Jeff was setting up a mini Wi-Fi hotspot. "All done."

Cross opened out the packet of various tools, gloves, and liquids that he and Bodie had bought from a nearby hardware store called Barnitts.

"I'm ready."

"A few more moments," Gunn said. "It may look easy in the movies, but accessing somebody else's system isn't straightforward. And they have decent security. Solid firewall. Extra monitors that I'm bypassing. All I have to do now is match my packet to the network rule set." He paused, then sighed. "And I'm in. As flawless as a Disney princess."

Cassidy tutted. "Incredible, Gunn. You *are* a Disney princess rolled in syrupy sweetness. You gotta let it go, boy."

"Is that supposed to be . . . like . . . smart?"

Bodie called them to order. They all knew this was a tough job, hastily cobbled together. The risks were high, but the rewards were so good they were practically unimaginable.

"Never lose focus," he said. "If they find us they'll kill us without hesitation. Are we together?"

The team came closer, as one.

"Family is a sense of belonging," Bodie said. "Stay with the plan. Work as one. And we'll meet again."

The team members bowed their heads and whispered the word "family." Bodie clapped Jeff on the back—the youth stood apart and looked a little awkward—and told him to be on hand to back up Gunn whenever the tech needed it.

"And keep a lookout," he said. "The more pairs of eyes we have, the safer we'll be."

They moved out from the small alcove they'd discovered in an alley, which was close to the back of the Illuminati house. The first hurdle was the enormous wall, but nobody would have to climb it. There was a door set into it that could be unlocked by a keypad.

Bodie knew how to build a radio device that could crack almost any alarm system using a combination of a microcontroller and a single-board computer. The device captured and replayed codes by eavesdropping on the radio frequency remote that most alarms were built with. The device programmer read the alarm, as well as the individual keypad's own microcontroller where the passcode was stored. The readout then sent it back to Bodie.

Stopping now, he hopped onto the local frequency, received the passcode, and punched it into the keypad. The door clicked. No worries. Jemma had warned them that this was now potentially the most hazardous part of the mission—no way of telling what lay beyond the wall.

Bodie eased the door open. Cassidy breathed easily at his side. Perhaps she was hoping for trouble, but he knew she was not someone to betray her anxiety.

Inside lay a concrete courtyard, unadorned, just a single flat expanse of gray. Nothing to draw attention.

Jemma had taken her time to locate initial blueprints of all the houses in the city archives, but even that kind of diligence had yielded little. The two entry doors should lead to a kitchen and a basement, the latter of which Jemma had suggested they try first, assuming the basement would have another exit.

Great plan.

Bodie moved swiftly to the door, Cross and Cassidy at his back. Jemma whispered in his ear, the comms loud and clear.

"On point so far. Gunn says nothing moving. He's accessing the interior and exterior CCTV. Wait!"

Bodie froze.

"Camera almost caught you then. Gunn managed to overlay a still frame just in time."

Bodie checked the new keypad. "Has he overlaid the interior? And checked the basement for sensors?"

"All good. As you step off the last stair, there's an infrared beam, a foot broad. Perfect placement, really. It'll catch anyone coming down that last step. Make sure you jump over two feet."

Bodie concentrated on the keypad, looking down. "You manage that, Eli?"

"You missing Agent Moneymaker, Guy?"

"Smooth." Bodie entered the passcode. "Smooth and sweet."

Inside, they used their flashlights, descended eleven steps, and jumped over the last. The basement was a huge storage area, full of boxes of food and drink, and wine racks. It smelled of spices and was clean and dry. Cassidy pointed out the exit.

"Another set of stairs," Bodie said through the comms. "We good?"

"All clear," Gunn came back.

The door at the top of the stairs opened; light flooded down. Bodie acted instinctively, moving with lightning speed behind a pile of boxes. Cassidy chose the wine rack and Cross an old armchair to shelter behind. Bodie shook his head. *Predictable behavior.*

It made him smile while the figure rustled around the basement, found what they were looking for, and headed back upstairs. Bodie allowed two minutes and then peered out.

"Let's move."

They ascended slowly, then used the device to get the interior keypad code. Earlier, Bodie had explained how his mind was working.

"Our old archaeologist didn't have access to this house, but someone else did. The Illuminati member that was expelled, the one who was helping him. That guy must have returned once more for the archaeologist, on some pretense, and planted the next waypoint."

Jemma had agreed, already revising her plan. "I see where you're going."

"Find out who it was. Hopefully he had an office right here."

It took a little digging, but the name Thomas Kilby came up. It turned out that the man had been a major part of the York Lodge, expelled for indolence. Nothing terribly serious, so he may have been readmitted at some point. Bodie reasoned it was another—and possibly the main—reason the archaeologist had chosen the York Lodge against any other, purely because he had a way to access the building under his enemy's nose and keep safe his next waypoint.

"Thomas Kilby," Bodie now repeated. "Second floor, third from the eastern end. Am I right?"

"Jeff cross-referenced the name Kilby with his footnotes, the part of the map where the archaeologist explained himself. All it says is TK, two up, three from east. Bullcrap to anyone that hasn't come this far, but makes sense to me. It's the location of his office."

"And it's the only York footnote," Jeff added. "It must be important."

Bodie nodded to himself. It made perfect sense. "Moving on."

Ensuring the readiness of his colleagues, he cracked open the inner door, steeling himself for anything. The corridor was brightly lit, the floors carpeted in beige, and the walls badly plastered.

"All for show," Cross whispered. "Wait until we reach the second floor."

Of course, the house had to be prepared to receive regular visitors. Confident in Gunn's ability to mask their movements remotely, the trio quickly traversed the corridor, stepped through an opening at the end, and ran down another. A set of stairs now twisted upward on its own small spiral, a brace of security cameras watching.

"Hope the geek got 'em all," Cassidy muttered.

Bodie grinned. "Me too, love."

"We have a problem," Gunn said seriously.

The trio froze. *"What?"*

"Every time Bodie opens his mouth the glare from his teeth interrupts my Wi-Fi jamming signal. Tell him to keep it shut."

Cassidy tried hard not to make a sound. Bodie kept a poker face, and Cross shook his head. They moved up, trying hard to keep it quiet on the metal staircase. This time Cassidy came up first, and her vision was filled with a shocked guard.

"Hey . . ."

The redhead moved like a striking snake, lashing forward and catching the guard around the head, sending him tumbling backward before he could react. Immediately the nimble woman had the upper hand.

He caught his balance and reached for his gun. Cassidy struck down, snapping the arm at the wrist, then smashed knuckles into his mouth before he could utter a scream. Not the best option for her skin and bone, but the fastest on this occasion. The man spluttered, head down. Cassidy delivered a blow to the back of his neck, which sent him farther onto his knees.

Lights out.

No movement.

"Did you kill him?" Cross asked.

"Maybe. Better check." Cassidy moved off, checking the remainder of the corridor. She turned back quickly with a thumbs-up.

Cross grunted. "Shit, yeah, he's dead."

"Bring him," Bodie said. "And his gun."

Cross looked up as Bodie moved off. "Ah, a little help?"

"Sorry, man. That's Thomas Kilby's office up ahead and he's our priority. Put yer back into it."

CHAPTER
THIRTY-SIX

"Jemma, we're inside Thomas Kilby's office."

"Good. Another step closer to getting away unseen."

Bodie looked at the guard Cross was dragging in. "Yeah, well, we have to assume it's been altered, redecorated, and God knows what else done to it over the years, so suggestions are welcome. Jeff?"

"I'd say pictures," he came back. "Pictures on the wall."

Cassidy was already on it. "Nothing," she said. "A few antique drawings of old York, the Viking encampment, the Roman fortress, and a modern aerial view. A letter and a certificate. Nothing here with Kilby's name on it. Not a surprise." She licked blood from her split knuckles.

"A safe?" Gunn suggested.

They lifted pictures and frames. They checked the carpet and the desk, finding nothing suspicious. Bodie checked the walls for hidden alcoves. Cross even looked suspiciously at the ceiling.

They paused and studied.

"Y'know," Bodie finally said. "The oldest things in here are those pictures. The discoloration underneath shows it. I say we have another look."

The dead guard groaned. Cassidy glared over at Cross. "'Kin 'ell, old man," she growled. "Not only are you slower than a long winter, you're losing your marbles too."

Cross licked his lips. "Shit, Cass, I was sure he was dead."

"Well, maybe my sensual personality brought him back to life." Cassidy walked over to the guard. "It's been known to happen, but in a different way."

Cross frowned. Bodie ignored them as he scanned the wall. Any little detail, even the York pictures, might be the key. He tried to imagine what an archaeologist and a fallen member of the Illuminati might come up with in the early 1900s.

It struck him.

The letter.

"Jeff," he said. "When exactly did our archaeologist friend embark upon his quest?"

"The year was nineteen hundred and ten," Jeff read aloud. "Part of the very first footnote. Is it a clue?"

Bodie couldn't stop the grin. "Damn right it is. This letter they have on the wall is a vital piece of Illuminati history. Yes, it's a copy, but I'd say they have it on every office wall in this house. It's a letter meant for all and addressed to the Antiquity Lodge. The date is 1910."

"So you're saying the unhappy member of the Illuminati, perhaps in his last act, wrote that letter with the intention that it would always remain on the York Lodge's wall? It has to be pretty powerful."

"It is," Bodie said. "They wrote this letter to the Antiquity Lodge that admits to many years of struggle and strife, that instead of them ceasing to exist they will accept the rule of this other lodge and are happy to be absorbed by it. Basically, it's the end of the York Lodge as an entity, the dissolving of their power, the end of an era."

"And a transfer of power, membership, and leadership to the Antiquity Lodge," Jeff said. "As you say, the most important document in their history."

"Not only that," Bodie said, "it's signed by Thomas Kilby."

Cross was shaking his head at Cassidy. "You missed that?"

"I'm a fighter, not a fucking nerd. That's why Bodie always double-checks me."

The master thief looked over at Cassidy. "Umm, thanks, I think."

"Take a photo, just in case," Jemma said. "Then get the hell out of there. Same way you got in, double time."

"Yeah, that's gonna be a slight problem," Bodie said. "We have a passenger."

The line went quiet, then Jemma said, "Dead?"

"On and off."

"On and . . . what the hell does that mean?"

"It means get yer sexy pants on, honey," Cassidy drawled, "'cause we're coming in hot."

Cross took the photos while Bodie helped Cassidy manhandle the unconscious guard. Once the redhead had him in a good hold, they were ready. Bodie cracked the door, checked outside, and waved them on. Soon, they were back at the metal staircase. Bodie went down first, surveyed the lay of the land, and signaled the all clear.

One more corridor and they were again in the basement, flashlights out and avoiding the sensor. Up the stairs and through the courtyard, locking up every door behind them. Gunn switched his overlay off, killed his monitoring.

Bodie gave the group a smile of intense satisfaction. "Perfect job, folks. The best team in the business just proved their worth."

Jemma pointed out the elephant in the room. "What about him? They're gonna know he's gone."

"He's Heidi's problem now. And yeah, you're right. But nobody saw anything, nobody heard anything. It's just another mystery."

"Under duress," Cassidy said, "I think we done good."

Bodie made to move away as the team gathered everything up. "Jeff," he said. "Any ideas on this Antiquity Lodge?"

"Oh yeah," he said. "It's the oldest lodge in the UK, the oldest outside of Germany, to be honest. It's another name for the Grand Lodge of London."

Bodie groaned. "Bollocks. You do realize that's where I was born?"

Jeff looked unsure. "I can't help where they founded a lodge hundreds of years ago."

"I know," Bodie said. "But it's gonna bring back some memories, and none of them are good."

"Skeletons in the closet?" Jemma asked.

"Enemies in the woodwork. Killers in the cupboard. You name it."

Cassidy cracked her knuckles. "Okay then. Let's move out."

CHAPTER
THIRTY-SEVEN

The train down to London was a rattler. Once a grumpy CIA handler had relieved them of the unconscious prisoner, the team caught a cab to the York railway station and bought six tickets to Kings Cross. The two-hour journey would enable them to rest and start a little research.

"Y'know what bugs me?" Jemma said, shivering on the exposed platform. "This poor archaeologist. We know nothing of him, of his motivations. Not even what happened to him. We don't even know how the map came to be at Olympia."

Jeff nodded. "That's been worrying me too. It's all good information, but what's the story?"

"We may never know," Jemma said as Cross came up the platform, loaded with sandwiches, energy bars, and bottles of water purchased from the cluster of shops inside the station. "Send the oldest for the heavy load," he said cheerfully. "I know the drill."

"Sorry, dude," Jemma said, peering past Cross at Cassidy as she approached. "But that's what I'm waiting for."

Bodie had been listening to them while turning the operation over in his mind, letting it mold and remold like a soft piece of clay. Now he turned and saw Cassidy walking along the platform toward them.

A comment almost leapt out of his mouth until he saw what she was carrying.

Coffee.

"Lifesaver," he said, and took a cup. The wind was indeed a scythe inside the station, whipping around as it sought victims. A predawn light was breaking in the snatch of sky they could see as they waited for the first train to Kings Cross.

"Where are we with the map?" he asked Jeff.

The archaeologist nodded around a mouthful of sandwich. "Good . . . hang on . . . good." He swallowed, sat on a metal bench, and pulled his thoughts together. "Obviously the further we get, the less I remember. I started at the beginning and didn't get much past York. We know the waypoint. The footnotes are a slice of history, nothing more. A way of backing up the writer's claims. I mentioned before there's something about Liege; we should check that. It says that the statue was moved to the Illuminati base of operations in the early 1900s, a mistake, I think. Also that this next waypoint is the last." He looked around. "It should point us to the location of the statue."

"And more importantly," Bodie said, "the Illuminati HQ."

"Yeah, sure."

Bodie shook his head at the archaeologist, guessing his thoughts. Since they'd saved his life, though, Jeff had proven invaluable. Maybe a relic hunter needed an archaeologist as a friend. Another gust of wind scoured the platform, testing their mettle.

"Following an ancient relic, seeking it out, to locate a modern-day version of an ancient murderous, secret organization is a little unorthodox," Cross said. "But you gotta hand it to Agent Moneymaker—she's driven, committed, and good at what she does."

Bodie nodded. "Yeah, she's impressive."

Cassidy tipped her cup at them. "Get a fuckin' room, boys. All three of you. Shit."

Jemma chipped in. "Cassidy's right," she said with a huge leap of intuition. "We don't know jack about her. She's CIA. A government employee. She may have saved your ass, Bodie, but she could easily shove you right back down the crapper."

The Londoner brushed at the stubble around his chin. "Ah, thanks for the image, Jemma. So far, we have no reason to doubt her, but you should all know by now that I rarely trust, and I vet my friends very, very carefully. Don't worry about me losing sight of the whole picture."

"Which brings us around to yet another rather large elephant in the room," Cross intoned gently. "Jack Pantera."

Bodie took a moment to sort through his feelings. This whole mission had been a whirlwind, keeping everything else on hold. He found that, despite all that had happened, he wanted to talk to Pantera—question his old mentor seriously about what had happened. Revenge wasn't Bodie's style. He needed to understand the situation and the motivations behind it.

"Jack is our next op," he said softly. "Make no mistake."

Cassidy cracked ten knuckles in a row. "Just choose a bone, my friend."

"Not like that, Cass. I went through hell with Jack. We bled together. I have to know why."

"He threw you in prison and left you to die." It was black-and-white for Cassidy Coleman. "Pure betrayal. It doesn't matter why."

"He was my father for more years than my real dad," Bodie said. "That counts for something."

Cassidy shrugged, taking a bite of her sandwich. The train pulled up and the team stepped aboard, locating their seats and falling silent. The train was at least half-full, and they knew ears always pricked up when a juicy conversation began.

Jeff sent a group message to say he was researching the Antiquity Lodge in London. Gunn piped up too, by text, to say he was already on it. The train rattled through some predawn English countryside, the fields often uniform and flat, the roads narrow and twisting. A barely discernible announcement went out regarding the food cart, stops, and arrival times, but Bodie was wholly unaware, sifting through the snippets and patches of life that he had been a part of these last few days and weeks. Life could certainly turn on a dime. Whoever said that got it spot-on.

Live your life while you can. Who knows what's around the corner?

He wondered if he'd actually been doing that. Foster families had poisoned him against friendships, turned him into a singular man that shunned social media and found fraternizing quite tough. He was standoffish, closed about his past with anyone except the tight circle that was his team.

Was that living?

They were winging it now, he knew. Heidi was away on some kind of side mission, God knew what. Jeff's memory of the map was imperfect. The best thing in their favor was that the Illuminati were unaware of how far they'd progressed.

Otherwise, Hell would be waiting for them.

Bodie tried to relax as the train carved through the coming day.

CHAPTER
THIRTY-EIGHT

Xavier Von Gothe sat alone, at the head of an enormous eighteenth-century table, his arms outstretched along its pitted surface to their fullest extent, his head lowered close to the dark oak, lost in a jumbled patchwork of thoughts.

First, Bavaria had been compromised. Agent Moneymaker's new team had found something at the museum, something his men could not find. Then all traces of them vanished, and Xavier felt something new steal into the darkest recess of his soul.

Fear.

Where were they? What did they find? The map, what he had learned from it, led from waypoint to waypoint, carefully keeping the locations secret. Footnotes they had found were little help. He already knew the history of the statue and the history of this blasted archaeologist that had turned out to be a thorn in his side. In the end, he knew, it was arrogance and procrastination that had put the Order in this position. If they'd never moved the statue—for their own pleasure—in 1910, nothing would have come to light. It was purely the moving of the statue that had triggered small events that eventually made the archaeologist aware. Then they had expelled a man, a traitor

Xavier now knew to be called Thomas Kilby. It was he who had helped the old archaeologist by opening doors.

A tall woman entered, her height exaggerated by her willowy figure. She wore a floor-length black robe, the hood thrown back and her black hair hanging free.

He glared. "What do you want, Calypso? I asked not to be disturbed."

His third-in-command didn't flinch even a little. She was an incredibly hard, tough woman with an unbreachable exterior. Unique in the Order, she had once been a Hood before being elevated to a leader. Xavier had smoothed the promotional process and now sometimes wished he hadn't.

"Calypso?"

Her eyes were ice. "We have learned, through our American contact, that Agent Moneymaker's team was recently inside the York Lodge."

Xavier stared at her. "Why then have we heard nothing?"

"The York Lodge has no idea," she said. "Still."

Xavier could barely believe it. It was a rare event that left him tongue-tied, but he could barely find words. "No idea? But . . . how?"

Calypso came farther into the room, her svelte figure moving gracefully beneath the long robe. "Our investigative team came back with the answers. Apparently the CIA is using a crack team of relic hunters to help them track down the statue."

Xavier stared.

"It gets worse. This team, they're more than just glorified thieves. They are covert infiltration specialists, possibly the best in the world. I have their files right here." She waved a collection of manila folders and then placed them on the table, sliding them over with one long finger.

Xavier was shocked to the core, but knew he couldn't let that show. Not to a subordinate and especially not to a subordinate so close to his position of power.

"I'll review and get back to you. In the meantime, delve into their histories, their families, their friends. Leave no stone unturned. Leave no weak and fragile place untapped. They started this war, but we will finish it. And Calypso?"

The beauty sent a chiseled glance straight through his eyeballs. "Yes?"

"They are heading to London now, yes? At least the map is clear on the third waypoint. Tell our brethren at the Antiquity Lodge to be ready. Tell them to prepare an event."

Calypso nodded. "And the scale?"

"Oh, make it incalculable. Immense. Make it horrific. My patience is now at an end."

Xavier somehow managed to calm himself a little while later. Slowly, he flicked through the folders Calypso had brought, meeting digitally printed images of Guy Bodie, Eli Cross, Jemma Blunt, Sam Gunn, and Cassidy Coleman. Their histories ranged from intense to boring, but all of their skills were noteworthy. Of course, they had come this far, which meant they had to be removed from the game. Permanently, and at all costs.

Xavier trusted Calypso to plan the London event. It would have to be good enough to take out a great team. They didn't know the Illuminati were coming.

Victory was assured. He picked up a phone to warn just a few of his London friends. No need to be rude.

CHAPTER THIRTY-NINE

Bodie led the way off the train, exiting into Kings Cross station. It was another drafty structure, and the wind tore at them, whistling down the platform. A bustle of passengers hurried around them, legs and heads bent forward, moving with purpose. The rolling thunder of suitcase wheels filled their ears, making communication practically impossible.

Bodie headed for the gates, slipped his ticket into the machine, and walked out when the barriers opened. The station gave way to a wide plaza with benches, statues, and kiosks dotted about. Soon, the rest of the team joined him.

"Knightsbridge," Jeff said. "Taxi rank is over there."

Bodie walked alongside the young man. "You have an address?"

Jeff reeled it off.

"All right. Let's grab the cab to Harrods and then walk. We're normal tourists, then."

Their taxi had double back seats, so the whole team fitted inside, if a little snugly. The drive took around forty minutes, Gunn fidgeting the entire time and Cassidy warning him to keep his elbows and knees to himself on pain of death. Bodie stared at the London streets, the diligent workers and bustling tourists, the unbreakable chain of cars and buses and vans, the industrious high-rises, hospitals, and hotels. He was ready for anything here today, and willing to take on a vile enemy to get the mission done and move on.

Another life awaited them all.

The taxi dropped them off outside Harrods, the area a nonstop stream of clamor and bodies, helping them blend in. They made their way along the Brompton Road side of the huge store, making a left at Beauchamp Place. This took them toward Pont Street, several quiet mews houses, and private schools. The traffic noise died down and an almost serene calm took over. Every time Bodie snapped a glance down one of the streets, he saw a curving road and houses with white frontages sitting in small sun traps amid the great city. An interesting contrast, he thought. An exclusive way of life. They passed Pont Street and moved into Chesham Place, an area where foreign embassies were prevalent. Several sleepy mews lay around here, and it was to one of these addresses that Jeff's GPS pointed.

He halted them at a quiet junction. "A short walk down there"—he nodded ahead—"and it's the first street on the right. The address covers four numbers, so it must be a big place."

"Quiet area." Jemma looked around. "Hundreds of windows. Security everywhere, enhanced for the embassies. Yeah, this should be easy."

Bodie herded them over to a bench. "Seriously, this is where a plan helps. It's time to earn your keep, kids."

Cross rubbed his hands. "I say let Gunn do the recon with Jemma. They can pretend they're married, say, wandering around London, sightseeing or something? Anything else would seem suspicious at this stage."

"They don't know we're coming," Gunn said, looking a bit perturbed.

Jemma pulled a face. "Gunn as a husband? Even I can't pull that off."

"C'mon, Blunt," Cassidy said. "You're desperate for a man, right? Well, Gunn's halfway there."

"Thanks." The tech geek ran a hand through his hair, the dry gel keeping it in place. "I'm pretty sure I can do this."

Jemma exchanged a glance with Cassidy. "Right then," she said. "Reconnaissance, then prep. You might want to find out where we can pick up some equipment," she told Bodie. "And quick, assuming we'll be going in tonight."

Bodie nodded. "I'll call Heidi right now."

His phone rang. Bodie stared at it. "Shit."

Cassidy stood up. "Is it her?"

Bodie stared suspiciously around and into the clouds above. "Yeah, that's bloody weird."

"Drone," Cassidy said with a smirk. "Has to be."

Bodie laughed and jabbed the green button. "Yeah?"

"It's me. Can you talk?"

Bodie replied in the affirmative and motioned for Jemma and Gunn to stick around. Cautiously, he switched to speakerphone.

"I've been kept apprised of your progress and appreciate the effort. You've done the best of jobs so far, but time is still against us. The good part is that it will be impossible for the Illuminati to move the statue and whatever else they have stashed away without weeks and probably months of planning, so again, this is our best chance to locate and catch them. More good news . . ." She took a breath.

"I'm liking this," Cassidy said. "She's just a frizzy little good-luck charm."

"My side mission was to root out a CIA mole. We got him. We put him down."

"Who was he?"

"His name isn't relevant. You don't know him. But this man was feeding information back to the Illuminati. Now, he isn't. I don't have one job to do, one team to cover. I have many."

Bodie felt a lift. "That's great news. Anything else?"

"Don't you want details?" Heidi's voice held a note of disappointment.

Bodie decided this was the best time to voice his feelings, despite it being over a telephone connection. "Be clear, Agent Moneymaker," he said. "Once this is done, once we complete this op, we are out. We're not government agents, lackeys, go-to guys. We're not consultants. Our association ends with the downfall of the Illuminati."

"I see," Heidi said. "You missed the part where you ask nicely."

"Believe me, that was nicely."

"And you seem to forget that I own your ass. Figuratively and literally. It's mine, Guy Bodie."

Cassidy flexed an ankle. "You sound like a boyfriend I once had to damage," she said. "Long time ago."

"We'll talk face to face," Bodie said. "But you know our stance."

"I do and we will. I'm sorry to hear it, since I thought we were gelling as a team. But I digress. Here's the bad news . . . our CIA mole was operational until just an hour ago. Yeah, we rooted the little bastard out, but he gifted you to them. They know you're in London and why you're there."

Bodie stiffened; Cassidy and Cross didn't need to be told to get their game heads on and scrutinize the area.

"You fucking kidding me?"

"No, I'm not. And I'm telling you to get the hell out of there. Right now!"

"What?" Bodie stared at the cell phone, suddenly wondering if this really was Heidi Moneymaker. "Why?"

"Why the hell do you think? They know! They've known for a while. If the lodge is in danger, if they think you're going to find the last waypoint, there's only one thing they will do."

Bodie experienced a terrifying, sinking feeling inside his chest. "An event?"

"No. *The event.* They will leave nothing to chance, Bodie. Nothing. Now do as I say and get out of London now."

"Out of *London.* Fuck's sake."

Bodie was on his feet before he realized what he was doing.

"Wait." Jemma held her hand out and placed it on his shoulder. "You pay me to be the thinker, so let me think . . ."

Even Heidi stayed quiet for about twelve seconds. "Bodie . . ."

"Wait," he said. "You forced us into helping you for a reason. And that reason is because we're the best at what we do. Give Jemma a minute."

The dark-haired American didn't need it. "Heidi, please, they're gonna attack anyway."

A short silence, then, "Why?"

"You know why. Because they want to make sure, once and for all, that the waypoint is destroyed. They can't find these waypoints, right? Even if they did, they might be scared of missing another. Believe me, they're gonna strike."

"You need to leave," Heidi said more quietly, unsure of herself.

"We need to hit it now. Hard. Fast. While they're hopefully still planning. We can't waste any more time." She stared around at every face, met every pair of eyes.

"We have no choice here. This could be our last chance to strike at the Illuminati and avenge all those innocents who died in Greece. A direct, sudden, forceful attack on that lodge is the best course of action."

CHAPTER
FORTY

"To the death, then," Bodie said.

"The event is expected by the CIA! Even by you!" Heidi cried. "You can't risk this. You—"

"Jemma. Jeff," Bodie said. "You've got three minutes to decide where we're looking. Cassidy, we have no weapons. You're in charge of handing them out after you take them away from the guards. Cross, you're the best trained. Stay on watch. Gunn—you're the cannon fodder. You're in first."

Gunn shook his head, resigned to the ribbing. The team made ready, preparing their minds and bodies for a fast assault. The truth was, of course, that if there was no tech work to do, he was essentially a loose end.

Jeff appeared even more frightened than Gunn. Bodie considered cutting him loose, or at least leaving him behind, but decided they stood a better chance taking him along. Besides, none of them intended to die this day.

"No blueprints. No history. No information," Jeff said. "I could find it eventually perhaps, but not in three minutes."

Gunn was furiously jabbing at his iPad. "Local council," he said. "The Royal Borough of Kensington and Chelsea has plans and they have archives." He dropped down to his heels on a patch of grass. "One second . . ."

Hacking was Gunn's specialty. "There's not much," he said in a deflated voice. "Buildings are built on a curve, two stories, big basements. At least fifteen to twenty rooms, not including toilets, closets, cupboards, etcetera. Only two front doors, not even a yard at the back. Damn, it's secure."

"'Secure' isn't even an option when we're here," Cassidy said. "We ready?"

"Smooth and sweet," Bodie said, sighing down at the cell phone still in his right hand. "Heidi? Wish us luck."

"I said—"

He ended the call, pocketed the phone, and joined his fast-moving crew. He wondered for a second what the hell he was doing, heading into a hostile environment without a real plan or any equipment, knowing they could die at any minute, but then remembered all who had died and suffered in the Athens museum, at the bus station, and so many more before that. A group that planned mass-casualty events to subdue the world was a group that needed to find extinction.

Cassidy was their asteroid. She jogged at the head of the group, entering the mews and wasting no time going around the slightly curved building until she reached one of the two doors. Nobody appeared to be around. The entire street was empty, quiet. Three cars were parked along its length and one bicycle. Between these narrow buildings, London and Knightsbridge seemed far, far away.

"Get ready," she said without turning. "This isn't gonna be quiet and it isn't gonna be painless. Time to get bloody."

She picked up a decorative bike stop—a lump of iron where a cyclist inserted their front tire—and hefted it. Then she launched it through the door's top window. Glass shattered, the noise alarming in the drowsy street. She knocked persistent shards out with an elbow and reached inside.

"Lock, done," she said. "Key . . . done."

She withdrew her arm, turned the handle, opened the door, and retrieved the bike stop. The team fell in behind her. They came first to a vestibule, and two men rushing straight for them. The men wore suits and white ties; they were clean-shaven and wide. Security guards. Muscle. But nobody did muscle like Cassidy Coleman. She launched the bike stop at the first; solid iron hurled through the air, smashing not only the man's teeth but his jaw as well. Cassidy didn't stop to check as the guard crumpled to the floor.

Guard number two was reaching for a holster. Cassidy let him get a hand inside his jacket before rushing in, elbow first. The blow broke his nose and sent blood washing over a nearby wall, but he didn't flinch. He pulled out his gun, only to have his fingers covered by Cassidy's powerful hand and crushed until either they broke or he dropped the weapon. He struggled. She clamped him hard, using her legs. Bodie was upon them by that time and helped by picking up the felled guard's gun and striking the second across the temple.

"Nice," he said as the man subsided.

"You're welcome," Cassidy replied. "Enjoyed it."

Across the vestibule lay a wide, high hallway. Wooden floors and expensively decorated walls met their eyes, and a wide staircase leading to the second floor. Gunn had already identified the second floor as the most likely to yield clues, but that still gave them a dozen rooms to cover.

More guards rushed from the right, three this time, their guns already drawn. Cassidy didn't stand on ceremony, pumping two rounds into the first. Bodie shot the second, and the third stumbled over his comrades, rolling and coming to a stop by their feet. Cassidy knelt and rendered him unconscious as Cross scooped up all their weapons.

He distributed them to the team.

Gunn looked aghast until Jeff caught his attention.

"If you don't want it, hand it to me."

"Really? Have you ever shot a gun before?"

"Have *you*?"

"I've *seen* people shot," Gunn said defensively.

"So have I." Jeff motioned to the dead guards.

"Shut the hell up," Cassidy said, moving on. "Fucking battle of the geeks."

Ignoring the right-hand offshoot, they headed for the stairs. A plush carpet helped muffle their footsteps, not that it would help. The Illuminati had known they were coming, but any chance of secrecy had vanished now. They pounded up the stairs. Cassidy met a guard at the top, flipped him over her shoulders, and hurled him down. Bodie watched the fall, tracking him with the pistol, but he landed with a loud crack and stayed still, barely breathing.

The corridor at the top was empty, for now. Bodie imagined Illuminati bosses searching for ways out like rats running from an explosion. Cassidy chose left at random, and with Cross's help, entered the room and scanned it for threats.

"Clear. Do your thing, people."

She watched the corridor from a covert angle as the rest of the team scanned walls and desks, taking pictures. It felt arbitrary, unsystematic. It felt somewhat desperate. But what choice did they have?

"Just a thought," she said. "They don't know where we are."

Gunn snapped a finger up at the room's CCTV camera.

"No. The security team knows where we are, but the Illuminati big-wigs don't."

"And the point?" Bodie asked, watching over everything and everyone as per usual.

"We grab one and beat the testosterone out of him."

"You think he'll know?"

"Well, he'll know where the statue is."

Bodie pursed his lips. "Wouldn't bank on it, love."

"Well, how about we put it to the test? 'Cause one just flew out of a room down the corridor and is headed this way with his Hood guard."

Bodie nodded grimly. "On your word." He backed her up.

Cassidy waited, then flung the door open into the Hood's face. The man hit hard and fell back, stunned. Cassidy stepped out, right in front of the running Illuminati chief. The man pulled up sharp, suit and coat flapping about him, polished shoes skidding on the floor.

"This is not—" the man began.

Then his Hood attacked, no longer dazed. Cassidy saw the leap and blocked it, but a busy fist managed to smash into her kidneys. She gasped, blocked some more, fell back. The Hood stepped past the door and Bodie hit him from the side, shoulder-barging at speed, and sent him crashing into the opposite wall.

The Illuminati chief backed off.

Bodie checked for other dangers, saw none. The Hood bounced back fighting. Cassidy sidestepped his lunge and tripped him right into Bodie, who took him hard with a raised knee. The blow made the man grunt, sent him to his knees, but even then he wasn't down for the count.

Twisting, rolling, he gained two meters of space. Cassidy pursued, Bodie a step behind. The Hood kicked out, feet like scythes. Cassidy got tangled and went down, but Bodie jumped over them both to land near the man's head. As the redhead hit the floor, hands breaking her fall, Bodie stepped on the Hood's neck, firmly but not with a crushing blow. He would never kill if he could knock someone out cold.

The Hood still twisted; Cassidy delivered three debilitating blows, taking the remaining starch out of him. Cross arrived with the others and used a belt he'd retrieved from one of the guards to bind the Hood's hands. Cross and Bodie dragged the Hood back into the office the Illuminati boss had exited, along with the man himself.

Before they could reach even that uncertain safety, another two guards rushed them. The house was livening up, the corridors and rat-runs turning as hot and lively as Leicester Square on a Friday night. Cassidy shot one, Cross the other, and the team managed to drag their bodies out of sight.

Bodie shoved the Illuminati boss backward, right into his own desk. "Where is it?" he cried, voice and word measured carefully to see what might spill.

"You'll never get it!" the man cried. "The journal is secure! Save your skins, save all of us and run!"

Journal?

"What have you done?" Jemma asked.

"Run!" The voice cracked with fear. "There is not time. We have to get clear."

"Hey, hey." Bodie snapped his fingers in the man's face. "Look at me. What's your name?"

"Voltar," he said, lips dry.

"I'll let you go," Bodie said. "I will. As soon as you tell me what I want to know."

"The journal, it is lost. It is hidden, you can't have it!" The man was close to raving. Jemma, Gunn, and Jeff spread out past him, checking the walls for pictures in the same way that had yielded success so far. No reason to believe this would be any different.

"Then you stay," Bodie said calmly. "Sit. Sit down."

He knew it was the last thing the man wanted. His nervous system was set to flight; he knew what was coming.

"Please . . ."

"Sit."

Cassidy took out the camera. Cross checked the door and the hallway, nodded with satisfaction.

"There's a reason they're not coming," Voltar suddenly piped up as if seeing another tack. "Do you not see? They're getting clear."

"Give me the journal and you can join them." Bodie waved his gun airily. "And the waypoint."

"I don't know any waypoint. We only have minutes."

Gunn looked around at that, Jeff too. Bodie saw on their faces that they weren't ready to die. Not this way. Still, he played it cool.

"I'll count the seconds if you like." He glared into Voltar's ice-blue eyes.

The Hood started to groan. Cassidy gave him a kick back into unconsciousness. Voltar saw it as his final defeat. "There is no time," he said.

"Give me the journal. The waypoint. I'll make sure you get out of here."

"They were waiting for you, you know. We knew you were coming. Then they activated the event and everything went to chaos. If they hadn't ordered the event, we'd have taken you quietly. Now, the place is pure bedlam, everyone running and thinking just for themselves, for their own lives and fortunes." He shook his head. "Why not me?"

Bodie saw Jemma double-take at something on the wall.

"The journal then," Voltar said. "It is in the safe behind the da Vinci there. Don't worry, it is a fake. Combination 905541."

Cassidy was on it, throwing the painting aside without a glance and jabbing at the keypad. "Better be no nasty surprises in here," she said, "or your face is gonna meet my boot. We good?"

Voltar nodded. "There are no surprises."

During his early career as professional thief, Bodie had encountered some marks who had planted small explosives within their safes, even one lunatic that left a grenade inside, the pin attached to the door. Cassidy unlocked the door and peered inside.

"What we looking for?"

"The black wallet at the back. The journal is inside."

"What journal?" Bodie said finally. "What is it?"

Jemma beckoned to Gunn, showed him what she had found.

An alarm began to shriek inside the building, leaving nobody in any doubt that they should be running for the hills.

Voltar was regarding Bodie with hatred and horror. "You said you wanted the journal. What do you mean?"

Bodie, spurred on by the alarm and the look on Jemma's face, shoved his gun up under the soft skin of Voltar's jaw. "Tell me everything right now, fuckwit, or I swear to God I'm gonna paint the ceiling red."

Voltar certainly had nothing to lose. "The journal belonged to that damned archaeologist that started all this. He drew the map you people have been chasing and following. The archaeologist called Roland Hunt."

"He left a journal?" Bodie stared over at Jeff. "We never knew that."

"The Illuminati of the early 1900s stopped Hunt in the nick of time. They confiscated his journal after he was captured, and then recaptured after he escaped. Later, they let him go again, but knew nothing of the map."

Bodie judged the man's words. "Why would they let him go?"

"The Illuminati are brothers. World shapers and savers. We are not the monsters you seem to think we are."

"If you believe that, mate, you don't know a thing about your bosses."

The alarm wailed. Cassidy brought the black wallet over, briefly showing him the journal inside. He kept his gun lodged under Voltar's chin and nodded at Cross.

"We good out there?"

"Yeah, all clear."

Bodie turned back to Voltar. "How long do we have, and what is going to happen?"

"From the start of the alarm? Ten minutes. That leaves us only seven to my count. And the termination event has been activated."

Bodie refrained from sighing. Cassidy tapped a foot. "Sounds bad."

"It is. They will bring the building down."

Jemma ran over, Gunn and Jeff at her back. "The picture on the wall there? When and how did you obtain it?"

But before Voltar could answer, the entire building started to shake.

CHAPTER
FORTY-ONE

"You tell us!" Bodie grabbed Voltar by the neck and pushed him up against the trembling walls. "Now!"

"Four minutes," Cassidy said.

"That one?" Voltar struggled to breathe. "With the rolled gilt edge? It is just a charcoal drawing we found among the effects of Roland Hunt. I guess the men of that time found it appropriate, relevant, and even properly fitting that it should be displayed so. He is the man that came closest and who they subdued so carefully."

Bodie eyed him. "And he is the man that will have the last laugh. What is it, Jemma?"

"It is a drawing, I'm sure, of the ancient Olympics. The place they were originally held, with the Statue of Zeus in the background."

Bodie struggled with it. "I don't get it. Roland Hunt drew that? Why?"

"Don't you see? It's the next waypoint. The final waypoint."

Bodie couldn't grasp the irony, the incredible, terrible depth of the Illuminati's final "fuck you" to the world. "You're telling me that these wankers, in their supreme arrogance, *returned* the statue to its original spot in the early 1900s? Oh, you bastards. You absolute—"

"They returned it to the very place the map was found." Cross shook his head. "So they could feel superior. Kings of the world."

"We didn't know that," Voltar said. "We knew nothing about the map until now."

"Roland Hunt did," Jemma said. "And he tried to tell us."

"Well, now we have this." Cassidy raised the journal. "And the map. Shall we do a Donald and get the duck outta here?"

Bodie grabbed Voltar. "Move."

They turned tail. Cross leapt into the corridor first, leading the way. The team followed hard at his heels. They swept down the corridor, Bodie dragging Voltar along like a big sack of shopping. They reached the top of the stairs just as a large contingent of Hoods and Illuminati raced from the other wing toward them, clutching papers, files, and thick folders in their hands, everything they couldn't afford to lose.

"Two minutes," Cassidy said.

"Crap." Bodie, last in line, waved them on down the staircase. As the Hoods approached, he threw Voltar at them, letting the man windmill his way among their ranks. Bodies tripped and fell awkwardly, screams rang out. Illuminati tumbled together, papers and wallets flying. For a brief moment, white sheets filled the air. Walls still shook, the ceiling cracked as something began to build, a device or primer bombs designed to weaken the structure.

"You people," Bodie said in disbelief. "You're destroying your own house."

He saw Cassidy staring up at him from the hall below as the others fled.

Then the building erupted.

CHAPTER
FORTY-TWO

Bodie heard the rumble as the ground shifted. The stairs buckled. A Hood leapt for him, grabbing his chest and coming in for a head-butt. Bodie flicked him around, shrugged him off down the stairs. Then he leapt straight after the man.

One stair, then another and another. The wood splintered and heaved, but he saw the way ahead. Another Hood was upon him, reaching for his collar. The swiftest of glances behind revealed the Illuminati struggling to follow, most of them scrambling or stumbling along. The top-floor railing twisted and fell, crashing to the floor below. Bodie saw a large patch of the ground floor just tumble away, a stream of wood, concrete, and rubble plunging downward in a lethal waterfall.

Another stair. Three from the bottom now. The Hood was uncaring of his peril, intent on impeding the intruder. Bodie put the brakes on for half a second just as the Hood lunged, and saw the man tumble headlong into another hole that had opened.

Through the new gap Bodie saw only emptiness and falling debris.

He paused on the last step, then took a flying leap and landed on the edge of the hole, teetering badly. His view ahead opened up and he saw the team battling the ongoing eruption to reach the front door. Gunn was down and then dragged to his feet by Cassidy. Jemma hit a wall and was steadied by Cross. Jeff fell and was scooped up by Cassidy's other arm. The team fought on.

Bodie flung himself to the ground on purpose, gaining traction, but then the hole started to broaden. He could hear individual explosions now as the house was deliberately, carefully brought crashing down. Not just that, it was disappearing into the earth.

What the hell is below us?

A pit, it seemed. Bodie saw another chunk of floor cave in to reveal a rock wall and a long drop. Something below, though. Something straight and hard, something familiar, now being covered by the rapidly disintegrating house.

A Hood must have leapt across the first hole, for now he struck Bodie's back, sending the thief sprawling. Bodie hit the edge of another hole and put a hand out, scraping his flesh on sharp rubble. Still on his back, the Hood pummeled Bodie's ribs from above. Bodie bucked and heaved, got into position, then threw the man over his head and straight down the hole. Not even a scream marked his flight path.

Up again. Knees burning, ribs aflame, and chest heaving. He was scraped bloody, and feeling raw. A terrible clatter and crash sounded from behind, and he assumed part of the first floor had come tumbling down. Smoke billowed all around him. A body hit some remaining paneling at his side and fell end over end with its own momentum, dead and flailing.

Now the walls were dissolving. Another explosion and another. Bodie saw one wall buckle at the base and fall away, bringing a huge part of the house crashing down on top of it.

He scrambled through the mess, the smoke, the rubble. Ahead, Cross threw Jemma out into the street—the door and adjacent wall were missing. Cassidy hurled Jeff after the American and then carried Gunn out.

All around them, the street bucked and heaved.

Bodie noticed the houses on the other side of the street beginning to sag as the chain of explosions reached them.

Oh no . . .

No way would he make it that far. He was unlikely to escape the house. A chunk of masonry the size of a car smashed down close by, rocking and shaking and bristling with rebar. He looked up to see the high ceiling falling in, deadly wedges of concrete and timber tumbling toward him.

Bodie had only seconds to think.

He looked back, saw the Illuminati pinned by wreckage to the ground by rebar and timber spears; he saw the Hoods that weren't crushed struggling valiantly to free their bosses even as a heavy, fatal cascade overcame them; he looked forward to see his team still free, still running; he looked left and right to see the collapsing, shattered world that remained.

And then did the only thing possible.

He jumped into the pit that had opened beneath his feet.

CHAPTER
FORTY-THREE

Bodie leapt into space, clearing the ragged edges of the hole with ease. Twelve feet down, and he hit the top of the pile, absorbing the impact with his knees. Spears of pain shot top to bottom, making him cry out. The rubble pile shifted, blocks, fastenings, and stonework falling away. A metal brace tore at his palm, drawing blood. He held his balance precariously atop the pile.

A small brick struck his back. Knowing it could just as easily have been a giant concrete ingot, he took his life into his hands, felt his heart soar into his mouth, and started to slip-slide down the sharp, uneven slope. A concrete block slowed him, a sawtooth-edged pillar ripped his jeans and flesh. He bounced farther, still fifty feet off the floor of what he now knew was the Piccadilly underground line. He'd seen the maps when they were still intent on infiltrating the house, knew the tube ran under here somewhere. Now the entire house was blown from below, creating at least two holes all the way through the foundations and down to the well-traveled rails. Bodie only hoped the authorities knew.

Hearing a noise above, he glanced up to see that another Hood was on his six.

"Bloody bollocks, don't you wankers ever give up?"

This Hood appeared to have a personality. "You try to be Jason Statham? Action hero? I show you what we do to action heroes."

He plucked out a heavy block and tossed it at Bodie. The Londoner scrambled to the other side of the pile, gripping rough edges to stop from tumbling. Around he went and then looked up again. The Hood was descending fast, with little regard for safety. Bodie dropped quicker, sliding down the pile on his side, one leg at full stretch, displacing dust, rocks, and wreckage. Twenty more feet and he looked up. The Hood was just above him, boot coming straight at his face.

Bodie took it on the forehead, absorbing and ignoring the pain. He reached up fast, grabbed the ankle, and yanked hard. The Hood fell, and was suddenly beside him. Bodie sent two quick elbows to his face, both men lying sideways on the fifty-foot-high rock pile, surrounded by shifting death and rained upon by collapsing pieces of house. The Hood was bloody, one cheekbone broken. Bodie was finding it hard to breathe and could feel blood flowing from several wounds. He let the Hood come at him, then brought a handful of rock straight into the man's face. The body flinched hard, the hands lost their grip. Bodie kicked out and sent him flailing down the rest of the pile, faster and faster and end over end until he struck the tracks below.

And then Bodie heard it.

The shrieking horn of an approaching train.

◆ ◆ ◆

Bodie felt raw fear, not only for himself, but for the passengers on board. Unable to help them, he reluctantly chose to help himself, sliding again down the rock pile, ignoring the bumps and rasps and scratches, skimming the side until he hit the bottom.

From here, the house looked a long way up. The train's brakes were screeching, the horn still blaring. Bodie saw its lights approaching, speeding straight for the blockage. He had ended up on the wrong side of the pile then, the dangerous side.

The train sped at him. Bodie moved away from the rock pile as several more lumps slid down and bounced away. An entire wall must have caved in then, for a tumbling cascade plunged down, the noise nightmarish and deafening. Bodie found himself pushed toward the train even as it rushed at him.

Brakes burned. The screech was a death knell, a keening cry of desperation. The light became blinding. Bodie didn't want to turn away, just shield his eyes. His new thought was to turn and run back to the pile, run up to get away from the train's impact, maybe even jump onto its roof.

But it was too close.

It was upon him.

And then stopping, brakes holding, drifting closer and closer until he had to take two steps back and its front end rested against his chest, the rock pile pushing up behind.

Desperately, he squeezed out and edged his way down the side, ignoring all the scared faces pressed to the window, found a ledge, and used it to clamber atop the roof.

That way, resting dazedly atop the underground train, he waited for rescue.

CHAPTER
FORTY-FOUR

Hours later, the team was nearing Olympia, Greece, in their government jet, with Heidi Moneymaker back in the mix.

"So," the CIA operative said into an unusual quiet that pervaded the plane. "Are we all rested?"

Bodie was laid half-reclined, arms and legs raised, staring up at the ceiling. He opened his mouth, but no words came out.

Cassidy filled the silence for them all. "Hard day at the office, Frizzbomb."

"Y'know," Heidi said, "from anyone else I would take that as an insult. But I can tell it's not meant that way. It's just *you*."

"Of course," Cassidy said, a bit surprised. "I don't need to insult. There's no agenda."

"I know."

Bodie didn't move, but continued to stare at the faux leather–lined roof as he spoke. "Talk to us about that journal."

"It's genuine." Heidi held it in her hands. "It's concise. And it's sad."

Jeff was seated beside her. "I read it. Gunn too. The Illuminati didn't keep it for any other reason than they are the dreadful, gloating scum of the earth Agent Moneymaker here has always said they were."

He stopped as his voice rose more octaves than he was comfortable with.

Gunn joined in. "For once, I agree with Jeff. They're hideous."

Cassidy was at Bodie's side, nursing her every muscle and with ice-packs strapped to at least three. "Give us the gist of it, boys."

"We know much of it," Jeff began. "Roland Hunt, our 1900s archaeologist, got wind of something big. He didn't know what it was. He pursued it anyway, followed his nose and the rumors flying around the very small world of relic examiners back then, and ended up in Liege, where there stands a large statue of the one and only Charlemagne."

"Our French king?" Bodie said, still prone.

"Yep. Hunt states that the closer he got, the more details emerged, although every scrap he found was mere rumor. Hunt was a terrier, a real go-getter. He rode the rumor down until it died kicking. He discovered that the Illuminati were much older than anyone gave them credit for, created in time immemorial and the forerunner of every single secret organization that came after. Charlemagne was a member of this group and came into possession of the Statue of Zeus sometime during his reign, which he was able to secrete at one of his many country houses. After his death, the statue was removed and stored underneath that very statue in Liege, where it stayed for a thousand years. They built an underground viewing room and a secret tunnel to come and go undetected. They are the epitome of sneaky, these Illuminati."

While Jeff paused for breath, Gunn continued. "All right, people. So Roland Hunt learned the statue was removed from Liege and taken somewhere at the behest of the new Illuminati leader of the time. Hunt tracked it down, following clues and people to Bavaria, York, and London. Later, he thought it would be good to leave waypoints at these places to help any who may follow."

"He saw his own death coming, then?" Jemma asked.

"In a manner of speaking. Hunt tracked the statue all the way to Olympia only to be caught by the Order, or their Hoods, and imprisoned. It was decided that they couldn't trust his assurances that he had told no one of his mission, so they found his family, put a herd of men into the village they lived in, and told Hunt if he ever declared the truth, his wife and daughters would die horribly."

Cassidy bit her lip. "Shit, of course they did."

"They kept his journal, but they let Hunt live," Jeff continued. "Live with all he knew and knowing there was nothing he could do about it—as a terrible lesson to him. Because they could. In the end, as he grew old and infirm, they poisoned him—a final message that his life was theirs to play with—so Hunt spent his final hours traveling to Olympia and making the map, which, on his deathbed, he buried in the ruins of one of the ancient temples, confident that it would be found at some point in the future. The Illuminati, of course, never knew. His family continued unaware . . . and here we stand."

Bodie thought it through slowly as the jet engines rumbled. "A classic case of the underdog never giving up. Captured, he lives on. Cowed, he seeks a way to sneak the waypoints into the Illuminati lodges and makes a map. Dying, he thinks to conceal it where it will be found. It would be inspiring if it weren't so sad."

The jet flew on, the team discussing their options as they headed toward an ancient lost prize and a world-shattering confrontation. Bodie questioned their numbers, and Heidi announced she had two special ops teams on the way.

"Rangers," she said. "Army Rangers."

Bodie knew enough about the US military to be impressed. "At least you're taking it seriously now."

Heidi smiled grimly. "I requested more. This is what's available. The damn suits and their military politicking will have America on its knees before long."

"Always been the same," Cross said. "They're happy to cry for dead troops, but cut the purse strings that might save them."

"Ah yes, I'd forgotten you're ex-military."

"Through and through, young lady. Through and through."

"The journal," Bodie cut in. "Is there more?"

"Hunt's final words center on the Statue of Zeus," Jeff said. "The ancient wonder that changed his life. Destroyed his life, some would say. The day he traced it was both the best and worst day of his archaeological career. To find a stolen ancient wonder of the world and then be captured and subdued by its owners had to be heartbreaking. The last passage is a description of the final path to the hidden lair of the Illuminati king."

"They're not called kings," Gunn said. "Novice. Minerval. That kind of—"

"Dude, they're all fucking baboons to me," Cassidy said. "King or not, they're gonna be kissing the end of my boot."

"The final path?" Bodie repeated, groaning as he sought to sit up now and all the aches and pains caught fire. "Hold that thought," he told Jeff. "Cross. Throw me that bottle of painkillers."

He caught it, swallowed some, hesitated, then decided on a few more. Finally, he nodded at Jeff. "Go on."

"It's twenty feet below the Olympia train station, and arrow straight," Jeff said.

Bodie's mind worked in a stealthy way, and he caught on immediately. "A tunnel?"

"Yep. The Illuminati built a tunnel underneath the station so that members could come and go as often as they liked, as covertly as they liked, and as easily as they liked. It's genius, really."

"And Hunt knew this how?"

"The expelled member, of course. Thomas Kilby."

"Incredible," Heidi said. "They expel a man and expect him not to harbor a grudge. Overconfident, egotistical asses."

"Hey," Cassidy grumbled. "Do not insult the ass."

"Yeah, sorry."

"So what's next?" Gunn put the journal down and turned to the window, where a fresh dawn was just starting to take fire.

"It all comes down to this," Bodie said. "We take them down now. Hit 'em hard and make them pay for every horrific thing they ever did. And Heidi?"

The CIA agent looked over. "Yeah?"

"Face to face now. After that, we part ways. Job done. Debt paid. Are we agreed?"

"Debt paid." Heidi nodded, then held his gaze. "But that still leaves you all as criminals."

"Crap, are you kidding me?"

"I'll agree to debt paid, Bodie, but you owe me more than that. The crimes you've committed. Some of the most audacious and clever in the world. If you're not working for the government one way . . ." She paused. "You will be another."

Bodie kept his temper. Jemma leaned over to Gunn. "She means in prison."

"I know that!"

"After all this . . ." Cross appealed.

Heidi never once stopped looking at Bodie. "What's it gonna be, Flash?"

He winced. "Flash?"

"Every time you open that mouth."

"Seriously?" Cassidy grumbled. "Can you two just go get a friggin' room? Work it out."

Bodie lay back. "Not in this life."

"Or in your dreams." Heidi pressed a button to consult with the pilot.

"C'mon, Bodie," Cassidy said. "It's as clear as that black microbe on your front molar. You two are into each other."

"Any more of that talk," Bodie said, "and you'll be taking the quick way down to Olympia. Understood?"

Cassidy turned away, smiling.

Heidi passed on the pilot's news. "We're about to start descending. You master thieves got any idea how to break into a secret HQ that's been unnoticed for centuries and probably guarded by hundreds of elite warriors?"

Bodie couldn't help but grin. "Yeah, CIA," he said. "Yeah, I've got a few."

CHAPTER
FORTY-FIVE

Xavier Von Gothe stood tall before the brethren, exalted and worshipped. He wore a goat's head and brandished a dagger that dripped blood. The ritual was complete, the victim dead. He started off the chant, an invocation to their dark deity. The brethren took it up, many masters and novices among them, so many gathered for the fight.

If it came to that.

Xavier ended the black mass with a prayer and a silent offering to the Great Dragon. He walked around the altar and shrugged out of his robes. He moved over to a podium and left the victim lying there in full sight, something to ponder for those who might even now be questioning their allegiance.

"If they come," he called out, "are we ready?"

A shout went up, a roar. Xavier didn't agree with stirring up the crowd this way, didn't agree that they should be allowed to see him so closely. Only one man stood above him—the High Minerval—and he had ordered Xavier to perform this task.

"If we are set upon," he said, "we will use everything we have to protect this, our home. Our museum. Our sanctuary." As he spoke, he was picturing the secret escape route and the other lodges that dotted the world. "The Order of the Illuminati," he said, "is a great, evergreen tree. You can smite it, you can hack at it, you can even sometimes chop it down, but a branch will always grow back. It is eternal."

The cheers flooded the chamber that lay two floors below the impressive headquarters his ancestors had built in the hills east of the Olympia train station. It had been a well-chosen site—the hills rugged and inhospitable and already hollowed out by underground streams. Once the site was chosen, they had made sure no planning permissions were ever granted, no invitations extended. The placement was both fortunate and perfect.

The statue simply had to be brought here, back home, where it belonged. His ancestors knew that too.

Xavier raised both hands once more, riding the crescendo. "We will battle to the last man. Blood for blood. And the Great Dragon will fight with us! We cannot lose! Now protect your home, rise up, rise up and fight!"

His satisfied gaze swept the assemblage. Nearby were Typhon and Calypso, his closest commanders, one thickset and hard, the other tall, willowy, and deadly. Even closer at hand was Baltasar, the man he had sent to collect the map, the best of the best, the leader of the Hoods.

We are the Illuminati. We cannot lose.

CHAPTER FORTY-SIX

Family is a sense of belonging.

Bodie felt it now, watching his team prepare for . . . what? Battle? An assault? Death? They were a covert infiltration team that also happened to know how to fight. Bodie could see how they were perfect for the job they were about to do, but remained unhappy being forced into it.

"Don't worry," Cassidy told him in inimitable style. "I can get us through this."

Bodie nodded. "You gonna make it, Eli?"

Cross scowled. "I'm forty-three, boss, not being forced to come out of retirement."

Jemma shuffled the sheaves of paper she was working on. "Almost done. Yeah, we're blind into the HQ, but we all know what a tunnel looks like."

"And how to hack a way into it." Gunn's fingers weaved a magical network upon his laptop's keys.

"And you, Bodie?" Heidi saw him watching over all. "You happy with the assault?"

"That's your word," Bodie said. "A government agent calls this an assault; I call it a masterful insinuation."

"Yeah, the only thing assaulted here's gonna be your penchant for shock and awe," Cassidy said. "Real agents do it noiselessly."

Heidi allowed a smile. "Sounds like you got a bumper sticker right there."

"We're waiting for a bit more gear," Bodie said. "Should be ready for tonight. Sunset."

They toiled away, fetching pictures of the Olympia train station and figuring out a good approach. Of course, the Illuminati knew they were coming, but this time there would be no event. Nothing would possibly be risked inside their own HQ, Bodie was sure of it.

Hours passed. Food and drink were brought. The Rangers were introduced and sat around the hotel room, checking and rechecking weapons. They were focused and deadly, and Bodie was glad they were on his side, not hunting him down. Jemma worked her maps, her figures, reworking the plan. Gunn helped her with information that might be stored privately online, including material that might exist on the dark web. Heidi made a point of missing that part, making a private call to her family back home. Bodie remembered she had an ex-husband and a daughter that refused to speak to her. He didn't know the details, but to see the CIA agent busting a gut to save innocent people made him sorry, and sad.

He walked over to her as Jemma announced she was almost ready. "Hey, no hard feelings, huh?"

Heidi stared at the cell phone she'd just placed carefully on the table. "What? Oh, yeah. I guess that really depends where we are this time tomorrow."

Bodie accepted that with a smile. "I guess you're right." He nodded at the phone. "Is everything okay?"

"I have an eleven-year-old daughter, Bodie, and I'm stuck in Greece. Trouble is—I want to be in Greece, and I want to be with her. I just can't seem to make it work."

Bodie scratched at a clean-shaven chin. "I wish I could help, but I'm an antisocial, untrusting thief who needs friends. Go chew on that for a while."

Heidi let out a brief laugh. "Thank God. At least you're not hitting me with honey-laden advice. Shit that never works."

"Nah, I'll leave that to the jerks. However," he went on, "if you ever need a pointer on how to break in to your local Walmart—give me a ring."

Heidi laughed harder, pushing the phone call aside. "Bodie," she said, "you and your team are good guys. I like you. I just wish we operated on the same side of the law."

Bodie felt the same. At that moment, Jemma called out, "We ready?"

He watched Heidi's game face replace the open countenance she was giving him. She took a deep breath and stood up.

"Let's go."

◆　◆　◆

The Olympia train station was a small, newly painted building bordered only by a few trees. The tracks ran past the entrance, with a small platform in between, and now, as the sun began to set, the place was sparsely inhabited.

Bodie watched a bright-white train come and go, disgorging just three passengers and admitting two. As a group, the team appeared suspicious, so they tried to split up and wander aimlessly. Jemma had briefed them on the station's layout, and they knew exactly where they had to go.

Comms were on. Heidi spoke up. "Everyone ready?"

Cross, who would pose as their Illuminati member on this mission, responded. "Just show me where to go."

Nobody responded negatively, so she gave the go. Turning from tourists into a cohesive team, they moved in.

Jemma walked with a powerful CIA-engineered tablet in her hand. "All right, I have authority over the security feed, thanks to Gunn. Sending it over to you now. Also got the tunnel's coordinates and measurements." She whistled. "It's almost one hundred and fifty meters long, retrofitted before the First World War. I see a guard station at each end, communication cables, two men at each end, and, no doubt, an elaborate way of gaining entry. Guards are . . ." She squinted. "Armed. I can't make out manufacturers, but expect firepower. And now . . . if I use the feed to follow the cables all the way from the guard station, I can estimate the entry point."

She looked up.

"Right there."

A door stood tucked away from the station platform. It was old, recently painted, unattractive, but looked sturdy, like a service door. It was fitted with a key lock, nothing more. Bodie looked away quickly to give the team as long as possible before they were made.

"First barrier," he said, reading out the blemished brass sign. "Supplies."

"Yeah, 'cause 'private' would invite the curious," Jemma said.

"Where's our Illuminati?" Bodie asked.

"I'm right here," Cross said, coming up to his shoulder and passing without acknowledgment.

"Perfect man for the job," Cassidy said.

The redneck ex-military man edged toward the door. Bodie saw no cameras around and assumed they may have attracted unwanted attention. The door was for key holders only, and Eli Cross was an expert at picking locks.

Eight seconds, and the lock clicked. Cross pulled the door open, and Bodie took a quick look inside. Sure enough, it was a supply room of sorts, full of boxes and equipment.

"Expect CCTV," Gunn said. "I'm getting some small feedback from inside that room."

Cross entered. "Far door," he said. "Keypad protected, card entry."

"Use the card."

Gunn, years ago, had prepared a credit card–style device that read codes by listening to the radio frequency of the keypad, mating microcontrollers. It snared and reran the codes within seconds using several built-in microchips, similar to but much more powerful than a standard credit card. Cross inserted his into the slot and waited a few seconds.

"Done."

Gunn hesitated no longer, but fed a loop into the CCTV system. The loop showed an empty supply room.

"Go team," he said.

"Hope your van's comfy," Jemma said, sounding a little nervous.

"Yeah, Jeff and I are needed back here. Sorry, cat burglar."

Bodie followed her into the room and walked over to where Cross held a door open. "Nothing to see here," Cross said. "Steady slope probably leads down to the first guard room. We ready for that?"

The entire team couldn't crowd in, so Bodie waved Cross ahead. "After you."

"This is where it gets tricky," Gunn told them. "Human traits can never be predicted."

"Explains why we know you so well," Cassidy said.

Cross was walking slowly down the tunnel. Gunn had no idea what the man might need to gain access to the deeper parts of the complex, but controlling the cameras and computers was a good first step. Bodie eased his way inside, knowing Cross would speak up the second he saw a camera.

"You ready to loop the tunnel feed?" he asked Gunn.

"Yep. It's on the same network, so good to go."

Ahead, Bodie saw Cross stop. Before him, filling the tunnel, stood a wooden hut with a glass window, almost like a ticket booth, with a door built into the side. A head poked out of the booth, staring at Cross.

The moment of truth. The team had reasoned that Illuminati members would not use an ID entry method; they would not carry cards or fobs or any kind of remote device. Instead, it would be a facial identification system, possibly fingerprints, run in-house and closed off from the outside world. Just one more way of keeping their secret.

"Good evening, sir," the guard said. "Have you visited before?"

Cross took a gamble, shaking his head. "No."

"Place your hand on the tablet."

Bodie couldn't see it, but assumed Cross had just been handed a small screen. As of now, the entire operation was up to Sam Gunn.

Seconds passed. The soldiers grew itchy. Bodie made himself breathe deeply.

"You're not in the system, sir," the guard said, suspicion packed into his voice.

"We go," Cassidy said. "Ready, boys?"

"Wait!" Gunn said. "Just got it."

"Try again," Cross said evenly. "I didn't come all this way to be turned around at the gate."

"Of course."

Twelve tense seconds passed, and then the guard apologized and admitted Eli Cross. The guard wanded him for weapons, patted him down, then let him through.

"Please proceed to the next station."

Bodie waited enough time for Cross to traverse the one hundred and fifty meters and then told Gunn to loop the feed. Cross would now be taking care of the far set of guards. Cassidy and the Rangers ran down the small slope, silencers fitted, shooting the first set of guards without warning.

The tunnel was clear.

The whole team crossed it quickly, coming through the far guard house and up against a final door, this one twelve feet high, black, and ornate. It looked to Bodie a little like the gate to hell.

"We're going in," he said.

CHAPTER
FORTY-SEVEN

A ceremonial barrier was all that secured the door. Bodie raised it, feeling the smooth gold against his palms, and rested it on the floor. Cross opened the door, peered inside, and waved them through. Beyond the door was a wide passageway, the walls covered in red silk. Bodie saw paintings high up, depictions of a being with horns holding sway over a large gathering and addressing a crowd. The artwork gave him pause.

What are we walking into?

The passage ended against another door, this one a double, higher than the first. Bodie took a moment to let the team fan out—the nine Rangers, Heidi, and his friends—and then pulled at a handle.

The door swung inward.

They saw a lavish hall, vaulted ceiling inlaid with gold filigree, rows and rows of plush chairs, all fronted by a stage and a podium. Some form of meeting chamber perhaps? Bodie saw it was currently deserted, and quelled a faint, disquieted sensation.

"Gunn?" he said.

"I'm watching the feed," Gunn said. "Don't worry. I've built up a pretty good picture here. The majority of folk are a level down, occupying a second chamber very similar to the one you're in right now. It's darker, though, and much worse. I see a man wearing horns on the stage and possibly a victim of some sort strapped to an altar. Whoa, that's pretty terrible. They're chanting, raising hands up. If I didn't doubt my eyes, people, I'd say that was devil worship."

Bodie thought back to the painting on the walls, the history of Illuminati and frat houses and a dozen other secret societies.

"Anyone on this level?"

"Yep, the whole gang hasn't been invited to Satan's party. Your chamber's empty, but corridors to the left and right are not. People in offices. A few guards. Some quiet rooms, whatever. But *beyond* the chamber is where it's at. I see the front parts of jail cells and after that, the motherlode."

Bodie clicked his tongue. "Get on with it, Gunn. We can't stand here all day."

"All right, walk straight forward, up the center aisle, and keep low, just in case. Take—"

Quickly, they followed Gunn's instructions, glad there was some kind of meeting going on downstairs, but worried about how the size of the chamber might corroborate the number of people.

"Hoods?" Bodie said. "They downstairs too?"

"Yep, a ton of them."

Shit.

Past the altar and a right turn, through another passage, and then they were among the jail cells. It struck Bodie as odd that the cells would be so accessible, in full view, but then he remembered the mindset of the Illuminati. No doubt they enjoyed gazing upon the faces of their captives.

Small cells with clouded vision panels and heavy steel doors sat on either side. This wasn't the time to check faces, so Bodie walked right past, coming upon the highest, widest curtain he had ever seen. It rose a hundred feet and disappeared in big folds to the left and right, as impressive and daunting as a brick wall. Bodie watched as Heidi passed by, losing herself in the folds as she tried to find a gap.

"Shit," came her muffled voice. "I can't find my way out."

"She's in the right area," Gunn said. "Look at the top. See the red banner? It's probably a marker of some kind."

Bodie spotted it and entered the curtain, encountering Heidi on the way. For a moment they were almost cheek to cheek, alone and feeling a little awkward, but then Bodie's questing hand found a thick curtain edge and pulled it apart.

His eyes were drawn by what was on the other side. And not just his eyes—his brain, his body, his blood. His entire concentration, the full scope of his imagination.

Nothing could stop him gasping as the sight took his breath away.

Wonders. Ancient and modern. The miracles of science and architecture, of stonework and clay, marble and brushstroke. The thief in him felt hunger, the man wonder, the person working for the government—great satisfaction.

"Their stash," he said.

"Stash?" Heidi echoed, her voice cracking. "I'd actually call this a phenomenon."

The floor ran away to the left and right to form a wide balcony, bounded by endless, high bookcases. An ornate rail ran all the way around, disappearing into the distance and the hollowed-out hillside. Alcoves dotted the balcony here and there, all filled with statues and carvings and immense works of art. The floor ahead descended gradually into an immense pit, rails to both sides to enable those worthy enough to tread its plush planks, the view of a lifetime to both sides.

The pit bristled with wonders.

"I don't know where to look," Heidi breathed. "I'm seeing tables of Fabergé eggs, more than what was thought missing. Three lost statues and two lost masterpieces that even I know of. I really, really don't know where to look first."

Bodie gripped her shoulders. "There," he said. "Right there."

He pointed and watched the CIA agent follow his finger.

"Oh, Lord."

The Statue of Zeus stood resplendent in all its glory, fully built and occupying the back of the pit, an honored and revered resting place. Ivory and gold panels glistened under the spotlights. Zeus's wreath sparkled atop his huge head, the gilded glass robe he wore burnishing the light and throwing it back like fire. The small chryselephantine statue of Nike, the goddess of victory, lay in contrast to the scepter and eagle Zeus clasped in his hands. The throne itself shone gloriously, inlaid with precious stones, gold, ebony, and ivory.

"Destroyed for over a thousand years," Bodie breathed.

"Not," Heidi said, deliberately blunt.

The others crowded around, equally impressed. Gunn commented over the comms while keeping a watch on their backs.

"Y'know," he said, "I'm inspired to say there could be parts of other ancient wonders in there. Parts of the Temple of Artemis and the Mausoleum at Halicarnassus. The head of the Colossus of Rhodes perhaps, and imagine what they might have from the Lighthouse at Alexandria? Oh, I wish I was with you."

"Me too," Jeff chimed in.

Bodie couldn't tear his eyes away from Zeus. The immensity of it was stunning.

"Shit," Gunn said, and the crude abruptness of it cut through everything.

"What?" Cassidy asked.

"Satanfest 2017 just ended downstairs. The dudes are filing out fast. Goat Head is shouting and waving his arms, and the Hoods are rising up. Guys and girls—" He went quiet a moment, then said, "I think you got made."

"Are you saying they're headed this way?" Heidi asked.

"Umm, not sure. But I do mean all of 'em. A hundred perhaps, with half as many Hoods and the main figures from the stage. They're running like hell, as if whatever they tried to summon down there actually made an appearance."

Bodie felt foreboding. "Please tell me they aren't running toward the exits."

"No, Guy, and that's the problem."

Bodie had figured that was a good thing. A break for the exits would have signified a coming event.

"Why is that a problem, Sam?"

"Because they're all running toward you!"

CHAPTER
FORTY-EIGHT

Bodie cast around for options, but Heidi and the Rangers were already scoping out a battle plan. For this, he would defer to their expertise. Everyone ran to conceal themselves in the pit, the Rangers covering them as they did so. They hid behind artifacts and relics, weapons drawn, waiting for the assault.

It soon came. The curtain must have been fixed to a remote because it started to swish aside with an electronic smoothness. Bodie crouched beside a bronzed statue sporting a sword and shield and wondered if he'd ever get his face-off with Jack Pantera.

Damn, I hope so.

Cross and Jemma lay low to his left, a steel chest covering them. Cassidy preferred half concealment, enabling her to aim better. The tall stallion she hid behind towered above her.

Through the curtain's widening gap, a ravening horde came. Bodie saw blood already on their hands and faces, a product of the black mass they had been performing. The angle of their run saw them attacking the ramp, with many heads glancing to the right, where Bodie suddenly saw a brick room fronted by a steel door.

Interesting . . .

The Rangers opened fire, felling three, and then three more. Those that saw the danger dropped low or fled along the balcony. Those that didn't surged straight for the ramp, rapidly closing the gap between them and the Rangers. Constant gunfire rang out, and some of the crowd fired back. Bodie aimed and shot, each bullet taking down a man who then slowed those behind. A roar filled the pit, echoing from the ceiling high above, the roar of the angered and the crazed, a roar of the aggrieved.

The Hoods came faster than the Rangers could pick them off. First the closest soldier and then the second in line jumped down into the pit, rolling and trying hard not to damage an ankle. The lessening firepower urged the attackers on, and then Bodie saw the Illuminati themselves at the back of the pack, trying to push through.

Cassidy fired shot after shot, reloaded in seconds, and kept the rush at bay. The first of the Illuminati were halfway down the slope now, driven by the fire their boss had planted in their hearts, spurred by the thought that they had always reigned supreme, never suffered a loss. Gunn's voice filled the team's ears, so they knew the Hoods were all inside and the true leaders were following fast.

"And guards," Jeff said. "The whole shebang."

The Rangers reappeared along the base of the pit, joining their colleagues. Several stray bullets passed them by, but the attackers didn't have enough firepower to make it count. Bodie again saw a dozen glances toward that brick building and acted on a hunch.

"Cross," he said. "With me."

They swerved past an ancient pillar, avoided a French Renaissance chair, and took just a few seconds to beat the lock. Door open, they peered inside.

"Ooh," Cross intoned. "Playtime."

"Not for us," Bodie said. "For them." He nodded at the Rangers.

"We have a mini armory over here," Cross said through the comms. "Jemma. Come help. We can distribute weapons to the Rangers."

They took what they could carry: rifles, semiautomatics, and magazines. Bodie unhooked a rocket launcher and two RPGs. They found knives and grenades. They found canisters with no name. Flashbangs and frequency jammers.

"Why here?" Jemma wondered. "Among their treasure?"

"Obvious, really," Gunn came back. "They'll have one on each floor. Maybe two. If the entire floor is a treasure chamber . . ."

"Yeah, okay."

"One other thing," Gunn said.

Bodie took that one. "Speak."

"These Illuminati are fired up, fighting for their lives. And they're plentiful. I advise cutting the head off the snake."

"Goat Boy," Cassidy said. "And whoever else. Can you pinpoint them for us?"

"Got a target on them since the beginning. I'm tracking 'em right now."

"It's a good idea," Bodie said, "but the Hoods won't stop. The Hoods are the real danger here."

The sound of gunfire filled the pit. Stray metal glanced off and dented a dozen artifacts, and smashed one glass figure to smithereens. Bodie, Cross, and Jemma moved quickly back to their places, ready to hand the new arms out.

Cassidy flicked an arm. "R P fucking G, now!"

Bodie cringed even as he slid it along the floor to her. The grenades went a moment later. Cassidy couldn't keep the grin from her face.

"Don't worry," she said, not trying to hide her excitement. "It's a final option."

"Yeah," Cross said. "As if. You don't even believe yourself."

Bodie slid what guns he could to the Rangers and Heidi, watching the others do the same. He kept a few spare mags for himself. The attackers had reached the base of the ramp now but were thinning out, bodies piled in their wake. The Hoods stepped on them and sheltered behind them, creeping forward. Today, Bodie saw, they all wore ceremonial robes and half masks, their traditional cowl thrown back, their feet bare. They carried daggers to a man, something customary for the ceremony perhaps. Maybe they all got to stab the poor victim.

Passing through the curtain, Bodie spotted the man with the goat head, saw him take it off. The leader unveiled right there at the top of the ramp, viewing and evaluating all he saw and no doubt fretting over the treasures he could not reach.

"I sure wish we had another team about now," Heidi said. "Someone to hit them from behind. Shit."

"Next time," Bodie said.

"Next time?" Cassidy cried. "Fuck that!"

She stood up, emptied her mag into the approaching mass. Several had reached the Rangers and were fighting man to man, going down within seconds but gradually overwhelming the soldiers through numbers alone. Heidi crept up to their side, now armed with a Glock and a knife. Bodie looked over to his team.

"Let's show 'em how it's done."

As one, they charged, Cross, and Cassidy, and Jemma, and himself, backing up the United States Rangers and the CIA, nobody easing off and nobody backing down, ready to use guns and knives and arms and legs and bone if need be.

Bodie kicked a man in the sternum, saving ammo, struck another over the bridge of the nose with an elbow, and one more with the butt of his gun. Blood sprayed, bodies fell. Gunshots laced the air and even bounced off the floor. The Hoods were upon them, and Bodie saw the first wave had been nothing but cannon fodder.

"Crueler than cruel."

Hand-to-hand combat broke out. Knives flashed. The Hoods were relentless and skillful, uncaring about their own survival. Bodie stumbled under a vicious onslaught only to see Cassidy haul the man away and throw him aside. He saw Jemma fall and dragged her clear.

He saw a Ranger die with a knife in his neck, another fall as he was repeatedly stabbed. He saw more Rangers come to the aid of the fallen, killing the killers. This was warfare in its rawest form: sharp and blunt and hot and cold.

A fist to the face sent Bodie falling over the body at his back. He caught himself, fired into the attacker, saw the bullet made no difference, and rolled. A knife embedded into the wood beside his head. He struck at the temple, three times, jabbed at the neck. The Hood fell away. Bodie removed the knife and buried it in the man, looked up.

Another Hood fell on top of him.

The team managed to rise, to back away. The Hoods came more slowly, trained to fight and look for the right moment. Cassidy waited until the first lunge, then toppled the table full of Fabergé eggs into the man's path. Screams went up from the balcony above. The man tried desperately to avoid the rolling, priceless wealth, but tripped over one and smashed three. He hit the floor. Cassidy finished him off. Heidi jumped up onto a statue as a Hood came at her, swinging around it and hitting him from the blind side. Her blow sent him into oblivion, falling and striking his temple against the statue's inflexible edge. She used her height advantage to jump onto another man's shoulders and take him down.

Bodie found a three-sided room of amber and felt a strong recollection of what it might mean. Before he could formulate the thought, two Hoods were on him. A knife slashed his sleeve, another stuck his shoulder, but only briefly. The wound bled, but the adrenaline meant he felt nothing. He leapt back, then, as the first Hood followed, toppled an amber panel onto him, bearing him to the ground. Another scream issued from above. Bodie saw the second Hood dive in with the knife high, and repeated the pattern, toppling the back wall onto this man's body, crushing bones.

He flitted away, running between relics and artifacts and coming around to a different vantage point. Another shot from the gun and a dangerous attacker fell. Four Rangers were down. Heidi head-butted a Hood and then lost her balance, falling to one knee. He smashed her to the floor, raised a knife, then spun as Cassidy shot him down.

Bodie recognized one of the Hoods who was flanked by what appeared to be three leaders watching over it all.

Bodie, Cross, and Jemma were driven back, away from the front of the pit and farther among the relics. A small horse found its way into Bodie's hand and ended up smashing the front teeth from a Hood's mouth. A knife took some flesh from the back of his hand. He leapt here and there, from bases to marble knees and bronze laps. He toppled a knight onto a Hood, flinching as the heavy armor crashed. He used a plush bed to scramble across and put distance between himself and an attacker, then unashamedly shot the man dead.

It was dog-eat-dog down here today.

All of a sudden the Statue of Zeus was at his back, and Cross was at his side. Two Hoods came at them. Bodie fired, but hit a blank chamber—empty. Cross kicked out. Bodie caught his man and flung him back against the statue's base, the thick white legs like a gigantic pillar rising above. The Hood delivered a kick-punch combination, sending Bodie to his knees, clutching his stomach. He managed to turn the Hood again, and held out a hand as a knife was drawn.

"Careful," he said. "Look up."

The Hood did, and blanched, not realizing the prize he fought and struggled against. All Bodie heard was one of the leader's voices, warning his men to be careful. The Hood hesitated. Bodie barged in with everything he had, driving the man back against a forged iron cauldron. In a stroke of luck, the blow felled the Hood. Bodie helped Cross with his attacker and then took a second to recover.

"To the end," Cross said.

"To the end, my friend."

They jogged back through the maze of relics, finding Jemma on the way, stuck beneath a dead Hood and a small statue. Bodie dragged the statue off her, and Cross helped her stand. "Thief," she said. "I'm supposed to steal these things, not count on them to overcome an attacker."

"Let's see where we are," Bodie said.

They stole closer to the front, some sixth sense warning them to move slowly. Bodie paused behind a gold sarcophagus that might have housed any number of Egyptian leaders thought lost to time, and peered out.

The Rangers were down to three. Heidi lay on the ground, bleeding. Cassidy fought three Hoods, valiantly standing her ground but making no headway. The Illuminati leader was walking down the ramp as if sensing victory, flanked by his chosen ones.

Heidi raised herself up on an elbow. "Damn, that looks like Xavier. One of the big bosses."

"Bodie," Jemma breathed with fear. "What are we going to do?"

And for once his perfect thief's mind was blank. The wit and brainpower, the skill and experience, that could read and act on every situation, was as dull as the sky on a rainy day.

"Not my expertise," he said. "Shit, what do we do?"

CHAPTER
FORTY-NINE

Cassidy saw them. "What the fuck are you waiting for? Nuke the bastards!"

Bodie was instantly galvanized, somehow knowing exactly what she meant. Play the Illuminati at their own game. *Give their fucking events right back to them.*

"Yeah," he said. "Oh yeah."

He looked around, knowing exactly what he needed.

Jemma tapped his elbow. "What are we doing, Guy?"

"There." He pointed at two dead Rangers. "Go get those grenades and be ready."

Cross was already creeping off, understanding the plan without being told. Three more grenades lay to the right. Bodie saw Cassidy and ran straight at her, catching all three Hoods' attention.

"Bollocks!" he cried, leaping at them, totally in the air and crashing down among them. They scattered, twisted away. Cassidy was free for several seconds and intensely busy.

"Ready?" she yelled, the question a bellow of rage and command.

"Ready!" Cross cried.

"Ready!" Jemma screamed.

"Fix this," she said and turned to the approaching bosses with the RPG launcher balanced across one shoulder.

Xavier's face twisted in fear and agony, but that was all he had time for.

Cassidy launched the first grenade, aiming for the wall above their heads and the bookcase and balcony alongside. Jemma threw her grenades one at a time, letting them explode among the artifacts and the huge pillars that held up the pit. Cross launched his too, concentrating on the pillars. Cassidy reloaded and fired the second grenade, this one high into the chamber, shattering the roof where it was least supported.

"No!" Xavier moaned. "You are mad. Mad!"

Bodie struggled with a Hood, kicked another in the face. An ominous groaning came from the pit's central support, and the brickwork looked like it was already buckling. More grenades were thrown, explosions occurring on the ramp and along the balconies, debris, fire, and rock blasting out. The remaining Rangers used their own bombs, sending blasts in all directions and disorienting the enemy. Bodie saw gouts of fire and wreckage in every part of the pit and up and down the ramp. Illuminati scattered, and Hoods raced after them. Cassidy returned and helped Bodie put down the three Hoods. Heidi shot two more.

"This is the main event," she said. "It's just a shame you bastards aren't down here to see firsthand the kind of terror and carnage you've wrought."

Bodie was first up, then the team was racing after the Illuminati, hitting the bottom of the ramp at top speed. Fires flicked at their ankles. A gas line exploded close by, causing an eruption of flame, a singeing torrent of fire that raged up into the heights of the chamber. Several bookcases toppled, sending their contents over the collapsing balcony in a surge of debris.

Bodie charged through the middle of it, ignoring the death and destruction on every side. A Hood leapt in from the right, evaporated in midair as a second gas explosion erupted beneath his body. Now there remained only Xavier and his acolytes, only three Rangers and the team. Not a man or woman among them was unmarked, not bleeding, not close to collapsing.

The chamber rumbled, the brick pillar support crumbling and waving from side to side. Part of the roof was falling in, the very skies of the Illuminati's wonder chamber falling down. Bodie was halfway up the ramp, his team at his heels. The Rangers pressed on, faster, and Heidi shouted that they should take the leader out.

The Hood that Bodie recognized turned, face as bleak as death and decay, signaling that he would not allow that. Heidi recognized him too, reached him first, and did not back down.

"Die hard, motherfucker," she said, and launched herself straight at his throat.

Baltasar twisted just a few centimeters, throwing her aside. She hit the railing, splintering three of the spindles. Bodie reached down and dragged her up. Now he saw two important-looking Illuminati turning, just behind Xavier, as he ran on to escape.

Xavier's scream cut through the clamor: "Calypso, Typhon, fight for me! Kill for me! And Baltasar, die if you must!"

"I got the thin bitch," Cassidy said, running past and attacking Calypso.

"We get the wide dude," Bodie said, pulling Heidi by the hand as if they were racing toward a theme park ride.

They stood toe to toe and fought for everything they held dear. Baltasar engaged the three Rangers, moving like fire and shadow, damaging them with scorching attacks, and then flitting away before they could react. Typhon faced Bodie and Heidi. Calypso moved in fast at Cassidy. The chamber and the pit burned around them, fire flashing and bookcases collapsing, tipping their contents into the fray in constant succession amid countless explosions and inferno-like chaos.

Just what the Devil ordered, Bodie thought wryly as he engaged his opponent.

They struck as one, Heidi and he striking at Typhon, then retreating to different sides. Their opponent blocked and fought back, but he was no match for their combined effort. Bodie jabbed between two ribs, causing the man to flinch, as Heidi delivered a strike to his midriff, forcing him to double over. Bodie's kick to the face sent his head snapping back and Heidi's push made him topple backward, his skull striking the floor with a loud crack.

He lay unmoving. Bodie considered dragging him clear—the knowledge his befuddled head contained could be invaluable—but looked to his friends first. Always his friends.

Cassidy was toe to toe with Calypso, the two matching each other blow for blow. Bodie saw a surge of books rushing down the slope, a lava flow of burning paper, flaming high, and flung himself headlong, tackling Cassidy about the waist and bearing her away. Calypso managed to see it at the last minute and hopped onto the railing, balancing there like an acrobat with a death wish as it passed. Cassidy flung Bodie away, not impressed, and kicked at the railing, splintering its entire length. The wooden beam twisted, but Calypso leapt off a moment before it fell, her right knee aimed at Cassidy's face, her shoulder rolling down for the follow-up. Bodie saw Cassidy slip underneath and help the woman on with a little shove, but Calypso twisted and turned, landing on her knees, facing the redhead.

Both women breathed for a moment.

The Rangers were fighting fiercely, but they had never faced such a competent and knowledgeable opponent as Baltasar before. The Hood had already cracked one Ranger's arm, made another limp, and broken the noses of all three men. But they hadn't taken it lying down. The Hood was staggering, his right leg badly bruised. Blood clouded his own eyes, and one of his fingers was broken. He struck now with a last-ditch effort. Bodie cast around again, worried that the man he now knew as Xavier had so long to get clear. That man could affect everything—their future, their lives, the entire world.

Cross and Jemma picked their way to his side. Heidi scooped up a heavy, splintered spindle and moved over to help the Rangers.

Bodie stared hard at the thief and the planner. "Family?"

They nodded in return. "Family."

All three spun and hit Calypso hard, just as the Illuminati leader sprung at Cassidy. The blows sent her tumbling, spinning, landing right at Cassidy's feet.

Out of sync for the first time. But it was all Cassidy needed. She knew the skills of her opponent and struck devastatingly hard and fast. A boot to the meat of the neck, a follow-up knee to the face, four hard punches to the solar plexus and abdomen, and then Cassidy was atop her, raining blows down. Calypso was already sinking into unconsciousness as Cross, Bodie, and Jemma came in to help. The fight was over in seconds.

Bodie stood up, held out a hand to Cassidy. "You okay?"

The redhead wiped blood from her face. "Shame she wasted those kind of skills. Could have been a great fighter."

"Wait," Bodie said. "Quickly, we have others to help."

They ran to where the three Rangers struggled to contain Baltasar. Heidi had drawn blood from his skull, back, and thighs, but was now on her knees, trying to recover from a knife-like kidney punch.

"You good?" He helped her to her feet.

"If good is agony, then yeah, I'm good," Heidi gasped. "Bastard caught me with a sharp one."

Cassidy bounded past her. "Let me help."

The addition of such an accomplished fighter signaled the end of Baltasar's advantage. Cassidy whipped in where the Rangers distracted the Hood, and broke bones with her punches. Bodie spun as flames washed over them, seeing the broken railing to their side catching fire. The entire length was burning, crackling. A chunk of ceiling crashed down, shattering onto the floor of the pit, but the brick support pillars appeared to be holding. Fires licked around random artifacts, and Bodie knew that if they wanted to preserve at least some of them they had to get help.

"I know we steal these things for a living," he told Heidi. "But I'm still fond of them. You gotta call in the cavalry."

"We have to get clear first." Heidi's face was strained with the rigors of her decision. "I hate the thought of leaving too, Bodie, but we have no choice."

"Then let's do it fast."

Baltasar had fallen, crawling now as Cassidy helped two of the Rangers up the debris-littered slope. The third Ranger rendered him unconscious, but didn't have the strength to drag his body clear.

Another stream of wreckage piled down the slope, augmented by a ceiling collapse. Most of the rubble landed on Baltasar, missing the Ranger who dived clear.

Together, the team rushed up the slope, battered, bruised, and bleeding. The curtains were engulfed in flame, a roaring sound around them like the battle of two dinosaurs. Parts of the material had fallen, and Bodie led the others straight through, past the empty jail cells, and through a final passageway. He didn't take it easy, didn't slow; there wasn't time, and if Xavier had the balls to arrange a plan or an ambush, then good luck to the little fucker.

Bodie helped Heidi while Cassidy helped the Rangers, with Cross lending a hand. Jemma backed Bodie up, running at his shoulder and scanning the terrain ahead. One more passage and they entered the silk-lined corridor where the far doors stood wide open to give easy access to the underground tunnel.

Through the first guard hut and then the second, they saw evidence that others had fled this way: cast-off folders and wads of money, a jewelry box full of diamonds. Cross reached down to grab the latter and Heidi growled at him.

"Careful there; I never miss a trick."

Cross held onto the box. The team raced as best they could, up and out, helping each other along. The last door ejected them into the darkness of late night, into the blessed relief of fresh air and wide spaces, into the choppy bustle that was the Olympia train station.

Bodie spied people running here and there, no doubt lesser Illuminati, guards, and other acolytes. What he didn't expect was the appearance of Jeff and Gunn.

Dragging Xavier between them.

A huge smile broke out on his face. "Now that *is* teamwork," he said. "You were waiting for him and backed us up. Great job."

"Think I broke a finger on his tooth," Gunn said, cupping a hand.

Cassidy snorted. "Join the club."

"Thanks," Gunn said, smiling now. "I will."

Jeff threw Xavier to the floor. The Illuminati leader had been tied by the hands and feet, belts around both. Bodie finally found the reason for the choppy noise that filled the station. A helicopter was waiting.

"We have to go," Heidi said. "Every rescue service in Greece is coming."

"We taking Xavier?" Bodie asked as he helped Jeff drag the man toward the noise.

"Damn right we are," Heidi said. "The leader of the Illuminati is a prize worthy of Zeus."

Xavier sneered through blood-smeared features as they forced him to move. "Leader?" he croaked. "No. I am not the leader. He left half an hour ago. Soon you will all scream his name."

"Wait." Heidi pulled up. "What?"

"Crap," Bodie said. "But it hardly matters. Your network is smashed. Your home ruined. Your lodges are no longer a secret, and your Hoods are all dead. Whoever your leader is, he can't recover from this."

Xavier glared in the direction of the wrecked HQ, but said nothing.

Heidi waved at the helicopter pilot. "Right, boys and girls, who's up for a journey home?"

CHAPTER
FIFTY

Several days later they found themselves at an impasse.

An obscure hotel in Nevada was their home; a large, overwarm conference room with questionable air conditioning and a smell like burnt waffles was their meeting place. Bodie and his team sat waiting, wired with impatience.

"Your frizzy girlfriend was clever," Cassidy told Bodie. "Getting us out of there on a chopper, and straight to America. She beat you just a little, not allowing us time to plan an escape."

Bodie tipped back a mug of coffee, savoring the strong taste. "Gotta say, I didn't expect that. She was a step ahead. Oh, and what the hell? She's *not* my girlfriend."

"Yeah," Cross said. "The name Heidi Bodie really doesn't work."

"Piss off, Cross."

"Glad to see you're all recovering nicely." Heidi walked in, a bunch of files under her right arm. "My own kidneys still ache, and I'm sure young Cassidy's hurt worse than she's letting on. But hey . . . we're all on the same side, right?"

"Young Cassidy?" The redhead blinked. "I like this woman."

"Still thirty, though." Cross leaned over, intoning the age in a deep voice. "Can't turn back the clock."

Cassidy glared. Jemma stepped in. "He can't help it," she said. "Once you get so elderly." She shrugged.

"Elderly?"

"First, the good news. Our friends in the Greek government, along with the rescue services, managed to save eighty percent of the artifacts and stop the chamber from collapsing. They're truly delighted the Statue of Zeus was found and saved." She sobered. "It helps in some very small way to ease the suffering of those lost in the events triggered by the Illuminati. Many of their secret papers are lost, either shredded or burned, or even carried away. But heads will roll, my friends. Heads will roll."

"That's great," Bodie said. "It truly is. I guess the bad news is that we're in America now, right?"

"Well, you're here now," Heidi said simply. "What are you going to do about it?"

Gunn whipped out his phone. "I got the blueprints to this place and the towns all around."

Jemma tapped the table. "And I could devise a plan of action in about ten minutes."

Heidi held up her hands, "Oh, I have no doubt you could break out of here. No doubt at all. But . . ." She paused. "You haven't."

"We thought we would sign off first," Bodie said. "I believe we're square. We held up our end, helped save lives. We figured, even though you're CIA, we can trust you."

"A big assumption," Heidi said, "considering I work within a chain of command and act on orders alone. Personal feelings can't interfere here."

"Personal feelings?" Bodie asked.

"Whatever. The fact remains that a decision was made among the higher agency echelons to break you out of jail, Bodie, so that your team could become the CIA's relic hunters. Particularly if those relics pose a threat to national or world security. We must act."

"You're offering us a job now?" Cross asked. "Damn."

Bodie knew that whatever they decided, it didn't have to be final. They were beyond competent enough to create their own future. What they didn't need was a CIA capture order hanging over their heads.

"We're persons of interest to several governments around the world," he said. "Are you going to smooth that over?"

"We can help with that." Heidi nodded. "And you people love your relics. What could be better than hunting them down for a living? Working on *our* side of the law." She grinned. "It's still a gray area, you know. The world we operate in."

Bodie laughed. "I do believe we already know that."

"We have some incredible jobs lined up," Heidi teased. "With secrets you just won't believe."

Bodie stared at his team, evaluating their reactions, but the truth was he knew them inside out. He knew their thoughts. Jemma would be assessing the offer and thinking it might hold some promise; she needed a stimulating future. Cassidy would be up for anything that Bodie sanctioned, and so, probably, would Cross. The older thief had been around the longest and probably saw this group as his last hurrah in the covert world. Gunn was Gunn, always along for the ride. Did the geek really have anywhere else to go?

Jeff, though. What would the young archaeologist do? The CIA couldn't exactly lock the poor lad up.

"If we join you," he said carefully, "it will be mostly on our terms. Every plan, every idea even, will be ours and ours alone to sign off on. If your CIA bosses try to change it, we're out."

Heidi nodded. "I can live with that. I'll take the heat for you."

"What's in the folders, Frizzy?" Cassidy asked, eyes searching the files. "Rewards?"

Heidi laughed. "New jobs," she said, splaying them across the table. "Take your pick, though the ones marked blue are more vital."

"New job?" Bodie felt a rush of gravity and turned a serious gaze upon Heidi. "I'm sorry. I thought you knew—the first job is finding Jack Pantera."

AUTHOR'S NOTE

The new installment of *The Relic Hunters* series will be available very soon. While it is a new series, it shares the same theme of escapist adventure, camaraderie, and cinema-style action as my Matt Drake series, starting with *The Bones of Odin*, which is also available for the Amazon Kindle.

Matt Drake #19 will release in October 2018.

If you enjoyed *The Relic Hunters*, please consider leaving a review.

And keep up with all the latest news and giveaways by following me on Facebook—davidleadbeaternovels—or at my website: www.davidleadbeater.com.

ABOUT THE AUTHOR

David Leadbeater has published twenty-three Kindle international bestsellers, and is the author of the Matt Drake series, the Alicia Myles series, the Chosen trilogy, and the Disavowed series. *The Relic Hunters* is the first in a brand-new series of action-packed archaeological thrillers and was the winner of the inaugural Amazon Kindle Storyteller award. David has sold over three-quarters of a million e-books on the Amazon Kindle.

For a list of his books and more information, please visit his website, www.davidleadbeater.com. You can also join him on Facebook for news and paperback giveaways: www.facebook.com/davidleadbeaternovels.